KILL MONSTER

KILL MONSTER

Sean Doolittle

This first world edition published 2019
in Great Britain and the USA by
SEVERN HOUSE PUBLISHERS LTD of
Eardley House, 4 Uxbridge Street, London W8 7SY.
Trade paperback edition first published
in Great Britain and the USA 2020 by
SEVERN HOUSE PUBLISHERS LTD.

British Library Cataloguing in Publication Data
A CIP catalogue record for this title is available from the British Library.

ISBN-13: 978-0-7278-8931-7 (cased)
ISBN-13: 978-1-78029-611-1 (trade paper)
ISBN-13: 978-1-4483-0228-4 (e-book)

All Severn House titles are printed on acid-free paper.

Severn House Publishers support the Forest Stewardship Council™ [FSC™],
the leading international forest certification organisation.
All our titles that are printed on FSC certified paper carry the FSC logo.

Typeset by Palimpsest Book Production Ltd.,
Falkirk, Stirlingshire, Scotland.
Printed and bound in Great Britain by
TJ International, Padstow, Cornwall.

For Kate and Jack
Worst Kids Ever

. . . but first, the true story of the minister, the rabbi, the creature, the water carrier, and the wreck of the steamboat *Arcadia*:

'We are glad to know that the only life lost on this unfortunate occasion was that of a mule, which would have been saved but for its own obstinacy.'

– *The Daily Missouri Democrat*
September 11, 1856

i. Beecher and Loew
Brooklyn, NY – Summer 1856

Six weeks after their first strange meeting, Beecher traveled by carriage to the far side of the city with a vial of blood from the Western frontier.

He arrived at a soot-blackened factory building an hour before sunset. He climbed the iron walkup and knocked on a grimy steel door. When the rabbi answered, Beecher glanced once over his shoulder, then followed the smaller man inside.

'It's authentic?' Rabbi Loew asked, appraising Beecher's vial between his thumb and one crooked forefinger. 'How can we know this?'

'Because we didn't pay for it,' Beecher said.

'You make jokes.'

'To the contrary, I daresay.'

'If there can be the smallest doubt, realize, please, that I cannot proceed.' The rabbi looked gravely at Beecher. '*Will* not proceed.'

Despite the theologically questionable business now at hand, Beecher found himself distracted by the shabbiness of the rabbi's living quarters – a meager watchman's apartment above a rope and cordage works on the East River. Loew's rooms were dim and musty, sparsely furnished, crowded everywhere with books. Some of the books looked very old indeed.

'Reverend Beecher? Are you listening?'

'A physician in the region is sympathetic to our cause,' Beecher explained. When the rabbi seemed eager for further elaboration, he added, 'The rest is a matter of some detail.'

'If your physician has access to this man Wolcott, why can he not perform the task himself?'

'Our physician may be a spy, but he's still a sworn healer. That means he's bound by oath to assassinate people only by accident.' Beecher sighed. 'It's also my understanding that he is himself now dead.'

The rabbi closed his eyes as he lowered the specimen, in the same motion concealing the vial in his palm. Beecher imagined an arthritic magician preparing a trick. Not far from the truth, perhaps.

'And if you'll forgive the reminder, Rabbi Loew,' he went on, 'it was you who first approached me.'

'So it was.'

'When shall I return, then?'

The rabbi straightened his shoulders. At full height, he almost reached Beecher's chin. 'Three days. With one of your boxes.'

'Very well.'

'And now, will you stay for wine?'

'Thank you,' Beecher said, 'but I believe that temperance remains one of the cardinal virtues.'

At this, Rabbi Loew laughed – a high cackle that startled Beecher mildly. The rabbi carried on laughing as Beecher showed himself out, leaving the steel door open behind him. Beecher could still hear the sound of the man's voice as he descended the iron stairs, a crow-like rasp somewhere over his head, drifting out toward the bay.

Three days later, Beecher returned to the rope factory as instructed, this time in a wagon, under cover of night. With him he bore an empty shipping crate marked *BOOKS*.

For more than two years, Beecher – with the help of his congregation, along with other monied allies – had been sending such crates fifteen-hundred miles west to the free-staters in the Kansas Territory. Though Beecher's crates were always marked *BOOKS*, or *TOOLS*, or sometimes even *BIBLES*, they always contained the same cargo:

Guns.

Sharps rifles, to be precise. Breach-loading, self-priming wonderments of modern accuracy and power. Just the tool to help give those right-minded Jayhawkers a leg up against the slave-mongering heathens from bordering Missouri. 'You might just as well read the Bible to buffaloes,' Beecher had been quoted as saying, 'as to those fellows who follow Atchison and Stringfellow; but they have a supreme respect for the logic that is embodied in a Sharps rifle.'

Perhaps he'd been unwise to have said so in Greeley's *Tribune*.

Whether for this reason alone, or by some otherwise unlucky combination of circumstance and treachery, Beecher's past three shipments had been intercepted en route to their destination. Two months ago, the opposition had sacked the abolitionist township of Lawrence. According to dispatches, a splinter gang led by the godless savage William 'Bloody Bill' Wolcott carried on wreaking havoc about the countryside even now. The pendulum, it seemed, had swung toward the enemy, and far in the distance, Kansas lay bleeding.

Then came Rabbi Zalman Loew to Beecher's door.

Beecher was given to understand that the rabbi had been ousted from his own temple some time previously. The two men had not discussed such details upon that first meeting.

Nor did they discuss such details now, six weeks and three days later, standing together in a dank hold of the rope works, surrounded by bales of coir and sisal hemp. The room smelled to Beecher of burlap and wet iron, with perhaps the faintest, rotten-egg tinge of sulfur somewhere beneath.

Rabbi Loew said, 'Let me now introduce you to a compatriot.'

The young, bearded man at Loew's side stepped forward, extending his hand in greeting. He wore orthodox garb, sidelocks tucked behind his ears. 'Reverend Beecher,' he said, 'I am Silas Wasserman.'

'It means *water carrier*,' Loew added. 'Reb Wasserman will accompany our cargo to the frontier.'

Beecher found Silas Wasserman's grip soft and somewhat clammy, despite the lingering heat of the day. But he nodded to the younger man with sincerity. 'For carrying our water, then, consider me your personal debtor.'

Wasserman stepped back, folded his hands before him, and turned his eyes respectfully to the floor.

'And our cargo?' Beecher asked.

The rabbi offered a smile Beecher couldn't interpret. Without further preamble, he shifted his gaze toward the dim reaches of the warehouse and spoke a phrase in Hebrew: '*Bo henah.*'

At Loew's command, a fourth man emerged from the shadows – a hulking figure, intimidating even from afar. As this fourth man shambled toward them, Beecher found himself transfixed by the giant stranger's brutish, menacing silhouette. Motes of dust swirled in the air as the figure crossed a beam of moonlight. In that fleeting, silvery moment, Beecher thought: *not a man.*

Crude. Lumpen. Faceless. Only just manlike enough in its shape – in its horrid, burdensome lurch – to be revealed for what it was: An abomination.

A blasphemy.

'The golem,' Rabbi Zalman Loew said.

'Merciful Jesus.'

The rabbi's eyes twinkled. 'Reb Wasserman, we have a new believer in our midst.'

Loew's creature was almost upon them now. Each approaching footfall sounded like a heavy sack of mixed cement landing upon the ground. Beecher could feel each muted impact beneath his own feet. He was nearly overtaken by a sudden, feathery lightness in his chest; he tried to call out, but his mouth had gone dry.

'A word of advice, Reverend,' Loew said. 'In your place, I would stand aside.'

Beecher stood aside.

A radiant chill touched his skin as the creature passed him by. From this distance, Beecher could see lumps, depressions, and fingermarks in the thing's otherwise featureless visage. It was like a small child's notion of a human adult, sculpted from a life-sized block of clay.

'In heaven's name,' he croaked, 'what is that smell?'

'Nothing of heaven,' the rabbi answered. 'You smell accursed earth. Mined from the Valley of Hinnom by my own mentor's hand.'

The creature lumbered to a halt at the open crate marked *BOOKS*. There it waited, motionless, a cane's reach away. A silent, soulless thing.

Loew placed a hand on Silas Wasserman's shoulder.

Wasserman, the water carrier, drew from his pocket a pair of smooth, emerald-green stones. With what Beecher interpreted to be trepidation, the young man approached the creature. Rising up on to the tips of his toes, he pressed the stones into the moist clay one at a time, endowing the inscrutable giant with a primitive semblance of eyes. Then he drew a hitching breath, cleared his throat, and said, *'Numa.'*

Like a barrel-bodied man stepping into a bath, Loew's golem climbed into its crate and sat down. Then it reclined – slowly, incredibly, molding itself to the dimensions of the space as it settled. The emerald-green stones receded into the thing, disappearing from view. Within moments, any observer might have mistaken the crate for what it appeared simply to be: a box filled to the lip with slick, mud-streaked clay.

Beecher whispered the first word that bobbed to the surface of his mind: '*How?*'

'How indeed?' Loew shrugged. 'Ancient teachings. Some of this, bits of that. And, of course!' He held up the blood vial, now empty, cloudy with rust-colored residue. 'This.'

Beecher opened his mouth to respond, then he closed it again. No further words presented themselves.

As Silas Wasserman set about fixing the lid on to the crate with a hammer and a fistful of ten-penny nails, Loew said, 'When the box next opens, the golem will awaken. It carries out its purpose: to find the man whose blood it shares. Only when that man is destroyed shall the creature return to the soil.'

With effort, Beecher wrenched his gaze from the crate and looked upon his odd little partner. He tried to gather his thoughts as Wasserman carried on hammering in the background. Finally, he said, 'And then?'

'And then? What *and then*?' Loew raised his gnarled fists to ear level and shook them in forecasted triumph. 'Then we make one for Atchison! And another for Stringfellow! Ha!'

'May God forgive us,' Beecher said.

'May God reward us!' Rabbi Loew unballed his fists and spread his hands. 'While we're waiting, shall we see about that wine?'

ii. Snag
Missouri River – Autumn 1856

For the rest of his penniless, disgraced, yet otherwise long and healthy life, Silas Wasserman would think back to the days he'd spent aboard the great white *Arcadia*, steaming up that great brown American river, absorbing an unspoiled countryside he'd only richly imagined theretofore.

At age twenty-four, Wasserman had never been farther west than Manhattan Island (and only rarely that far). But from the familiar street corners and alleyways of the Brooklyn he knew, never could he have imagined – no matter how richly he may have tried

– the particular smell of cow shit on the St Louis levee; the sounds and sensations of the river churning beneath the *Arcadia*'s massive side wheels; the size of the sky over the vast Great Plains.

And the sheer breadth of humanity in the characters he'd encountered on this journey surely rivaled Ellis Island itself. There was, for instance, the beefy Swede named Frisk – one of his more jocular fellow passengers.

'Big Muddy,' Frisk said one evening, above deck, in a toast to the river. 'Too thick to drink, too thin to plow. Cheers, *compadre*.'

'*L'chaim*,' Silas reciprocated. He allowed himself a nip of the schnapps he carried in a small copper flask in case the evenings cooled. He was forced to acknowledge that this particular evening hadn't cooled much as of yet. But Silas found the gregarious Frisk easy to join.

According to Frisk, a general goods man like himself could find plenty of demand in Council Bluffs selling supplies to Mormons. He'd boarded in St Charles with his family, a good mule, and enough dry merchandise to get a respectable outfitting post up on its feet. Also, according to Frisk, they were all in mortal danger every moment they spent aboard the steamboat *Arcadia*.

'That's why it's an adventure,' he said, taking another long gulp from his much larger whiskey flask. 'Also what an educated man calls an irony.'

'Ah. Yes, I see.' Silas went against his better judgment and had another short sip of schnapps himself. 'An irony in what way?'

Frisk gestured toward the massive, churning paddle-wheel. 'Whatcha think turns that big ol' thing?'

'Steam?'

'You betcha, steam. From those great big boilers belowdecks. What makes the fire that heats those boilers? Wood. And plenty of it, believe you me.' Another gulp from the flask. 'Where do you think all that wood comes from?'

Silas thought carefully before answering, not wanting to foolishly mistake a complicated question for a simple one. 'Trees?'

'Trees!' Frisk bellowed, spreading his arms to indicate the many old oaks, maples, and elms lining the riverbank. 'Now tell me this, my young Hebrew friend: what else do those trees do, sooner or later?'

To this question, Silas found himself at a loss. He had another taste of schnapps to help him think. Again, just a small one. But he began to enjoy the sensation of liquid warmth spreading out from his belly to his limbs. He was already beginning to feel a bit looser in his joints.

'They fall in the water, that's what they do,' Frisk said. 'They fall in the water, sink down beneath the surface, and put holes in steamboats. Believe you me, even your best pilot can hit a tree snag.'

'Goodness,' Silas said. All of a sudden this voyage did seem more adventurous to him. He wouldn't have thought that were possible.

Frisk laughed, tipping his flask again. 'There's your irony. The steamboat runs up and down the river on trees. The river cuts the bank away. The trees fall in the river and sink the boat.'

Which was, to Silas Wasserman's lifelong chagrin, precisely what happened later that very evening, not long after the schnapps was – somehow – gone.

First, a sound like cannon fire.

Then a horrendous judder. A terrifying lurch from stem to stern.

Then came the rising chorus of gasps and screams as the ship's heavy timbers trembled, as Silas and his fellow voyagers were thrown from their feet to slide about the deck like so many tenpins.

When he did think back, Silas often would think: *perhaps*.

Perhaps if not for the effects of the alcohol he'd consumed. Or, perhaps, if he'd followed Rabbi Loew's dire instruction never to leave his cargo's immediate presence. Perhaps if he'd upheld any number of charges with greater dedication, he would have been able to perform the sacred duty required of him in the unthinkable event of just such a catastrophe:

To take his post in the *Arcadia*'s heavy-laden cargo hold.

To retrieve from his pocket the special object Rabbi Loew had crafted specially for him. A charm, of a kind – formed from a measure of the creature's own clay, mixed with a vial of Silas Wasserman's own blood. A magical *shem* for the water carrier alone, the only instrument capable of bringing the awakened creature to heel: the Shepherd Stone.

And, finally, to wrench open the crate marked *BOOKS* and decommission the terrible thing inside. It was a power vested in

only one human soul on God's earth. This was the responsibility
– the privilege! – Silas had accepted.

But by the time he'd gathered his wits, the great white *Arcadia*
had already listed starboard, her larboard paddle-wheel raining
muddy river water, gallons more of the same pouring into her holds
and over her rails.

Chaos. Panic. Humanity en masse. Even as he groped for the
nearest railing and struggled to regain his feet, Silas felt that he had
one of two choices: move along or be trampled flat. And though
he may have edited the details slightly in his eventual telegraph to
Rabbi Loew back home, the honest truth was this:

By the time he paused to consider the monster in the box
somewhere below him, Silas Wasserman had already clambered,
hatless, atop the upper cabins along with everyone else.

Crewmen and locals took them away from the foundering ship in
rowboats. By the time the last of the *Arcadia*'s passengers had been
ferried safely ashore, only her smokestacks, and a thin white sliver
of her pilot house, remained visible in the moonlight.

Silas did return at sunrise the following morning. He came, like
all the others, to see what could be done about the recovery of
property.

But all was lost to the river by then. To stand on the land and look
at the water, it was almost as if the *Arcadia* had never existed at all.

As he trudged away in shame, Silas overheard Jesper Frisk
speaking to a newspaperman on the bank. He couldn't help thinking
that, at least at a glance, the big Swede looked rather none the worse
for wear, despite his heavy losses – not least, his family's prospects
on the frontier.

'God as my witness, I tried to save her,' Frisk was telling the
man with the journal and pen. 'But the blasted stubborn beast
wouldn't budge. I'll tell you, pots and pans are one thing. But believe
you me: it would sicken any man to lose such a good mule.'

iii. Arcadia
A Cornfield in Kansas – Present Day

Randy James Bierbaum's last day alive was filled, right up until his
final moments, with elation.

Throughout that morning and afternoon, Randy enjoyed a seemingly relentless succession of exhilarating thoughts. Thoughts like: *Oh my god*, and *Yes! Yes! Yes!* and *This is unbelievable!*

And, on the heels of these: *Take THAT, Myra.*

'RJ,' a voice called. 'Look here.'

Randy made his way toward the stern-end of the dig site, mud and heavy silt sucking at his five-buckle overshoes. He came upon his kid brother, Dickie James Bierbaum: fifty-four years of age, covered in mud and smiles, standing shin-deep in a puddle alongside a handful of volunteers.

'Brandied cherries,' Dickie said, handing over a clear bottle stoppered with paraffin and cork. He followed this with a second bottle. 'And pickles!'

Un . . . be . . . lievable, Randy thought again. Somehow, miraculously, after all these decades, the cherries were still red. The pickles were still bright green. It was like holding Christmas in his hands.

Take that, Myra.

'This is making me hungry,' Dickie said. 'Anybody else?'

The volunteers reported levels of agreement ranging from *starving* to *You don't mean* that *stuff, right?*

Randy was hungry, too, but he couldn't bear the thought of leaving the site before dark. In fact, he didn't want the low autumn sun to set at all. For the past five years, Randy and Dickie Bierbaum of Kansas City – co-owners and operators of Bierbaum Refrigerated Trucking, Inc – had spent every spare minute away from their livelihoods in pursuit of a day just like today. Part of Randy was convinced that if he closed his eyes, even for a moment, it would all be gone.

'Bring me a cheeseburger and fries,' he said. 'I'll stay back and make sure the pumps don't quit.'

'That's dinner!' Dick shouted, projecting his voice over the constant drone and chug of the generators. Beaming, he slapped Randy on the back and slogged toward the rim of the excavation.

'Extra pickles,' Randy called after him, still gazing at the fine old bottles in his hands.

According to Randy Bierbaum's painstaking research, many dozens of commercial vessels had been lost on the Missouri River during the heyday of the great paddle steamers. Among these extinct behemoths, *Arcadia* had been more or less average in size: 180 feet long,

60 feet across the beam, with 30-foot wheels on either side. She'd been capable of carrying 200 tons of cargo, all of it bound for settlements west.

All of it now buried in an eighty-year-old Kansas farmer's cornfield.

This cornfield *had* been river, once upon a time. At least until the fickle Big Muddy cut itself a new channel and changed course, leaving *Arcadia*'s mysteries entombed under fifty feet of modern farmland. And while Randy and Dickie weren't the first treasure hunters to locate her bones, by God, they were the first to truly find her.

They'd spent a full two years convincing the grizzled old farmer to grant them permission to tear apart his field. They'd each spent every last dime of their personal savings – including insurance and retirement accounts – battling logistics and groundwater.

They'd coped with the weather, seasonable and unseasonable. They'd battled groundwater. They'd jostled with come-lately competitors. They'd battled groundwater. They'd endured countless minor setbacks, mocking naysayers, know-it-all experts, one extraordinarily expensive geographical miscalculation, and even sabotage. They'd battled groundwater.

Along the way, Randy's grown children all decided he'd gone batshit crazy and gradually stopped calling the house. His bride of thirty-five years had thrown up her hands and walked out on him (for their marrow-sucking tax accountant, no less).

Dickie, for his own part – never married – had sold his bass boat, his Road King, and finally his home, he'd been sleeping in Myra's former sewing room for a year. At least that's where he'd slept until they'd broken ground on the dig, at which point the two of them had taken to staying on site together in the single-wide trailer they'd hauled in for the purpose.

Through all of that and beyond, at last came the day – that glorious, shining September day – when their core auger first breached *Arcadia*'s hull, just as that old submerged oak snag had done in her prime.

And what treasures had waited for them inside!

Clothing. Footwear. Whiskey. Tools. Buttons made of wood, brass, and horn. Bolts of blue silk from China; crates of gold-rimmed china from France. All these items by the pound, and others, an improbable number of them undamaged. All perfectly preserved in the anaerobic mud for more than a century and a half.

In the past three weeks, Dick and Randy Bierbaum had uncovered, along with the lost *Arcadia* herself, enough pristine antebellum artifacts to fill a museum. Which so happened to be Dick and Randy Bierbaum's long-range plan.

But, for now, every thrilling minute carried a potential new discovery. And Randy had never had more fun in his life.

One of the last actions he completed in the short time left to him, after Dickie and the volunteer crew had cleared out, was to wrench open the latest crate and find a more-or-less solid block of mud inside.

The bottom must have broken out of this one, Randy surmised. He rinsed off the lid and tried to make out its faded markings in the sunlight. He found a legible *B* and rinsed some more, uncovering what he thought was a *K*.

Books, he thought, smiling to himself. They were probably goners, but you just never knew. This mud, they'd found time and again, was filled with surprises.

And because Randy James Bierbaum had already stooped to retrieve a margin trowel from a tool bag, he wasn't even looking when the mud opened its eyes.

IT'S ALIVE

ONE

Ben Middleton mistimed his post-lunch flatulence so that the odor had already begun to rise up around him well before the department printer had finished spitting out his pages. It was no place for a person to be standing. Naturally, the new girl from marketing chose that moment to pop around the corner and into the supply alcove.

'Oh, hey,' she said. She had a vaguely aquiline nose, the tiniest glint of a stud in one nostril, and the greatest crooked smile. Then her nose twitched. A slight frown crinkled her brow.

Ben leaped into his side of the conversation too quickly. 'Hey, how's it going? Settling in?' *Stop talking*, he thought. *Run.* 'Did Ajeet get all your graphics stuff installed?'

'He did, thanks. Thirty.'

'Sorry?'

'Ajeet told me you wondered how old I was. I figured you must be shy, so I'm telling you: I'm thirty.'

Note to self, Ben thought. *Murder Ajeet Mallipudi with bare hands.* Meanwhile, the way she was hanging around to chat confused him. And her expression now seemed at ease again. Maybe she really hadn't noticed anything unpleasant?

'Anabeth, right?' He'd set up all her new-hire accounts before she'd started. Anabeth Glass. 'Do you go by Ana, or Beth, or . . .'

'I prefer Anabeth, actually. Or Abe.'

'People call you Abe?'

'People I like. Which I guess is most people.'

'I'll call you Anabeth until I know I'm safe, then.'

'Ha. You can call me Abe.'

'I'm Ben.'

'Middleton, yeah. Ajeet said you set up my network account.'

'Did he.'

'Speaking of which, I think I forgot to lock my workstation when I left my desk. I'll come back. See you around, Ben.'

Another thing he liked about her smile: her eyes.

See ya, Abe, he started to say, but she was already half-gone. As she rounded the corner, Ben glimpsed her raising a hand. At first he thought she was waving goodbye to him. Then he realized that she was blocking her own nostrils with the back of her index finger. He was pretty sure he heard a light gasp.

Good God. *It wasn't me!* he wanted to call after her. *Somebody else must have been here first!*

Then he noticed that the printer had stopped whirring. All done.

Ben sighed, scooped his performance appraisal out of the paper tray, and continued on to his manager's office. What the hell, he thought. Might as well get it over with, as long as he was on a roll.

'Look, your work isn't the problem,' Corby McLaren said. 'We both know your ticket stats are rock solid, and people seem to like the way you carry yourself. You don't make them feel stupid like the others do.'

'Uh huh,' Ben said, only half-listening. He was thinking about Anabeth Glass and the fact that, at thirty years of age, she was fewer than ten years younger than him. That meant that he was still – at least for a little while longer – within the numeric decade of a person who struck him as cool and interesting. It was almost enough to cheer him up a little.

'Don't get me wrong. The other guys, they can fix a server.' McLaren, who was five years Ben's junior himself, seemed to wish that he didn't have to be the one explaining all this again. 'They could probably build their own space shuttle if they wanted to. The point is, they look down on everybody.'

'That's true.'

'It's not completely their fault. Life hasn't kicked any of them in the balls yet, not really. That's why simple human manners are beyond them.'

'If you say so.'

McLaren pointed with his pen. 'That's also why I need you to be more of a leader out there.'

'Because I've been kicked in the balls by life?'

'Because when you say things, they listen,' McLaren said. 'They look up to you.'

Ben laughed before he could stop himself. 'Corby, if you think any of those guys wants to be where I am when they're pushing forty, you're high.'

'I said they looked up to you. I didn't say they wanted to be you.'

'I guess you didn't.'

'Nobody in their right mind wants to *be* you.'

'Thanks, I get it.'

'I don't think you do,' McLaren said. 'That's my whole point. You keep on doing 1- or 2-level work, yet for the second quarter in a row, I've had to rate you as a 5. Why the heck is that? In your opinion.'

'Because you insist on ranking a five-person team 1 through 5?'

'It's not ranking, it's rating.'

'Not when you give us all a different number, it isn't.'

'Now, that comes straight from corporate.' Corby showed Ben his palms. 'Company mandate. My hands are tied. You know that.'

What did your boss rank you? Ben thought. But he only said, 'Sure, Corby. I know.'

'Then why?'

'Because I'm not being a good leader.'

Now it was McLaren's turn to laugh. 'You're not even being a good follower. You never turn in your time sheets. Each and every week I have to remind you to submit your activity reports. You come in late, you take long lunches, and I don't think I've heard you speak up at a staff meeting in six weeks. You even missed your quarterly review.'

'What are you talking about? I'm right here.'

'This meeting was scheduled for yesterday!'

'Oh.' After an awkward beat, Ben added, 'Sorry about that.'

Corby McLaren took a long, slow breath through the nose. 'Listen. I'm not saying I'm in love with the way things are right now. But you've been to the town hall meetings. You understand the challenges we're facing as a company these days.'

'Sure,' Ben lied. 'I get it.' The truth was, he'd worked here nearly two years and still didn't completely understand what the company did or made. Mostly he just reset people's passwords and made sure their email worked. It was a paycheck, and one he sorely needed, but that didn't make it any easier to pay attention to what all went on here.

'Let me bottom-line this for you.' McLaren pushed a piece of paper across the desk. 'In case you haven't been doing the math, you're basically hosed at this point. But if you can find a way to finish Q4 with a 1-rating, that'll average you out to 3.75 for the year, and I'll be able to go to bat for you with corporate. Anything less than a 1?'

McLaren held up his hands again, as if to indicate that Ben's fate would officially be out of them.

Ben nodded at the paper in front of him. 'What's this?'

'That's your growth plan.'

'My what?'

'Consider it a good-faith agreement,' McLaren said. 'Read it over, then sign at the bottom to indicate your understanding that, as of today's review, you're officially on notice. The requirements are spelled out in the bullet points.'

Ben pretended to read the bullet points. 'I see.'

'Again, this doesn't come from me – this is directly from corporate. But I have to tell you straight up, face-to-face, one grown man to another: we're not talking about the difference between riding the bench and starting varsity, here.'

'Figuratively speaking.'

McLaren extended an imploring grimace. 'Are you taking my meaning, Ben, or do I have to say it out loud?'

'Nope, I got it. In order to keep paying my bills, all I have to do is sign this piece of paper, then climb over four other guys until I'm a 1 and somebody else is a 5. Then, next quarter, the five of us do it all over again, making it easier for *you* guys to identify who gets it in the neck the next time layoffs come around.'

McLaren sighed. 'I suppose that's one way of looking at it.'

'Can I take this with me?' Ben picked up the sheet. 'I'd like my legal team to review the bullet points.'

'Oh, be my guest.' Sitting there on his side of the desk, Corby McLaren looked so defeated that Ben almost felt sorry for him. On the other hand: what a crock of horseshit.

As Ben rose to leave, Corby tilted his head wearily and said, 'I'm trying to help, you know. You really do seem to be your own worst enemy.'

'My ex-wife would agree with you one hundred percent,' Ben said. 'But don't forget the bright side.'

'What's that?'

'At least my work isn't the problem.'

*   *   *

'Ben,' a voice behind him called. 'Ben! Hey. Wait up.'

Ben looked over his shoulder to find Ajeet Mallipudi hustling toward him. He walked faster.

'Slow down. My legs are shorter than yours.'

'The answer is no.'

Ajeet pulled up alongside him. 'But I didn't even ask you anything.'

'It's still no. I don't want you nerds trampling all over my property all weekend.'

'But we want you to trample around with us.'

'Are you kidding? That's my best time to be away from you people.' Ben glanced at him. 'And I know you sold me out to Anabeth, by the way. Thanks a lot, Jeeter.'

'Who?'

'The new girl. From marketing.'

'You mean Abe? You're quite welcome. She's awesome.'

'How do you know she's awesome?'

'She joined our *Halo* team. We finally smoked those goofs at Facebook.' Ajeet nodded rapidly. 'She's designing us t-shirts.'

'I swear I'm living my life all wrong.'

'She's coming too, by the way.'

'What do you mean?'

'This weekend.'

Ben stopped walking. 'What. To your paintball thing?'

'She was totally and immediately down for it.'

'Seriously?'

'That is, if we *had* a place to do paintball.' Now puppy eyes.

It drove Ben crazy to find himself rethinking this all of a sudden. He had absolutely no business concerning himself with Anabeth Glass.

Shit.

'All right, fine,' he said. 'You can do it at my place. One condition.'

Ajeet pumped his fist. 'Name it, bossman.'

'First thing Monday, all you guys have to email McLaren and tell him in writing what a super team-building exercise this was. And how the whole thing was my idea.'

By four o'clock, Ben had a headache that started at the base of his skull, vined up around his ears, burrowed in through his temples, and attached itself to his eyeballs. At four fifty-nine, he packed up his stuff and endured a hero's farewell from Ajeet and his other workmates in First Floor IT. At seven minutes past five, he turned around and went all the way back to lock his workstation – one of McLaren's numerous bullet points. Finally, at five thirteen, he said goodnight to Gary at the security desk.

'You have a good night, Benjamin,' Gary said, then snapped his fingers. 'Almost forgot. There was somebody here asking for you.'

'Me?' Ben didn't mind stepping out of the stream of quitting-time foot traffic. He liked Gary, a retired EMT and former barman who had continued to work part-time into his seventies. Gary told great stories and could greet every person in the building by name. From memory. He said he liked the exercise. 'When was this?'

'Around two this afternoon,' Gary said. 'I tried to leave you a message, but your voice mail was full. Email too.'

Crap. Two more of McLaren's bullet points. 'Was her name Christine?'

'It was a him, and he wouldn't give me his name. I sent him packin'.'

'What did he look like?'

'Come on around, I'll show you.'

Ben stepped through the hinged counter into the control area. He looked over Gary's shoulder at the monitor bank. Gary pecked out a time code on his keyboard, twiddled the cue knob on the deck, then pointed to the lobby feed, which now displayed a frame of frozen video.

On screen, a young man stood on the other side of the desk, gesticulating to a three-hours-younger version of Gary. The stranger – probably mid-twenties, somewhere around Jeeter's age – wore white canvas sneakers, cuffed jeans, and a messenger bag cross-slung on one shoulder. His dark curly hair poked out from beneath a White Sox cap.

'Hmm,' Ben said.

'Friend of yours?'

'Nope.' He didn't mention to Gary that he'd seen this guy exactly three times in his life: once this morning, at Caribou Coffee; again at the sandwich place where he'd picked up a meatball sub for lunch; and once on this monitor right now.

'Didn't think so,' Gary said. 'He tried to leave some kind of package for you. Fat chance, buddy, that's what I told him. Not without a name and some ID. Besides, he seemed a little off to me.'

'Off like how?'

'Like kind of an asshole. Pardon my French.'

'That sounds about right today, actually.'

'And kind of jittery.'

Whatever. Ben was too tired to think about it. 'Maybe I'll see him at coffee in the morning.'

'What's that now?'

'Nothing.' He clapped Gary on the shoulder and headed along his way. 'Thanks again, Gare. You're a hero.'

'Fly low, fella.'

'I try.'

Ben pushed out through the revolving doors and into the crisp October evening. The days were getting shorter, midtown leaves starting to change, and he could taste the faintest hint of wood smoke on the breeze. He took deep breaths through the nose as he walked to his car, letting the autumn air clear out the inside of his head. He pressed on through the bustling main lot, cutting a diagonal line toward the farthest corner, feeling lighter with each step he took away from the building. Soon he became a lone figure crossing the asphalt.

By the time he reached his new car – a used Chevy Corsica with 189,000 miles on the odometer and an 'I ♥ My Granddogs' bumper sticker shaped like a chew bone on the trunk lid – Ben was thinking, *See, life isn't so bad.*

Then he noticed the note tucked under the driver's side windshield wiper:

YOUR LIFE IS IN DANGER.
(over)

Ben snatched the paper, which had been torn sloppily from a narrow-ruled legal pad. The handwriting was a hurried scrawl from a pen clearly running out of ink. He flipped the page over and read the second message on the back:

NOT A JOKE!
CALL 708-555-5108

Ben looked up and scanned the parking lot. He looked at the page again, front and back. To nobody in particular, he called out, 'You couldn't have fit all that on the same side?'

This time last season, Lance Baxter and Arnie Dillon had gone in together on a deluxe tree stand from Cabela's for the purpose of bow-hunting whitetail deer. The unit featured fold-out seating, a full 360-degree canopy in forest camo, integrated heating coils powered by a deep-cycle marine battery, and whisper-quiet cooling fans powered by the sun. They'd installed the whole magnificent shebang in a grove of old oak timber along a brushy creek bottom on Arnie's neighbor's land. It was a secluded, peaceful, off-the-track spot, which could be accessed any time of day simply by calling in sick to the nuclear power plant in Brownville, where Lance and Arnie had worked together for years.

Which was exactly what Lance and Arnie had done today – the kind of clear, glowing fall day made in God's own workshop for taking an October buck or, short of that, spending a weekday afternoon getting shitfaced up a tree.

For the latter task, they were well-provisioned. Lance had personally retrofitted the tree stand with a hinged floor panel that opened on a collapsible beer cooler. This year, Arnie had done him one better, inventing his own two-liter gravity system that dispensed rye whiskey with the turn of a thumbscrew.

So they weren't exactly at their sharpest when Lance almost shot the stranger.

'Hold hold hold!' Arnie hissed, gripping Lance's string hand a split second before Lance let fly.

At that same moment, what had sounded like a real bruiser of a buck crashing through the underbrush – a twelve-pointer easy, maybe better – turned out to be a man.

A large man.

A large man built like a Chiefs middle linebacker. Covered head to toe in mud. Flecked all over with leaves and twigs.

'Holy shit,' Lance breathed. Fingers trembling, heart pounding in his throat, he took a deep breath and lowered his brand-new compound bow. 'Holy shit, holy shit.'

Arnie gave a nervous chuckle, patting him on the arm. 'You're OK.'

'Holy shit, that was close.'

'Sure as hell sobered me up.'

From above, they watched the guy trudge out of the brush and plod into the small clearing beneath their tree. Right into their kill zone.

'That's some camo,' Arnie said.

Lance was still shaking all over. 'Boy, that was goddamned close.'

Arnie cupped his hands around his mouth and called to the ground. 'Hey, idiot! Private property! Wanna know how close you just came to getting your dumb ass killed?'

When the guy looked up at them, Lance's heart skipped a thud.

The mud-covered man had no face. Only a pair of bright, eerie, green eyes.

Arnie recoiled beside him, saying, 'What the sh—'

Before he could finish the thought, the mud-covered man lumbered over, hugged the ladder attached to their stand, and reared back with an almighty powerful heave. There came a bright, wrenching sound of metal on wood.

The next thing Lance knew, he and Arnie were falling. They hollered and grabbed each other all the way down, crashing to the forest floor in a splintering, tumbling, bone-rattling jumble.

The next few moments after that flickered past in a blur.

First, Lance regained consciousness in a rubble of planks, braces, and camouflage netting. He could smell the sharp tang of spilled whiskey. He could hear ruptured beer cans foaming into the leaf bed beneath him.

Next, he became aware of somebody screaming. He recognized that the *somebody* was Arnie Dillon, twenty feet away.

While Lance struggled to disentangle himself from the wreckage of their mangled hunting stand, he stared at his best bud, who was down on one knee, bow at the ready, an arrow nocked and drawn.

Over him loomed the mud man.

The mud man lurched forward. Arnie screamed again and let loose.

Lance heard the arrow whicker through the air and strike home with a heavy, wet-sounding *splud*. It was a kill shot, he could see that immediately; the arrow stuck out of the stranger's chest just off the center line. If Arnie hadn't drilled this crazy stranger bang through the heart, this crazy stranger didn't have one. That, Lance thought with a mixture of horror and pride, was just how good Arnie was with that bow of his, even sailing three sheets to the wind.

And now they were going to have a dead body to explain after all.

He was sort of surprised that the arrow hadn't ripped completely through the dude, though. Especially at such close range. He was even more surprised when the mystery man underneath all that mud didn't fall down. Or even stumble.

He's cranked out of his mind on something. It was the only explanation Lance could think of for the pure bull strength it must have taken to pull a whole damned tree stand out of a whole damned tree with nothing but a pair of arms, never mind the fact that the berserk sonofabitch was somehow still standing upright on two sturdy-looking legs.

But then the green-eyed mud man did something that no amount of drug-induced amplitude could have explained:

He sucked the arrow the rest of the way into his chest cavity.

Just like that.

Lance watched in disbelief as the exposed length of arrow shaft slowly shortened, finally disappearing with a moist smack, fletching and all.

Meanwhile, Arnie looked up at his attacker, his face twisted in panic. He struggled to nock another arrow.

But he wasn't nearly fast enough. In one barbaric, unstoppable motion, the stranger swept Arnie's bow aside, stooped, and took Arnie's head in both . . . hands? They were certainly hand-like appendages. But not like any human hands that Lance Baxter had ever seen. More like rock formations.

When they pressed together, Arnie Dillon's head split open in a pulpy *splurt* of brain and bone. Lance saw colors – a great mist of red, globs of gray, gleaming shards of white – as he watched his friend's skull collapse like an overripe pumpkin.

Arnie's dead body fell amidst the leaf litter, limp as a rag. Lance heard more screaming.

This time the voice was his own.

Then the mud man turned toward him.

Lance doubled his efforts to get himself the hell out of there. But his boot was trapped, and he was stuck fast. He could feel faint tremors in the ground beneath him as the mud man tromped his way.

Those sons of bitches, he thought bitterly. *They lied to us*. A few years ago, when the river flooded, and the power plant had to close, and the Nuclear Regulatory Commission had wandered around in spaceman suits every day for a month, everybody had sworn to high heaven that there hadn't been a leak. Full containment, no cause for alarm. Back to business, everybody.

But Lance Baxter was looking at the obvious proof to the contrary right in front of him: some kind of horrible, killer mud mutant, thundering closer by the moment.

The sons of bitches lied to us all!

With one final, terrified shriek, he pulled back with every last ounce of his strength, throwing all his body weight against his leg. There came a flash of blinding, white-hot pain as his ankle snapped inside his eight-inch Danner boot. He'd gotten these boots the same day he'd upgraded his bow. Even through the agony, he thought: *And I was worried about blisters*.

Then a dark shadow fell over everything. The god-awful, foul-smelling mud mutant stood over him, framed by fiery trees and dusky sky, blotting out the low red sun.

As the thing drew back its block-like fist, Lance noticed something odd protruding from the spot where a normal man's knuckles would have been. He had just enough time to identify the small object he spotted there: a HellRazor broadhead arrow tip, still attached to the shaft.

Somehow, impossibly, the arrowhead – its triple blades sharp enough to shave with – now stuck out of the mud man from an entirely different spot than where it had gone in. And pointing in the opposite direction, too.

Hey, Lance thought. *That's Arnie's.*

Then the blocky fist pistoned toward his face.

There was no telling what other things Lance might have thought, or believed, or eventually refuted to the authorities – not to mention his foreman at the nuke station – had the HellRazor not lived up to its legendary penetrating and lacerating capabilities on its way through his prefrontal cortex. But one fact remained, with or without Lance Baxter's ongoing input: Arnie Dillon always had sworn by the things.

TWO

The next time he needed to set aside his entire life to fulfill a generations-old family duty to protect a complete stranger from a supernatural kill monster, Reuben Wasserman thought, he wouldn't do it in a lime-green Dodge Challenger with black racing stripes.

It was impossible to go unnoticed in the thing, for one reason, which was at least half the point of owning a car like this in the first place. It was also the reason why Reuben was sitting in an Arby's parking lot, a full city block off-site, spying on a guy named Ben Middleton through a pair of high-powered binoculars. Corporate security at Middleton's workplace had rousted Reuben a second time after he'd been ejected from the building; the old-timer behind the front desk must have called out the golf cart patrol. Now they had the Challenger on their radar.

Which was fine. Reuben Wasserman didn't want any trouble. All he wanted, really, was to get this over with and go back home to his girlfriend, Claire; his parakeet, Van Damme; his Volcano vaporizer; and his MBA thesis, which he was set to defend in five short weeks.

If only he knew what the hell he was supposed to be doing, or how he was supposed to go about doing it.

Through the binocs, Reuben watched Middleton grab the note from under his windshield wiper. He watched Middleton flip the page over, look all around the parking lot, then holler something at the sky.

The guy had a fitting last name, Reuben thought. He wasn't skinny, wasn't fat, stood more or less average height. Had the kind of basic look about him that Claire would have called 'Goy 1.0.' Middleton with a capital Middle.

Rueben watched the way he crumpled the paper into a ball and tossed it into his car, as if a strange note warning him about his personal safety were no more or less irksome than a parking ticket. Then Middleton got in behind the wheel, backed out of his lone spot in the hinterlands, and headed for the exit.

Rueben lowered the binoculars. He looked unhopefully at his phone in the dash cradle. It continued not ringing. He watched Middleton turn out into the street, fart a gray cloud from his tailpipe, and bimble away.

Now what?

Reuben sighed and fired up the Challenger.

Eli would have known what to do. Eli wouldn't have wasted all this time following Middleton from a distance, trying to work up his nerve. You wouldn't have seen some beet-faced rent-a-cop chasing Eli around a parking lot in a golf cart.

Eli had been the first-born. He'd been older, tougher, calmer, and wiser. This was supposed to have been *his* job.

If I don't come home, promise me you'll take this seriously. That was what Eli had said to him, the night before he'd shipped out to the Gulf. *Promise me, Rubes.*

Of course Rueben had promised. More than a hundred and fifty years' worth of Wassermans had passed this idiotic responsibility down to their first-born sons, and not one of them had ever been called upon. Not one! Not since great-great-great-great-granddad Silas – the big schlemiel who'd cocked the whole thing up in the first place. Reuben hadn't really believed the old stories anyway, not since he'd been nine or so, and besides: of course his big bro would come home. This was Eli he'd been talking to.

Eli, who hadn't come home after all.

And so, all these years later, here was Rueben: in Omaha, Nebraska, of all places. Trying to remember if they'd said anything in Hebrew school about how many lengths you were supposed to stay back in a hot green muscle car when you were tailing a guy whose days, probably, were numbered anyway.

He hoped Claire was remembering to feed the bird.

'Oh – hey,' Christine said as she opened the front door. She'd either come in from a run or was heading out for one: trainers, leggings, a fitted zip-up, her hair pulled back in a colorful band. 'You just missed him.'

'Who, Tony?' Her new husband. 'That's OK. We're playing eighteen at the club tomorrow.'

Christine narrowed her eyes in a way that immediately made Ben wish he hadn't led off by provoking her. What was wrong with him? 'Now that you mention it, he took Charley to Guitar Center,' she said. 'They'll probably be gone for hours.'

'Ouch.'

'You started it.'

'You're right. I'm sorry.'

'Look, whatever. Tony's out of town until Sunday, for your information. And Charley's still not here.'

'That's OK. I came to talk to you, actually.'

'Did you lose your phone again?'

'Yes, but that's not why I dropped by.'

'Leaving the mystery of your unexpected visit as yet unexplained.'

Ben sighed. 'I wanted to chat parent-to-parent, that's all. Can I come in, or what?'

'I was just about to hop in the shower.' It was a cursory objection – something to say as she stepped back into the house, pulling the door open with her.

Ben rubbed his hands together as he entered the soaring, cinnamon-scented foyer of the Mr and Mrs Antonio and Christine Montecito household. 'Fell right into my trap,' he said. 'Phase One complete.'

'What's Phase Two? Borrow some money?'

'Wow. You're shooting to kill tonight.'

'Sorry. You bring it out of me.'

'I don't know why.'

'You never did,' she said, leading him toward the Queen Anne living room. 'Want anything to drink?'

'That's not very funny.'

'I meant like water,' she sighed. 'Or I can make tea. I think there's diet soda.'

'I'm good, but thank you.'

She plopped down on the sofa and crossed her leg over a knee, pointing the toe of one fluorescent running shoe toward an expensive-looking wingback chair. 'So.'

Ben eased himself into the chair, which propped him in an overly vertical, almost royal posture. He felt royally silly. 'Charley's fourteenth is coming up,' he said.

'That rings a bell, yes.'

'I thought of something you and the new hubby could get for him. It's 100 percent guaranteed to please.'

'What are *you* getting him?'

'That's the beauty. Your present would go perfectly with mine.'

'Well, I'm stumped.'

'Promise to hear me out?'

'Now you're making me nervous.'

'This rock-and-roll camp in Cleveland,' he said. 'It's all he talks about when he's at my place.'

Her face saddened almost immediately. 'I'm sure it is.'

'You know he was gutted to miss it. But they just announced a winter session. Between the holidays. Technically it's already full, but I know one of the guys on the board, and he said he'd make an excep—'

'Ben.'

'I know, I know. I haven't said a word to Charley about it, I swear. I keep telling him to get his grades up.'

'You're aware that we caught him ditching summer school?'

'He mentioned it, yeah.'

'Which he wouldn't have had to attend in the first place if . . .'

'If he were holding up his end of the deal. I know.' Ben nodded to indicate how much he understood. 'But this is something he's actually into, and it's a killer opportunity. Who knows? Maybe it'll help turn things around. Give him something to work toward.'

Absently, Christine grabbed a nearby throw pillow and put it in her lap.

'You could always think of it as my birthday present, too,' he offered. 'One-stop shopping.'

'Is this about him turning fourteen, or about you turning forty?'

'Jesus, Christine. Are you pissed at me about something in particular, or just generally?'

'I'm not angry with you about anything.'

'Then why are we already arguing about this? I sort of thought you'd agree with me.'

Her stepdaughter Francesca came into the room just then, decked in teen wear, popping out an earbud as she moved. 'Can I go to Markisha's?'

Christine shifted gears smoothly, smiling at the girl. 'Homework?'

'All finished.'

'Home by—'

'Ten. I know. Hi, Ben.'

Ben shook his head. 'Stepmothers. Am I right?'

She grinned. 'Bye, Ben.'

'Later, gator.'

'Have fun,' Christine said.

'Peace,' Frankie answered, popping the earbud back in and departing the room as breezily as she'd entered.

Ben looked at Christine. Christine looked back at him. Francesca's final word seemed to hang in the air between them: *Peace*.

Rueben sat under a tree down the street from the big brick house, wishing he'd chosen a different spot. Or that a different kind of tree had grown out of this one. Acorns kept falling, large ones and small ones, pinging off the Challenger's hood and the roof over his head. Lord only knew what they were doing to the paint job.

While he waited, he pulled out his laptop and downloaded the long-range digital shots he'd taken of the cute suburban mom-type Middleton had come to visit at this address.

It really was quite a house. Owned by somebody named Antonio Montecito, according to the county assessor's website. Reuben felt an energizing spark as another puzzle piece fell into place. He spent a few minutes on his phone, cross-checking the new photos against a Facebook page he'd already bookmarked. Then he consulted his notepad, where he'd scribbled the word *Affair?*

He crossed the word out and wrote a new word beneath it: *Ex-wife.*

Christine Montecito – formerly Middleton, maiden name Hubble – represented a branch on the other tree now dropping bothersome acorns all over Reuben's life: the family tree leading from Ben Middleton all the way back to a bloodthirsty frontier-era *meshugener* named William Wolcott.

So absorbed in this minor deductive triumph was Reuben that he almost didn't notice the teenage hottie pulling out of the driveway in a Subaru sportwagon. He pulled the bill of his cap down over his eyes and scooched down behind the wheel, not sure why he felt such a powerful urge to hide, feeling silly when the girl turned out of the driveway and drove off in the opposite direction. He could see her singing along to music inside the car, not an evident care in the world, least of all the strange car sitting under the oak tree in her rearview mirror. *Get a grip on yourself*, he thought.

Then he jumped inside his own skin at the sound of something hitting the car overhead. *Ping!*

Stupid acorns.

'Look, it's not just his grades.'

'What else, then?' Ben said. 'We both know he's not a bad . . .'

'You don't see the way he is around here,' Christine said. 'Disrespectful to me. A straight-up shit to Tony. And Tony tries to connect with him, believe me. He bends over backward.'

Ben didn't want to hear about Tony Montecito bending over backward. But he didn't want to fight, either. Anyway, he was intimately familiar with Charley's attitude toward all three of them these days. 'The kid's had a weird couple of years. And now he's made of zits and testosterone. It won't last forever.'

'I'm not so sure about that.'

'Trust me, I've been there.'

'That's not what I mean. There's more.'

'Lay it on me.'

Christine paused, as if she'd started down an unintended road and was uncertain whether to proceed or turn back. 'Promise you'll hear me out?'

'Now who's making who nervous?'

'It's Tony.'

'Who?'

She glared at him. 'That's not funny, goddammit.'

'Sorry, sorry. We were talking about Charley. I thought you were going to tell me you found a joint in his sock drawer or something.'

'I'd know how to deal with that. Plus I'd have a joint for later.'

'So what's going on with Mr Superdude, then?'

'Tony has an opportunity of his own,' she said. 'A career opportunity.'

'Good for him.'

'At your company.'

'I won't even ask if you're kidding.'

'That'll save time.'

Ben couldn't help chuckling. This news made perfect sense,

somehow. 'Your new husband is taking a job at the company that's about to fire me? Sure, why not?'

'Well, it's not . . . wait. What did you just say?'

'Nothing. So! Hubby's the new VP of Humiliating Ben Middleton, huh? Solid choice.'

'If he accepted the offer, he'd be your new chief financial officer.'

'That's the guy who decides when to lay people off, right?'

'Among other things,' she sighed. 'But it would mean he'd work in the head office.'

'Naturally.'

'Where your company's headquarters are located.'

'It's good and rubbed in now, thank you.'

She seemed to be watching him too closely. 'Which is in—'

'Hey, wait,' he said. 'My company's based in, like, Alabama or somewhere.'

Christine nodded slowly. 'Atlanta. Yes. That's why he's out of town, in fact.'

At last the penny dropped. Right to the bottom of Ben's stomach. 'You're talking about moving,' he said.

'I'm not supposed to be talking about it at all, yet. Nothing's official.'

'You're talking about moving a thousand miles away.'

'God only knows how Charley's going to react,' she said. 'He already hates me. I don't know how—'

'You're talking about moving a thousand miles away with Charley.'

Christine finally dropped her eyes, hugging the pillow a little closer. 'I've been wanting to speak to you about all this. But Tony hasn't even accepted the offer yet, and we're still—'

'What about *your* job?' Somewhere in this giant house, she had her own photography studio. Weddings and high school graduation portraits, mostly. The odd local band, corporate head shots for rising CFOs-in-waiting, that sort of thing. But she did her own personal work, too. She usually kept at least a few art prints rotating at a co-op downtown, and they'd always sold steadily. Once upon a time, Ben had done all her framing for her.

'I can do my stuff anywhere,' she said. 'Believe me, I know how big a deal this is. And I don't want us to end up in court again. That's absolutely the last thing I want.'

Ben was having trouble hearing her over the sudden seashell echo in his head.

'Say something,' she said.

'I don't think that would be wise.'

'Ben . . .'

He stood up from the couch. 'You're right. I should have called.'

'Look, don't just leave. You wanted to talk to me alone; you're here, we're alone. Let's just sit a minute and—'

'Seriously, Christine. If you want me to react to this right now, it's not going to go well.'

She caught up with him again at the front door. 'Can I ask you one thing at least?'

He stopped and waited, one foot already on the stoop.

'What are you getting Charley? For his birthday.'

'I was making him something.'

'What are you making him?'

Ben didn't feel like talking about it. He pushed out on to the stoop.

He was about to head down the front steps when he heard Christine say quietly: 'Are you making Charley a guitar?'

When he turned to look at her, she was standing in the doorway, one hand on the inside knob. It occurred to Ben that they were standing now in more or less the same position as when they'd started this visit. Back to square one, as usual. He didn't answer her question.

'I thought you sold off the workshop,' she said.

'Been buying a few things back.' He shrugged. 'Doing repairs on the side. No big deal.'

Ben didn't notice that her eyes were wet until she wiped them.

'He'll be floored,' she said.

He nodded. 'I know the feeling.'

Though Reuben may have been fulfilling his promise to his big brother now, he hadn't exactly kept up with the homework along the way. The most recent intel the Wasserman family had compiled more or less stopped where Eli had left off when he'd shipped out, leaving the past ten years of Ben Middleton's life something of a dark spot on the radar. But an afternoon on the Internet, along with $89 in background-check fees, had filled in a few of the blanks.

For example, Reuben had been able to find where Middleton lived and worked easily enough. The guy had what amounted, in this day and age, to a reclusive streak – no active social media accounts that Reuben could find – but Reuben had managed to Google up a few scattered personal photos related to a defunct business called MiddleTone Labs: Middleton sanding a piece of wood; Middleton at a soldering bench; Middleton standing with various tattooed degenerates who appeared to be happy customers.

There had been a personal bankruptcy five years ago. A DUI the year after that. Followed by divorce records filed the year after that. A tough patch for middle-aged Middleton.

And now this.

Reuben honestly felt sorry for the poor schlub. Not sorry enough to enjoy a single moment of this fool's errand, no, but sorry enough to see it through. He would, against every personal instinct, continue taking this seriously. Just as he'd promised Eli he'd do.

Meanwhile, Middleton emerged from the big brick house again, pausing on the front steps. He turned and said something to his ex. Reuben tossed his notepad into the passenger seat and put on his seatbelt. At least it was time to move again. Thank god.

When he looked up, however, he saw something unexpected in the street that seemed, in his judgment, like cause for immediate alarm:

Ben Middleton walking directly toward him.

Stalking, more like. Fists clenched at his sides.

'Oh, shit,' Reuben Wasserman said.

THREE

Ben pounded on the driver's-side window of the radioactive-green Dodge. 'Hey, asshole,' he barked.

Inside the car, the driver cowered behind the wheel, fumbling with his keys.

Ben knew that he should keep his volume down – it wouldn't do to make a scene in front of his new CFO's house – but the day had finally gotten the better of him. 'I see you in there.' *Pound pound pound.* 'Open up or prepare to be boarded.'

The driver's shoulders slumped. He pulled the brim of his Sox cap low over his eyes and gripped the wheel with both hands, as if pondering his next move.

Ben pounded on the glass one last time. The guy finally rolled the window down, looking sheepish. 'I guess you knew I was following you, huh?'

'Gee,' Ben said. 'I don't know how I ever remembered seeing this same car three times since this morning. Plus Gary showed me your picture.'

'Who?'

'Exactly.'

'I . . . huh?'

'Who the hell are you?'

'My name is Reuben Wasserman.' He reached across his body, extending his right hand through the open window. 'Wasserman means *water carrier.*'

'And Reuben means sandwich. What do you want?'

'Um, that's kind of a long story.' Wasserman retracted his unshaken hand. 'Do you think we could go someplace and talk?'

'I do not. And I turned your little note over to the police, by the way. They said it looked like a threat to them.'

'Wait – no, you didn't. I followed you all the way here.'

Ben gritted his teeth. 'Followed me why?'

'I realize this is a little strange. You don't know me at all, but if we could just . . .'

'You know what? Never mind. Scram, waterboy.'

Wasserman didn't seem to want to go on sitting there in his flashy hot rod, not scramming. Yet that was exactly what he appeared to be doing.

Ben felt like an idiot standing there. He supposed that he probably should call the police for real, which would have been easier if he knew where he'd misplaced his phone. It occurred to him that walking up to this car in the first place had been a terrible idea. How was he to have known that the owner wasn't the type to pull out a gun when confronted?

The truth: it wouldn't have mattered. He'd been guided by a single thought alone: *this son of a bitch followed me to the house where my son lives.* Now that the adrenaline had subsided, he found himself wondering how Corby McLaren might handle a situation like this.

'Let me bottom-line this for you,' he told Reuben Wasserman. 'If I see you or this car again, together or separately, I'm not sure what will happen. But I can't promise that I won't become unreasonable.'

Wasserman seemed to have reached the conclusion that he was not in immediate physical jeopardy. 'If you don't mind me asking, do random strangers warn you that your life is in danger very often?'

'You're the first in recent memory.'

An acorn bounced off the car's roof. Wasserman flinched at the sound of it. 'And you're really not curious enough to know why that's happening now to give me half an hour of your time some-where other than under this tree?'

Ben's head was spinning. He wanted very badly to be alone. And for this day to be over. 'I'm curious about lots of things,' he said. 'That's not the same as giving a shit.'

'You maybe sort of should on this one. Trust me.'

Ben glanced over his shoulder and saw that Christine had re-emerged from the house. She stood in her activewear between stately white columns, arms crossed, watching the whole exchange from the portico. When she saw that Ben had finally noticed her, she raised her palms as if to ask, *What's going on out here?*

Ben turned his attention back to the creepy little snoop who called himself Reuben Wasserman.

'It's, like, super important,' Wasserman said. 'I promise.'

Another acorn pelted the hood of the car.

Ben sighed.

Lexi Cortland couldn't remember the last time she'd crossed the north pasture without Lord Vader trying to kill her to death.

'I thought you said something exciting was supposed to happen,' Chip hollered, raising his voice above the growl of the ATV beneath them.

'Just wait,' she called over her shoulder. 'And keep your head on a swivel back there.'

Vader, their black Brangus bull, was 2,200 pounds of bad mood. He had great knotted shoulders, a villainous-looking neck hump, and balls the size of buttercup squash. Her dad would probably kill her if he knew that Lexi was out here playing matador on the four-wheeler again; on the other hand, he might think it was better than Chip trying to figure out how to unhook her bra through her flannel shirt. To be 100 percent honest, Lexi still hadn't decided which activity she preferred. She knew that scaring the ever-living crap out of Chip would be fun, though.

'It'd be a lot more exciting if I was the one driving this thing,' Chip yelled.

'You just wait,' she yelled back, jouncing over a series of ruts. Wild sage and brome grass whipped at their jeans. She sort of wished he'd put his hands back on her hips like before, but Chip had decided he was too manly for that, apparently. Ha.

Meanwhile, Lord Vader was nowhere to be seen. The sun had already dipped below the western tree line, setting the horizon afire, and it would be full dark soon. The rest of the cattle were grazing the bottoms at this hour, the cows all getting drinks from the river with their fall calves, but Vader rarely left the pasture. Which left their arena wide open, which made this a perfect time to put on a show for Chip. But the KingQuad had a busted headlight, so it was also getting to be a little bit dangerous.

Lexi goosed the ATV up to the top of the next rise and idled there, scanning the pasture in the dying light. Where the heck *was* the grumpy hunk of beef?

She felt a hand slide around her waist and smiled to herself. Then another hand patted her on the shoulder. In her ear, Chip said, 'What's that?'

Lexi looked down his arm, following his pointer finger to a dark shape in the grass a hundred yards away. Her heart sank immediately. *Oh, no*, she thought. *Surely not.*

She cranked the handlebars and thumbed the throttle lever, pointing the KingQuad down the other side of the hill. At the sudden lurch, Chip grabbed on to her waist with both hands. Lexi smiled again, thinking: *That's more like it, tough guy.*

When they reached the spot, she saw that her immediate first thought had been correct: Lord Vader, the great and terrible ruler of the north pasture, had finally kicked the bucket. It was amazing, unexpected, and a little bit sad. Lexi hadn't thought she'd ever see the day.

But something looked wrong.

She killed the motor and climbed off the four-wheeler. The tangy, vaguely sickening smell of butchered meat touched her nostrils as she neared Vader's motionless form. When she got there, it took a few moments of gawking in the dusk, listening to the sound of buzzing flies, before she understood what she was seeing:

Vader's head was gone.

Completely.

Like, not there anymore.

The grass all around was matted with syrupy bull blood. In this light, the blood looked almost as black as Vader himself. Lexi Cortland still half-believed that her senses were playing some kind of trick on her. Because their old bull's neck had been a foot thick if it was an inch, with muscles like bridge cables. And something, somehow, had torn his head clean off.

Not cut, not sawn: torn. And not clean off, actually.

Not the least little bit clean.

'Oh, wow,' Chip said at her side. 'I guess this is kind of exciting after all.'

'Chip,' she said. 'What is this?'

'It looks like a dead cow.'

'Bull,' Lexi said.

'No, really,' Chip said. 'It looks like a dead—'

She punched his arm. 'Don't joke around. This is . . . what the heck is this?'

Chip squeezed her shoulder, then left her, following a trampled path in the grass. Ten feet away, he stopped abruptly. 'Here it is.'

Lexi turned and looked. The path continued on past the spot where Chip stood, a narrow matted line extending all the way across the pasture, like a deer trail. 'Here's what?' she called.

Chip stooped, grunted, then straightened again, obviously lifting something heavy.

'Wait,' Lexi said. 'I don't want to—'

But Chip had already turned and raised Vader's massive, horn-less, disembodied head up by the ears. A bunch more goopy blood poured from the ragged neck stump, spattering the grass in front of him. Probably his boots, too. He yelped and jumped back, dropping the head.

'Ugh,' Lexi said, feeling her gorge rising in her throat. She swallowed hard, turning back to poor Vader's headless carcass.

No help for her there. She bent at the waist, hands on her knees, trying to breathe without smelling anything. In another few moments, she felt Chip's warm hand on her back, patting gently.

'You OK?'

'I don't know.' She wished she could talk without opening her mouth. She was starting to feel dizzy. What on earth had trampled that path through the grass?

A sudden flash of light illuminated a glimpse of raw glistening meat and torn gristle three feet in front of her face. She saw a round white eye in the midst of it all: a cross-section of Vader's severed spinal column. Some part of her brain simultaneously identified the electronic shutter sound of Chip's camera phone.

'Good God,' she said, straightening quickly. She looked at the darkening sky and gulped the fresher air above her head. 'Chip, what could have done this?'

'Dude, I have no idea.' Chip shook his head, his face uplit from below. He was already working at his touch-screen with his thumbs. 'But it's for sure gonna get me followed on Instagram.'

The quickest way home was the interstate. The quickest way to the interstate from Christine's house led back past the office. Near to the office was a sports bar called Small's Balls, which Ben had never personally entered, but where other people from work congregated regularly. If he turned up murdered tomorrow, he reasoned, it might give the cops a leg up if at least a few folks remembered seeing him with his killer the prior evening.

Plus he hadn't eaten yet.

'You don't drink beer?' Wasserman asked him after the waiter left their booth, raising his voice enough to be heard over the boisterous Thursday night crowd.

'Among other things,' Ben answered.

'How come?'

'None of your business.'

Wasserman looked at the pitcher of Goose Island he'd just ordered as if wondering what he was supposed to do with all of it.

'Oh.'

'Look, man, I think you probably need some help,' Ben said. 'And I'm not a completely unsympathetic person. But you and I are not teammates.' He gestured at the major league play-off game

duplicated on screens everywhere around them, indicating people
who were teammates. 'And we're definitely not going to be drinking
buddies. So start over at the beginning. What's a grommel?'

'Golem,' Wasserman said.

'Big *Lord of the Rings* fan, huh?'

'No. That's Gollum.'

Ben felt his headache coming back. And he was starting to feel
shaky. He sipped his ice water, wishing his burger would hurry up
and arrive.

'A golem is an artificial man,' Wasserman said. 'Created by magic
to serve a master.'

'Uh huh.'

'I know how it sounds. I didn't believe it, either.' Wasserman
shrugged. 'Then again, some say that Adam was technically a golem.
At least until the big guy gave him a soul.'

'Who?'

'Adam,' Wasserman repeated. 'Mr Eve?'

'Oh,' Ben said. 'That Adam.'

'I'm not on medication, if that's what you're wondering.'

'That's exactly what I'm worried about, actually.'

Wasserman hauled his shoulder bag up into his lap and started
unfastening the buckles. 'In that case, I'm not sure this will make
you feel any better. But if I'm crazy, then so was my brother, my
father, my grandfather, and his grandfather, all the way back to—'

'Whoa.' Ben held up a palm like a traffic cop, hearing Gary's
voice in his head: *He tried to leave some kind of package for you.*
'What are you doing?'

'I want to show you something.'

'Whatever it is, I don't want to see it.'

Wasserman ignored him, pulling some kind of thick, banded folio
out of the bag. Like a scrapbook. Or a photo album. He dropped
the book on the table between them with a heavy thud.

Ben said, 'What's this?'

'That's the Middleton file.'

'The *what* now?'

'Well, your part of it, anyway. See for yourself,' Wasserman said.
'For the record, most of the stuff in there was gathered way before
the book came to me. I guess all of it, really.'

Ben looked at Reuben Wasserman for a long time.

Finally, against his better judgment, he sat forward just enough to slip the elastic strap free of the album's leather cover. He leafed through the first several pages, felt springs pop loose somewhere in the gears of his brain, and then sat there, staring. A strange sensation rose in his chest.

He looked at Wasserman again. Back at the book.

'Oh my gosh,' a voice behind him said. 'Is that *you*?'

Ben glanced over his shoulder to see Anabeth Glass, still in her work outfit, now holding a beer in each hand. In this context, it took him a moment to recognize her. She laughed and craned forward, clearly delighted to get a closer look at the photograph he'd landed upon: a grainy, black-and-white portrait of his own Little League baseball team.

This picture had run in Ben's hometown newspaper just over a quarter century ago. Alongside the team photo was an action sidebar of a game-tying home run caught in mid-swing. The caption below the batter's box read: *Ben Middleton, age 11*. He remembered the moment well. It had been his only hit of the season.

'Look at you go,' said Anabeth, beaming. 'I'll bet those middle school *chicas* didn't stand a chance, did they?'

Ben felt as though he'd woken up in an unfamiliar room. He couldn't seem to gather his thoughts. 'What's happening?'

It was probably natural enough for Anabeth to assume that the question was directed toward her. She tossed her head toward a far-corner booth and said, 'Team meeting. We're battling Google tomorrow night. I believe that with the correct mission planning we stand an excellent chance of mowing their doodle-making asses down systematically.'

Ben followed her gesture, spotting a few familiar faces crowded together: Ajeet Mallipudi, Gordon Frerking, Devon Miller, and Jeremy Zwart, the other four members of the First Floor IT crew. Ajeet grinned and waved. The others raised their beers.

'Who's your friend?' Anabeth said.

Reuben Wasserman piped up, handling his own introduction. 'The last name means *water carrier*.'

'Hi, Reuben. Anabeth Glass. I guess my last name means *water carrier*, too. Or, you know,' she raised her hands an inch, 'beer.'

'Pleased to meet you, Anabeth.'

'Call me Abe.'

'I'm not feeling well,' Ben said. He pushed out of his side of the booth, jostling Anabeth unintentionally as he made a beeline toward the exit. His hunger had turned suddenly to nausea, the burger he'd ordered now forgotten.

Halfway to the doors, he turned around and went straight back to the booth. Anabeth stood where he'd left her. She looked baffled, her wrists and forearms still wet from sloshed-over beer.

Reuben Wasserman brightened. 'Hey! You came back.'

Ben ignored him. He grabbed a wad of napkins from the table dispenser, dabbed Abe's wrists lightly, and said, 'Sorry about that. Knock 'em dead tomorrow.'

Then he grabbed the so-called Middleton file from the table and took it the hell with him.

FOUR

On Friday morning, Reuben camped out at Caribou Coffee until past nine o'clock. He didn't hold out much hope that Middleton would stick to his usual routine – not after the way they'd parted company the previous evening – and he didn't honestly know what he planned to do even if Middleton did appear on schedule. All Reuben knew for certain was that he hadn't yet fulfilled his promise to Eli.

Screw that noise, a voice inside his head insisted. *You told this loser everything he needs to know. Warning delivered! If you start driving now, you'll be back in Hyde Park by dinnertime.*

But another voice – Eli's voice, it sounded like to Reuben – said: *You know he still doesn't believe you.* Which led Reuben Wasserman to wonder:

What had he really promised in the first place?

While he pondered that question, Reuben drank six Americanos and scoured the online editions of every newspaper he could find between here and Kansas City.

Two news items jumped off the screen at him.

The first story concerned the brutal murder of two deer hunters near the town of Brownville, Nebraska. The strange killing of Lance

Baxter and Arnie Dillon was a matter of ongoing coverage by the *Omaha World-Herald* and the *Lincoln Journal Star*, as well as the local network television affiliates. More than one reporter had landed upon the word 'barbaric' to describe the violence that had befallen the hunters, though investigating authorities so far had announced no suspects, no leads, and, indeed, no official mechanism of death.

But then, how could they?

The second item was a small story from the *Nebraska City News-Press* about mutilated livestock on a local farm. Reuben might not have noticed this one at all if not for the eye-catching adjacent banner ad for a rural go-go bar called Cow Patty's, which had drawn his eye. That was probably an example of irony.

He plotted the locations of all three incidents on his phone's GPS map, beginning with the killing of Randy James Bierbaum – the treasure hunter found with a crushed trachea at the *Arcadia* dig site three days ago – and ending with the heaping pile of steak tartare in a pasture just north of a small farming town called Peru. In connecting these dots, the GPS map plotted a line that followed the Missouri River valley north, jogged northwest at the end, and finally pointed, like a finger, directly toward Ben Middleton's house.

If Reuben's calculations were accurate, the creature appeared to be covering approximately forty-eight miles every twenty-four hours. This worked out to slightly less than the average walking speed of an adult human male, if that man walked continuously, around the clock, never stopping.

Which meant that the creature – barring unexpected complications, such as a nuclear strike, or perhaps a lucky meteor – ought to be arriving in their lives any day now.

Presuming, of course, that the creature didn't know how to run.

On Friday morning, Ben woke up alone in the childhood home he'd inherited: a creaky, rambling farmhouse on fifteen wooded acres overlooking the Platte River valley.

He called in sick to work. While the coffee brewed, he put out some food and a pan of fresh water for the dozen-odd feral cats that lived in the timber. Reuben Wasserman's scrapbook remained on the scarred kitchen table where Ben had left it the previous night. He pretended he didn't see it there.

He pulled on a fleece, poured a cup of coffee, and sat outside on the porch for a while, steam rolling from the mouth of the heavy white mug in the chilly morning air. It had been ages since he'd risen with his head so full of noise. Or with such a powerful urge to trade in the java for something strong enough to quiet down the racket in his brain.

Instead, he watched a whitetail doe and three spotted fawns grazing a stand of fiery red sumac along the shelterbelt. After the deer bounded away, he tightened his focus to a woolly bear caterpillar inching its way along the porch railing. The caterpillar's fuzzy bands of brown and black undulated purposefully, presumably unhindered by inner turmoil. Ben thought about what his mother used to say: *when the brown bands are narrow like that, get ready for a tough winter.* He'd read somewhere that the brown part of a woolly bear caterpillar didn't actually predict anything at all – that this was just some old chestnut the farmers pulled out when the days started getting shorter. Still, he made a mental note to make sure that he had plenty of gas on hand for the tractor and the snow blower.

When the last of his coffee had gone cold, Ben dumped the dregs into the bushes and went back inside. Wasserman's scrapbook still hadn't moved from the kitchen table. Part of him had begun to hope that he'd dreamed the events of the previous day, but there the evidence waited for him: leather-bound, banded shut, chock-full of psychosis.

Right?

Still thinking about the caterpillar on the porch, Ben filled a Thermos bottle with coffee, traded the fleece for a Carhartt work jacket, and went out to the workshop to put in a few hours of honest work on Charley's birthday present.

Contemplating that steady blue line on the GPS map turned out to be more than Reuben could bear sitting still. So he packed up, paid up, emptied about a gallon of used coffee into a men's room urinal, and took the Challenger back to Middleton's office. He trolled the parking lot for half an hour, unmolested by security, searching for Middleton's turd-mobile.

No dice.

Which made it time to do what Reuben ultimately had put off

doing last night, given Middleton's demeanor when he'd stormed out of the sports bar. One final, last-ditch effort:

A house call.

Just as Reuben made it onto I-80, heading roughly southwest out of town, his phone rang in the dash cradle. His heart rose for a moment, buoyed on the hope that Middleton had finally come to his senses. Then he noticed the caller ID on the stereo read-out. He thumbed the call button and spoke to the empty car.

'Morning, sweetie. How'd you sleep?'

'Where are you?' Claire said. Her voice – normally one of the warmest things about her – came over the Challenger's Bluetooth system like shards of ice.

Reuben didn't understand her tone. 'Still in Omaha, unfortunately.'

'Is that a fact?'

'I know, I know,' he said. 'I'm really sorry. I meant to call last night, but yesterday was brutal, and I was pretty well toasted by the time I finally—'

'Uh huh. How's your uncle doing?'

'Not great,' he said, doing his best to sound natural. He didn't want to get too fancy. He was a business student, not a thespian. 'He took a turn yesterday. I'm on my way back to the hospital now. Between you and me, I don't think he's going to last through the weeken—'

'You don't have an uncle in Omaha.'

Stab of panic. Sudden, deafening roar of blood in his ears.

Reuben gripped the wheel and said, 'What?'

'Your sister just called your apartment, looking for you,' Claire said. 'I told her where you've been all week. Wait, let me correct that: I told her where you told *me* you've been all week. And why you claimed to be there, too.'

Oh, no.

Shit.

'Claire . . .'

'She was fundamentally confused by that information, let me assure you.'

'Claire, listen—'

'Oh, I'm listening,' Claire said. 'Because I'm absolutely dying to hear you explain this.'

A car horn blared just off his port side, informing Reuben that he'd drifted a few inches into the passing lane without realizing it. He overcorrected, swerving abruptly back to his own side of the dividing line, tires moaning against the roadway. The other driver kept on the horn all the way past him, and Reuben thought: *Up yours, cock-knocker.*

Only he must accidentally have said it aloud, because Claire's response surrounded him like an armed posse: '*What* did you just say to me?'

'Not you, sorry, not you.' Reuben had never heard her sound so pissed. 'Hang on a sec.'

He pulled to the shoulder and braked, decelerating over the rumble bars, his tailbone vibrating in unison with the rearview mirror. He piloted the Challenger to a short, skidding halt through the grit scattered along the edge of the pavement.

Shit shit shit.

He took a shaky breath and started over. 'Claire, listen to me. You're totally right. I haven't been telling you the truth, and I can't even imagine what you must be thinking. But I promise there's no possible way you're anywhere close to being right.'

'That's supposed to reassure me?'

'There *is* an explanation. I swear.'

'Great, I'm still listening. For about the next ten seconds.'

An eighteen-wheeler roared past, buffeting him with its slip-stream, rocking the Challenger on its springs. He didn't know what to say.

'Somebody here needs me. That's the only way I know how to put it.'

'Ha!' Claire said. 'What's her name?'

'Ben.'

'I see. Even better.'

'It's not like that,' Reuben insisted. 'At all.'

'Then what's it like? By all means, fill me in.'

'I . . .' Reuben paused as another big rig pummeled him with wind and noise. 'I just don't know how to explain this over the phone, honey. But the second I get home we'll sit down, just the two of us, and I'll tell you every single thing. OK?'

'Are you sure?'

'Absolutely. Every last detail.'

'In that case,' she said, 'I won't be here when you arrive.'

'Claire, no, please,' Reuben said. He could feel his heart racing. 'Just wai—'

'Feed your own stupid bird,' she said.

The Bluetooth system beeped at him, and Claire's voice disappeared. The loneliest, emptiest, most abandoned-sounding dial tone in the world filled the car.

Reuben put his head back against the seat and closed his eyes. After a moment, he reached out and killed the tone.

Five seconds later, the phone rang again. Reuben sat up like a man electrocuted, jamming this thumb painfully while jabbing at the call button. 'Claire, thank god. OK. Just give me one chance to—'

'Ruby, I'm so sorry!' a completely different voice said. 'I had no idea. I just blabbed without thinking.'

Reuben sighed heavily, sagged back into the seat, and closed his eyes again. 'Hundred percent not your fault, sis. Don't worry about it.'

Long silence.

Then, tentatively, his kid sister Sara said, 'Are you telling me this means there really is a monster?'

Once upon a time, Martin Middleton – Ben's father – had earned his living as an electrical engineer for a mid-sized architectural firm. On his fortieth birthday, he'd cashed his 401(k) and taken an unexcused absence from his family, striking out to 'follow his bliss' via unencumbered travel and nonspecific adventure. Marty Middleton's parting gift to his young son, then eight years old, had been a do-it-yourself ham radio kit and a three-line note: *If you can build this, you'll always be able to reach me. I'll see you again. Dad.*

Both these claims had turned out to be spectacularly untrue, of course, as bliss-following Martin had managed to kill himself three weeks later while hang-gliding somewhere in New Zealand. He hadn't been a bad guy at heart, Ben's mother always said – just the last in a long line of scoundrels, screw-ups, and general shmuckos that had comprised the male of the Middleton species for generations. *But that was before you came along,* she'd told Ben. Even as a kid he'd been skeptical of that. But he'd gone ahead and built that radio anyway.

Meanwhile, Susan Middleton had carried on doing what she'd been doing before single motherhood had landed upon her newly widowed shoulders: being a well-liked high school music teacher.

She performed part-time as a cellist with the Omaha Symphony Orchestra and gave private lessons on the side, teaching out of the house for extra cash on her spare evenings and weekends. It had been entirely from his mother that Ben had inherited his love of music, if precious little native talent for producing it himself.

Years after his parents' separate but equally untimely deaths, Ben had combined his maternally bred passion with his paternally forfeited trade skills – along with some unexpected woodworking Zen he'd first discovered in high school shop class – to gradually teach himself the finer points of luthiery and signal routing, eventually launching a dream of his own. He'd called it MiddleTone Labs: a boutique custom shop specializing in solid-body electric guitars, hand-wired effects pedals, and vintage-style tube amplifiers, all of Ben's personal design.

The company had looked like an energizing success that somehow matured into a towering failure, ultimately crashing to pieces like a middle-aged electrical engineer in a cut-rate hang-glider. It never occurred to Ben to question where he'd inherited his business sense.

He'd moved what little remained of MiddleTone headquarters out to the sturdy old barn that still stood on this acreage, even though it had been decades since a Middleton had farmed the surrounding land. There he made the most of his fake sick day, trying his best to limit his thoughts strictly to the work at hand.

Ben finally came in around mid-afternoon, after he'd grown too hungry and distracted to carry on without slicing off fingers – or worse, screwing up the neck pocket on Charley's guitar. He made himself a sandwich and sat down with Reuben Wasserman's scrapbook again.

It began with a family tree, pasted right inside the cover on old-looking onionskin paper. Perched at the top: Ben's great, great, great, great grandfather, a genuine Wild West marauder named William Wolcott. Here, at least, was something Ben could say for his father: Marty Middleton may have been a self-absorbed fool. But at least he hadn't been a slobbering, kill-crazy maniac.

He'd come from one, though.

It was an old gallows joke in the Middleton family that the men had all been sired by an outlaw. Privately, Ben often had wondered if this tired old claim were actually true, or just an offhanded way of writing off decades of idiotic behavior. But according to history books, the man himself had been real enough. In his day, William – who had gone by the storybook-sounding handle 'Bloody Bill' – had murdered women and children and burned at least one small prairie town to the ground. And here again was the name. In hand-scripted ink. Heading up the genealogy chart Reuben Wasserman and his family had painstakingly compiled, tracing its ever-thinning branches all the way down to Ben himself. If the Middletons had been a monarchy, it occurred to him now, it would be just about time to sell off the throne.

As for the rest of the material collected within, Ben's own personal papers weren't as comprehensive. Included in these pages was every piece of public information about his first twenty-five-odd years a diligent person would be able to find, all of it dug up and slipped under plastic by complete strangers. His birth notice. His wedding announcement. Even his high school sports stats. He found a string of local newspaper articles about the highway crash that had taken his mom six months before Charley had been born – stories so painful that Ben had declined saving any of them for himself.

Curiously, things more or less dried up there. Ben couldn't help thinking that if anyone were to use this scrapbook, as it stood, as the definitive guide to Benjamin Allen Middleton, they'd be forced to imagine a promising, young(ish) man with his prime years still ahead of him. So it was good for a few laughs, at least.

But Ben still didn't know what to do about any of it.

He didn't know how or why this crazy Wasserman clan had developed their breathtaking obsession with the Middletons. He didn't know how the woman he still loved could possibly consider – even after all he'd put her through – moving their teenage son to the other side of the country.

He didn't know why he hadn't already reported Wasserman to the police. He didn't know what he was going to do for work after the end of the quarter. He didn't believe for a single, solitary moment that a 150-year-old mud monster was coming to kill him . . .

. . . and he didn't know what was making the faint noise he heard coming from somewhere inside the house.

FIVE

A nswer: his lost cell phone.

It had fallen down between the sofa cushions. Ben fished the phone out with his fingertips, looked at the caller ID, sighed, and put the phone to his ear. 'Hey, Jeeter.'

'Hi Ben,' Ajeet Mallipudi answered, sounding chipper as usual. 'How are you feeling?'

'I'm fine,' Ben said. 'Just a stomach thing, no big deal. Thanks for checking up on me.'

'Oh sure, sure,' Ajeet said. 'We missed you at work. Are you sure you're OK?'

'Feeling better already.'

'That's great. Cool.'

Ben sensed that there was more coming, so he waited.

After a pause, Ajeet said: 'So we can still have paintball at your place tomorrow?'

SIX

E *nough is enough*, Reuben Wasserman thought. He told himself that Eli would have understood. It probably wasn't true, but honestly . . . did it really matter?

Eli was gone. And, look, Middleton wasn't going to listen to him until it was too late, anyway. He could have stayed home and sent an email for all the progress he'd made. Meanwhile, his own life was falling apart at the seams.

It was time to go home.

So he checked himself out of the Settle Inn, set the cruise control five miles an hour above the posted speed limit, and aimed the Challenger back toward Chicago, where he belonged. Every so often, maybe once per hour, he replayed Claire's latest message over the car's sound system. It must have come in while he'd been staring down his own reflection in the bathroom mirror back at the motel.

I lost my temper. I'm sorry. Her voice sounded damp and vaguely swollen, as if she'd been crying. It killed Reuben to know that it was all his fault she sounded this way. And here she was, the one apologizing. *If you come home right now, I promise I'll listen. I'll come back to your apartment after work and wait for you there. But only today. So . . . please come home.* A long pause. *This is Claire.*

Something about that parting attribution overfilled Reuben's heart with affection and remorse. Of course it was Claire. Who else? Sweet, unpresumptuous Claire. He didn't deserve her.

And so he drove, stopping only for fuel and coffee, clocking time and distance in his head all the way. He lost an hour to road construction around the Quad Cities, finally nosing his way across the Mississippi River much later than planned. He opened up the Challenger's big hemi V8 after that, gobbling up gas and gambling with the state patrol as he tracked imaginary lines across the collar of Illinois with his Michelins. He hit late traffic coming into Joliet, by which time his joints had grown stiff, his bladder full. Reuben pressed on, mile by creeping mile, ignoring his mounting discomfort as he plowed through the 'burbs, into the heart of the South Side.

It was just after eight o'clock by the time he finally pulled into his parking spot behind the three-flat apartment building where he lived, on a leafy Hyde Park side street, not far from campus. Reuben could smell cooking food as he lugged his suitcase up the creaky wooden staircase to his door. Burning food, more accurately, but what did that matter? It was heaven to be home.

And Claire was here, just like she'd promised. She was attempting to prepare them a meal. Reuben Wasserman was damn well going to make all of this up to her, just like *he'd* promised.

'It's me,' he called on his way through the door. 'Claire?'

'I'm right here,' she said.

Sultry voice. Lights low in the apartment. Two very promising signs.

She was sitting with a glass of red wine at the dinette table off the kitchen. And she was wearing his favorite of her work outfits, too: the charcoal pencil skirt, the white blouse with the high collar, the black kitten heels. As an added bonus, she was wearing these things in his very favorite configuration of all: blouse untucked, top button open, heels kicked aside. Hair down. He thought of it as her 'in for the evening' look.

Reuben dumped his bags by the door and tossed his keys in the dish and went straight to her. He ignored the pain in his straining bladder. He didn't even bother to close the door behind him.

'God, honey, I'm so sorry,' he said. 'You look fantastic. It smells great in here. Thank you. Thank you for giving me this chance.'

She didn't rise to meet him, but that was OK. Reuben fully expected he'd have to work for this. Fair was fair.

But as he approached her, the track lighting in the apartment came up, as if on cue. The effect was confusing. Like he'd walked into a set on a theater stage.

In the climbing illumination, Reuben noticed several things at once, in no particular order. Each detail seemed to overlap the others in a series of snapshots, a disorienting collage:

Claire's eyes were deeply bloodshot. Her face looked slick, glistening with nasal discharge and tears.

The wine was a prop. She was handcuffed to the arms of the chair.

The note he'd heard in her voice was not seduction. It was terror.

Van Damme's cage was empty.

'Ah. You made it. Wonderful,' a strange voice behind him said. 'We've been waiting for hours. It's almost time to eat.'

Reuben spun around as a man stepped out from behind the open apartment door. The man was very tall and very slender. He wore a dark, ill-fitting suit and black leather gloves. The man had perhaps the most alarming face Reuben had personally ever seen on another human being.

'My name is Malcom,' this man said, smiling a smile that made Reuben's testicles want to crawl up into his body and not come out again. 'Malcom Frost. How do you do?'

'I . . .' Reuben started. But that was all he could come up with.

Malcom Frost stood perhaps six and a half feet tall. If his suit had been soaking wet, he might have weighed 160 pounds. His face and scalp were a webbed mass of scar tissue topped by patchy wisps of white-blond hair. He looked like a man who had survived a house fire. Or possibly a napalm strike.

'Reuben, I presume?' Frost smiled again. His dishwater-gray teeth looked underdeveloped. Almost like baby teeth. 'Reuben Wasserman, the water carrier?'

'I . . .'

'Why don't you sit down?' Frost suggested. 'Take a moment to collect yourself.'

Reuben heard a sound and looked at Claire. She was crying again, working hard to control her sobs. She worked as a loan officer at the Fifth Third branch on East 53rd. Reuben had always been amused by that confluence of street address and business name. They seemed meant to be together. Just like he and Claire seemed meant to be together.

What was happening? What was happening? Why was this happening?

'I said *sit down*!' barked the man who called himself Malcom Frost. Then, almost as quickly as he'd erupted, he softened again, tilting his head kindly. 'Oh dear. My apologies.'

Claire lost her battle with the sobs, then. Reuben looked down, pulsing with a hot blend of relief and shame. He didn't want to see, didn't want it to be true. But the lights were up now. There was no denying reality.

Reuben Wasserman, the water carrier, had pissed himself.

They sat together in a triangle at the dinette table: Reuben in his reeking, sodden Levi's, Claire in her handcuffs, and Malcom Frost.

Two other men in dark suits had emerged from the bedroom hallway to place table settings for all three of them. These men – thick faces, thick necks, general thickness – now busied themselves in the kitchen. Both wore impenetrable black sunglasses, as if they'd seen too many movies. Not movies about kitchen help, per se.

'What I can't quite bring myself to imagine,' Frost was saying, 'is how you managed to mobilize before we did. Will you tell me your secret?'

'Google Alerts,' Reuben said. 'Now can you take those cuffs off her?'

'I can. And I'd like to. I don't enjoy making people suffer.' Frost smiled again with those unnerving little Chiclet teeth of his. 'I suppose that's perhaps not entirely true, but I do like this Claire of yours. Believe it or not, Mr Wasserman, I have no personal issue with you, either. You two seem like a cute couple. When one of you isn't running off telling the other one lies, that is.'

'Please,' Claire said, regaining her composure. 'Just tell us what you—'

Frost crooked a single thin finger, cutting her off as if flipping a switch. 'Hush, now. Reuben knows why I'm here.'

'But I don't!' Reuben said. 'Who are you?'

'Let's not retread the introductions. But I understand you've been taken off-guard.' Frost chuckled, shaking his head. 'Google Alerts. Can that really be true?'

'Look, I set one with the keywords "Steamboat *Arcadia*" when I was about fifteen years old, OK?' Reuben said. 'It started popping off about six months ago.'

'Extraordinary.'

'What do you want?'

'Simply put, I need your help.'

'*My* help? With what?'

'Collecting a package. It's going to require more travel on your part, I'm afraid.'

'But I don't know anything about any of this.'

'Now, that's not strictly true, and we both know it.'

'I never even believed those stupid stories!'

'Never?'

Claire said, 'What stories?'

'Maybe when I was a kid,' Reuben said. 'When I was a kid I believed in Santa Claus, too.'

'Had you been here in Chicago when we arrived,' Frost said, 'carrying on about your usual Friday class schedule as I understand it, I'd be inclined to believe that. Imagine my surprise to discover that the water carriers really have kept tradition alive all these years. And in this day and age!'

'Reuben, what stories? What *steamboat*? Please tell me what this is about.'

Frost ignored her as if she hadn't spoken. 'It's commendable, really. Or at least mildly heart-warming. Not that it particularly matters to the task at hand.'

Reuben couldn't hold the man's pinched, hooded gaze. He looked at Claire instead. She met his eyes, waiting. But he said nothing.

What could he say?

'You're scaring me,' she said. '*Please* tell me what this is about.'

'Ah,' Frost interrupted. 'Here we are now.'

One of his men – henchmen? Would you call them henchmen? – brought a covered platter to the table. Reuben recognized it as the silver serving tray his Nana Edie had willed to him. He'd never used it before. In fact, he'd sort of forgotten all about it. It looked pretty tarnished. You'd definitely want to give it a once-over before using it for company.

'Thank you, Lucius,' Frost said, as Goon One placed the platter on the table. 'Aberdeen? The wine?'

Goon Two came over and filled Reuben's glass from the open bottle of Malbec. Claire's glass remained untouched in front of her. Reuben thought, *How does he expect her to eat with her hands cuffed to the chair?*

And with that thought, certain details about their present circumstances began to clarify in Reuben's mind. He thought of the odd, vaguely unpleasant smell he'd first noticed coming up the outer stairs. He thought of the empty parakeet cage.

'You look like a white-meat man to me,' Frost said, lifting the silver lid from the tray. 'Do I have your number?'

Reuben felt his gorge rise at the sight of Van Damme's small carcass, plucked and charred, positioned in the center of the large platter. It looked preposterous. Like the Thanksgiving turkey at a child's tea party.

'And you, dear?' Frost picked up his knife and fork, gesturing to Claire with the utensils. 'Don't be shy. I'll do the carving.'

Across the table, Claire gawped, then gulped, then squeezed her eyes closed.

Frost tilted his scar-wrinkled head. 'Not hungry?'

All at once she leaned to the side until she was practically hanging from her handcuffs, then vomited on to the carpet.

'You asshole,' Reuben said, standing up. A rough hand shoved him straight back down again. He shrugged the hand away and glared at Frost. 'You cooked my bird?'

'And here I thought you were about to defend poor Claire's honor.' Frost winked. 'None for you either, then, I take it.'

Claire heaved again. Reuben heard the contents of her stomach splattering the wet carpet. Now the smell of it rose up, mingling with the aroma of burnt parakeet. He felt light-headed.

Frost looked back and forth between his two goons. 'Lucius? Aberdeen? No?'

The goons shook their heads, folding their gloved hands in front of them.

Frost seemed disappointed.

Then he shrugged. He picked up Van Damme's carcass by one tiny blackened foot and popped the whole thing in his mouth. He began chewing, bones and all.

'Oh, God,' Reuben heard himself say. The room seemed to tilt. His vision started to wobble. He placed his hands on the table to steady himself.

'Actually, you're right,' Frost said, grimacing in displeasure. He kept chewing, speaking around his crunching mouthful. 'Tastes . . . domesticated.'

Reuben became aware of the sensation that he was sinking, slowly, as if on a pillow of air. Somebody seemed to be dimming the lights in the apartment again. But who? The last things he remembered seeing were Lucius and Aberdeen standing off to the side, expressionless; Claire, slumped across the arm of her chair, hair hanging around her face like a curtain; Malcom Frost, across the table, still chewing.

Then everything warped, faded, and went dark before his eyes.

SEVEN

Half an hour before dusk, Ben stood on the porch and watched a dark, ominous-looking 1983 GMC Vandura climb the lane toward the house, trailing streamers of exhaust and rock dust behind it.

Within a few moments, the van swaggered to a stop in the turnaround, and the rear panel door slid open. Out piled Ajeet Mallipudi, Jeremy Zwart, and Devon Miller, all dressed head-to-toe in army-surplus camouflage. Ben headed down the steps and across the leaf-strewn grass to meet them.

'Ben!' Ajeet called. 'Hi!'

'Hey, Jeeter. By tomorrow, I figured you meant tomorrow.'

'I know, this worked out great! Now we can set up camp tonight.'

'Battle commences at dawn,' Devon announced, catching the cuff of his pants on the door latch as he climbed out of the van, nearly pitching himself face-down on to the rock-topped lane.

Jeremy laughed at him. 'I told you to blouse those.'

'Blouse your ass,' Devon muttered.

Meanwhile, Ben tried not to perk up too visibly as Anabeth Glass hopped from the front passenger seat. She wore her hair under a black kerchief, long thermal sleeves under an ancient-looking Queen t-shirt, and form-fitting tactical trousers. Unlike Devon, she touched down with poise and clear athleticism. She also looked much better in combat boots.

'Hey there,' she said, smiling at Ben. 'How's the tummy?'

'Much improved, thank you.'

'You weren't really sick, were you?'

'Not really,' Ben admitted. 'But I was out of comp days.'

'I knew it,' Jeremy said.

'Tell Corby on him,' Devon said. 'I dare you.'

Ben ignored them both. To Anabeth, he said, 'The clowns from Google didn't show, huh?'

Abe clucked like a chicken – a comment on the mettle of their slated opponents, he gathered. 'They got off easy, am I right, boys?'

Ajeet, Jeremy, and Devon raised their fists in unison.

Amidst this exchange of *esprit de corps*, the van's owner, Gordon Frerking, made his way around the front bumper to stand next to Ben. Gordon crossed his arms and said, 'Well?'

Ben crossed his arms too, doing his best to match Gordon's pose. He looked at Gordon – shaggy mat of black hair, bookish spectacles, unfortunate chin whiskers – then back at the van. 'So this is it, huh?'

'This is *her*.'

'Paint came out nice.'

Gordon nodded. 'Wait'll you see the inside.'

For the moment, they appraised the exterior of the vehicle together. A majority of American television owners Ben's age likely would have recognized the van, with its charcoal-on-black color scheme and slashing red body stripe, as a true-to-life replica of the signature vehicle used in the 1980s program *The A-Team* – a show to which Gordon Frerking, Ben knew, was far too young to have been personally exposed. Ben credited late-night cable television reruns and a big-screen reboot. There was something so inexplicable about the time and expense Gordon must have pissed away on such a project – something so baffling about its ultimate purpose – that Ben couldn't help admiring it. Part of him envied these dopes.

'Well,' he said to Gordon, 'you're obviously not familiar with the value of a dollar, but if you're asking for my reaction, I say bravo.'

Gordon dipped his head coolly in acknowledgement.

Jeremy piped up: 'We gonna pitch these tents before it gets dark, or what?'

Claire's cheeks were streaked with drying mascara. Having been granted five minutes alone together in the spare bedroom Reuben used as an office, she couldn't seem to decide whether she wanted to kill him or never let him go. Urgently, she whispered, 'Could this have anything to do with how much online poker you've been playing? Do you owe these people money or something?'

God, how I wish, Reuben thought. 'It's nothing like that.'

'Then why won't you explain? Why aren't we dialing 911 this minute?'

'Because explaining would take all night, and we've only got two minutes left.' Raising his voice to be heard beyond the closed office door, Reuben added, 'And because at least one of those gorillas from Men's Wearhouse is standing outside this door right now, listening to every word we say. I can hear him breathing with his mouth open!'

He heard rustling movement just outside the door. Was that Lucius standing guard out there? Or was it Aberdeen? Reuben didn't honestly know which goon was which. All Reuben Wasserman knew, down in the innermost part of his gut, was that he couldn't breathe a word of the truth to Claire after all.

Not now. And not simply because she wouldn't believe him.

'What stories don't you believe?' she asked him again, as if reading his thoughts. She'd always been good at that. Usually better than Reuben was at reading his own.

'Boogeyman stories,' he sighed. 'At least I thought so.'

He tried to fold her into his arms, but Claire wasn't budging. She jerked away and covered her face in her hands. 'Who *are* these people?'

'I swear on my life, sweetie, I absolutely do not know.'

'I don't believe you. What did he mean about water carriers? What tradition? What package are you supposed to help them collect?'

'It has something to do with old family business, that's all I know for sure. It doesn't actually have anything to do with me. God only knows it has nothing to do with you.'

'Then why have I been handcuffed inside this apartment so long that my ass feels like cottage cheese and my wrists are still numb? And why, why, why, why, *why* are you actually thinking of *leaving* with that freak show? For Christ's sake, Reuben!'

'Claire, listen to me.' He took her by the shoulders, craning to look her in the eyes. 'I don't know the answers, and right now, I don't care. Right now, my only priority is keeping you safe.' Big talk. But he truly meant it. 'That's the only thing I care about.'

'I don't need you to keep me *safe*, I need you to make *sense*.' Claire squeezed her eyes closed again, shaking her head vigorously. 'I don't accept any of this.'

A heavy hand pounded on the door, followed by a male voice: 'Mr Wasserman. Please step out of the room now. Alone.'

'I hear you,' Reuben called. 'I'm coming out.'

'No!' She grasped at his arm. 'Stay right here. With me.'

He pulled her close. She didn't fight him this time, seemingly unconcerned by his soiled trousers, still damp with accidental urine. He squeezed her tightly, drawing in a deep breath through the nose, filling his lungs with the scent of her hair. Before letting her go, Reuben put his lips close to her ear and whispered: 'The minute we're gone, drive straight to the police station on Cottage. Tell them I threatened your life and that you need protection. I love you.'

He broke away then, turning without looking at her, knowing that if he looked at her again, he really wouldn't be able to leave. He opened the door and slipped out of the office to find Frost and his henchmen waiting in the hall.

'Excellent,' Frost said. He towered over Reuben like human scaffolding, taking him by the elbow in a hard, bony grip. When Frost stooped close, his breath smelled like charred parakeet. 'If you continue following my instructions with this same sort of readiness, the two of us will get on just fine.'

* * *

Ben took First Floor IT west of the house, maybe three hundred yards out in the timber, to a clearing he'd probably have used himself, in the astronomical event that he ever felt inclined to go camping on his own property.

He had Gordon park the van at the edge of the shelterbelt and helped them haul in their gear on foot. Then he figured what the hell – as long as he was out here, he might as well stay and lend a hand.

So he clicked together tent poles for Anabeth until the other dummies started snickering, then he checked to see how Jeeter was making out. Then Jeremy couldn't find his rain fly, and Devon ran out of stakes, and Ben finally ended up roving around the camp with a spotlight in his hand like some kind of supervising field comman – well, like George Peppard from *The A-Team*, he supposed.

It was a pretty October night, if nothing else: crisp clear air, starry sky. A bright silver moon made gnarly silhouettes of the half-bare trees. At some point, Frerking sidled up beside him, uncovered a pinner joint and said, 'Any chance these woods are 420-friendly?'

'I don't see any cops,' Ben told him. 'Just don't burn anything down, OK?'

'Cool.' A raised eyebrow. 'You in?'

'Nah. I'm on duty.'

'Right on.' Gordon palmed the joint and returned to the snarl of nylon and threaded fiberglass that would, somehow – hopefully at some point in the near future – become a tent. Meanwhile, speaking of burning things, Ben pulled a folding camp shovel out of somebody's duffel bag and dug them a pit for the fire they'd surely be wanting out here in another hour or two.

When they were finally all set, he declined the opportunity to go out on 'Night Ops' with them. In fact, considering the rugged, hilly, unfamiliar terrain they'd be encountering in the dark, he recommended that they all do their more breakable leg bones a favor and stand down for the evening themselves.

Instead, they gathered around him in a loose semicircle, decked out in headlamps and full battle gear, bristling with CO2-powered small arms.

'Come on, man,' Jeremy said. 'It'll be fun.'

'It's a great way to vent your frustrations,' Devon agreed.

Ben looked at him seriously. 'Do I seem frustrated?'

'Ummm . . . no?'

'Oh, please,' Abe said, benevolently taking Devon's side. 'Who isn't?'

'Yeah,' said Ajeet. 'And, also: don't worry. It doesn't really hurt that bad once you get going.'

'That's true,' Jeremy said. 'See?'

He leveled his weapon and, from a distance of perhaps four feet, fired a paintball directly into Devon's crotch: *thwap*. Devon folded up like a cheap suit, collapsing to the ground in a camouflaged pile.

'You asshole,' he groaned, clutching himself.

Jeremy laughed. 'I told you to wear a cup.'

Devon coughed out a war cry and fired a half dozen return shots as fast as he could pull the trigger, stitching Jeremy from belt to eye goggles: *thock-thock-thock THWAP-THWAP-THWAP*. The mist from exploding paintballs drifted in their lantern beams like blood squibs in a B-grade war movie.

Gordon became overwhelmed by the giggles and had to stoop to catch his breath, hands on his knees.

'What's so funny?' Abe said, and shot him once in the ass: *thwap*.

'Oh, no,' Gordon said. 'You did not.'

Soon the four of them were charging around the clearing, whooping and hollering, lighting each other up from all sides. Ben stood with Ajeet just beyond the fray, observing the candy-colored carnage in the lamplight. 'You're right. This is fun,' he deadpanned. 'I'm glad we did this.'

'I hope we don't run out of ammunition before tomorrow,' Ajeet said.

As if in reply, Jeremy unleashed a barrage of rounds from behind the limited shelter of a nearby bur oak: *thoka-thoka-thoka-thoka*.

'Eat, drink, and be merry, *muchachos*!' he called out. 'For tomorrow we *diiiiiiieeeee . . .!*'

There was no need to gather anything. Reuben was packed already. He offered zero resistance as Malcom Frost escorted him to his own front door, where he'd left his bags.

'Mr Frost, I'll go anywhere you take me,' he said. 'If it's within my power, I'll do anything you ask. If it's not within my power, I'll kill myself trying. Just please. Don't hurt her.'

Frost relaxed his talon-like grip on Reuben's elbow. Just a little. Reuben willed himself to look up into the man's pale, ruined face. He tried his best to meet his new captor's hooded eyes. With all the sincerity he could express in a single word, he spoke that single word one more time: '*Please.*'

Frost finally offered a beneficent smile. Reuben could have sworn that he detected a trace of pride in the man's crepe-tissued expression – like a father noticing for the first time that his son had become a man. In a gesture so deft and fluid that it didn't even occur to Reuben to flinch, Frost removed one glove and placed a cool, moist palm upon Reuben's cheek. Reuben thought of the fleshy, feather-gilled salamander he'd been forced to handle in high school science class, and it took everything he had to suppress a shudder.

'You have my word,' Frost told him. Then he leaned closer and added, softly: 'She won't feel a thing.'

At that same moment, Reuben caught sight of one of Frost's goons peeling away, striding in the wrong direction, back down the darkened hallway toward the office. Drawing a silenced pistol from beneath his jacket as he moved.

'*No!*' Reuben shouted, shoving his way past Frost as the goon opened the office door and stepped inside.

Reuben heard the sound of Claire's startled gasp. Heard the soft click of the latch as the goon – Aberdeen? Was it Aberdeen who'd poured the wine? – gently pulled the door closed behind him again.

'No! Stop!' Reuben shrieked again, his blood turning to icy slush in his veins. '*Claire!*'

He heard her scream from behind the door.

With that sound, his mind went blank. He heard his own roar, felt his throat tearing itself raw. Reuben clawed his way between Lucius and Frost, managing perhaps three running steps before a dark shadow fell upon him from above. The world's biggest, nastiest wasp stung him deep in the side of his neck.

He must have gone unconscious in his tracks this time, Reuben would think later – half-wishing they'd killed him right there, half-wishing he'd taken one last look around this longtime, well-loved apartment, which he'd never again call home.

Either way, he'd have no recollection of hitting the floor.

EIGHT

A round six thirty on Saturday morning, Ben awoke to a faint but urgent pounding downstairs. He came down in his t-shirt and boxers and headed toward the door off the kitchen. There he found Anabeth Glass prancing on the chilly back porch, her breath coming out in puffs.

He opened the door. 'Bathroom?'

'Sorry!' she said, pulling such a face on her way in that he probably would have laughed if he'd been more than half-awake. 'Is this OK? I like being one of the guys but I gotta draw a line.'

'Down the hall on your left,' he said, pointing the way. He looked at the clock, looked at himself. 'I'm gonna put on some pants.'

His alarm was sounding by the time he got back to his room upstairs. Ben threw on a pair of jeans and a flannel shirt, came back down again, and got the coffee going. He was padding around the kitchen in his moccasins when the plumbing rattled in the old lathe and plaster walls. Abe returned from the bathroom, her nose and cheeks still flushed from the chill outside. She looked much relieved.

'A thousand thanks, sir. That coffee smells wonderful.'

'Care for a cup?'

'I should get out of your hair. You have war soon.'

How the hell did I let myself get talked into that, anyway? he thought, taking two heavy white mugs down from the cupboard. 'Sun's not up for an hour. And I made a whole pot.'

'In that case, yes, pretty please.'

'How do you like it?'

She took a seat at the kitchen table, stripping off the fleece earband she'd worn on the way in. 'Strong and black. Just like my fiancé.'

'You're engaged.' Ben filled her cup on the table in front of her, ignoring a quick but undeniable flutter of disappointment.

'Ha – not really. I was just curious to see how you reacted. Although I did used to be married.' She took her first careful sip of coffee, sighed in approval, then warmed her hands around the thick ceramic. 'It didn't last.'

'You either, huh?' Ben raised his own mug in solidarity. 'What was his problem?'

'Nothing. He was pretty great, actually. It was me who couldn't grow up.'

'You either, huh?'

'By the way, did you know that there are about a dozen fairly hardcore-looking cats circling around your porch out there?'

He took a quick peek out the window. Still too dark to see much, but he knew they'd be there. 'One of these days they'll finally get in the house while I'm sleeping,' he said. 'Back in a minute. Help yourself to more coffee.'

He excused himself down the back stairway, where he kept a fifty-pound bag of dry Purina, then went out to throw some food in the pan. He noted a paper-thin shard of ice floating in the old ice cream bucket he used as a water dish and wondered if the first hard frost of the season had finally arrived during the night. He could smell wood smoke, saw a flicker of pale orange out in the trees. First Floor IT had managed to keep the fire going, at least. Ben imagined they'd needed it.

He came back inside, rubbing his hands together, and found Anabeth right where he'd left her, sitting at the table with her coffee.

She was paging through the Wasserman scrapbook.

'Oh,' he said, louder than he'd intended, stepping over too quickly. 'That's—'

'None of my damned business.' She lifted her hands away from the book as if it had squirmed. 'I'm so sorry. Way too nosy. Character flaw.'

'No big deal.' He collected the book from the table just the same – closed it, banded it, tossed it on the counter behind him. 'Just a bunch of old news.'

'Sure. I have plenty of that myself.'

He joined her at the table. They exchanged high-level overviews on marriage break-ups: hers (inevitable, best for everybody), and his (devastatingly painful, financially apocalyptic); about places they'd worked previously (her, all over; him, nowhere special); about outside interests (Abe: meeting new people, reading old books. Ben: building guitars, thinking about building guitars). They didn't get especially deep or private, not at half-past six in the morning, but he did enjoy chitchatting with her, maybe more than he'd enjoyed talking to anyone in recent memory. Before he knew it, the window over the sink faded in with a dim view of the sheltered belt in the first light of dawn.

'Well,' she said, 'time to get my battle face on. Thanks again for the java, this was nice. I love your place out here. See you in the trenches?'

He rose with her. 'Guess I should tag along before I lose my ambition.'

She looked him up and down, appraising the red checkered flannel and faded denim he'd dressed himself in. 'Is that what you're wearing?'

'And a jacket.' He nodded toward his Carhartt as he stooped to pull on his boots. 'What's wrong? Too fancy?'

'You don't have, like, a hunting coat? Something that says stealth?'

Ben didn't hunt. He'd never possessed an interest. He kept an old shotgun in the back stairway, but that was mostly for scaring off coyotes; they came up to eat out of the cat pan sometimes, particularly when the cats were around to sweeten the deal. 'I guess I must be more of an indoors kid at heart.'

She chuckled, shaking her head. 'Your ass is so grass. Come on, then – I'll try to watch your six. No promises.'

He deposited their empty mugs in the sink and followed her out the door. A cold, sunny morning awaited them, everything tipped in frost, ropes of mist still hanging near the ground. On their way across the porch, Abe reached down and – to his utter amazement – casually tousled the chin of the one-eyed feral tom by the food pan as if he were a lazy house cat. Ben had tried to touch that cat once and it almost ripped his face off.

They heard the sound of distant laughter then, followed by shouting. Followed by a sudden eruption of semi-automatic, air-powered gunfire out in the trees: *thocka-thocka-thocka.*

'I guess the revolution started without us,' Ben said.

Abe laughed. 'Sounds like it. We'd better hurry.'

Had we? Ben thought, then straightened with alarm as the mechanical clack of paintball guns ceased abruptly, and the sound of laughter turned to screams.

NINE

For the rest of his life, Ben Middleton would cope with recurring nightmares about the next ten minutes. Although even as those minutes unfolded – seemingly an hour at a time – he couldn't quite seem to convince himself that he wasn't dreaming already. Because nothing about what he saw, as he and Anabeth crashed into the clearing at a dead sprint, stood to any kind of waking reason he'd experienced in his time on earth thus far.

Amidst the jackstraw rubble of the ruined campsite stood a hulking, man-shaped thing. The unclothed figure had no face. No genitals. No immediately distinguishing features at all, except for its undeniable stench, which Ben picked up on the breeze even at fifty paces. It was the smell of an open sewer pipe, of week-old garbage, the sulfurous tinge of freshly struck matches.

The smell of corruption.

Presently, this interloper was encircled by a clutch of camo-clad, twenty-something network administrators with GoPro cameras strapped to their heads, all of them screaming, shooting at the thing with paintballs. One of them – Gordon Frerking, Ben guessed by his shape – waved a stick of flaming wood from the campfire.

Ben almost laughed, finally understanding that he was the victim of the most elaborate prank he'd ever seen: this character who called himself 'Reuben Wasserman' was actually some old college buddy to one of these idiots. They'd called him in as payback for the time Ben had taped down all the hook buttons on their desk phones at work.

A bit of quick visual math revealed that somebody was missing from the group, which meant that one of them – probably Jeeter, Ben surmised, judging by the remaining sizes and shapes of the battle-armored silhouettes now putting on a show for him – was zipped inside a rubber monster suit. (A rubber monster suit that smelled like it had been dipped in shit, but a rubber monster suit nonetheless. Where on earth had they gotten such a thing?) In that passing, too-brief moment, he actually felt better than he had all week.

But then he noticed the way the paint splotches began to shift across the thing's dull, clay-colored surface, the various colors blending together in a hypnotic swirl. The effect was other-worldly. Vaguely . . . celestial. Like nothing you could rent from a costume shop.

Ben stood there, transfixed by this strange aurora glissading across the thing's broad back. He found that he couldn't look away. Could not, in fact, seem to muster the will to try.

Little by little he became aware of somebody screaming his name from the fuzzy periphery. Only then did he manage to wrench his gaze toward all the shouting. In doing so, Ben finally pinpointed the whereabouts of their missing group member. It was the first time he noticed Ajeet Mallipudi's motionless body in the grass at the thing's feet.

Jeeter. His heart skipped a beat. Then he finally understood.

This wasn't a joke. The guys weren't playing a game.

Reuben Wasserman was no imposter. He wasn't crazy, either.

His golem was real.

And it had finally arrived.

The creature turned slowly toward Ben, as if sensing his presence. Ben felt his blood run cold. The swirling colors disappeared instantly, as if the thing had sucked them up through its . . . skin? Meanwhile, two eerie green slots appeared in the creature's crude, blank face.

Now it had eyes. When those eyes fixated on Ben, he felt it like an impact. All the strength ran out of his legs, and he stood like a prey animal, frozen in place. He couldn't make himself move.

The creature charged.

Beside him, Abe shrieked at the top of her lungs. Ben glanced and saw her moving past him, toward the creature, armed with a rock the size of her fist. Without thinking he intercepted her, shoving her out of the way just as she hurled the stone, pushing her as far out of the creature's path as he could. Abe tripped and fell. Her rock sailed ineffectually over the onrushing monstrosity, skittering away somewhere in the trees.

The creature kept coming, straight toward Ben alone. The impact of its loping footfalls shook leaves from the nearest trees. Ben could feel the ground trembling beneath his feet as the creature cut the distance between them in half. He could hear his compatriots from First Floor IT screaming something at him, saw them waving their arms wildly. It took him a precious, costly moment before he finally understood that they were begging him to run.

He pulled himself together and complied, turning and sprinting back the way he and Abe had come. He thought of the twelve-gauge in the back stairway. Had he ever remembered to pick up a new box of shells for winter? He could feel the impact tremors growing in amplitude behind him and wondered if he'd even make it in time. Ben dared not look behind him: he could *smell* Wasserman's creature gaining ground.

Amidst the terrified shouts from the others, his mind became a clanging foundry of protests: *This can't be happening. This can't be happening. This is not true.* An actual monster had not slept in the dirt for a century and a half, then followed Bloody Bill's bloodline all the way here.

And yet it was inside this single, soul-chilling realization that Ben found the strength to ignore his burning lungs and run faster. He stopped asking questions. Stopped hearing the terrified shouts now receding into the background. In that moment, he even stopped worrying for poor Jeeter.

From that point on, even as the ground trembled at his heels, Ben could think only of a family tree, hand-marked on parchment, with a single name missing from the list. The next name after Ben's in Bloody Bill's lineage:

Charley.

TEN

Ben hit the back door amidst a spreading pool of shadow. Something in that beat of sudden silence – a momentary, breathless gap in which the thunderous sound of the creature's pursuit disappeared, replaced by the rustle of dry leaves in the breeze – told him what he could have lived happily not knowing, if perhaps not lived for very long. Wasserman's creature had closed the final distance between them by launching itself into the air. Ben looked up at the hulking silhouette plummeting toward him from above, blotting out the low morning sun. The puddle of shadow around his feet grew rapidly larger. It seemed to generate its own magnetic hum.

He yanked open the screen door and shoved into the cramped back stairway by the skin of his ass, throwing the heavier inner door closed again behind him. The earth beyond seemed to shatter, rattling the whole house with the force of an impact somewhere between crashing jetliner and fallen asteroid.

Ben snatched the Mossberg from its perch across the coat hooks. Had he kept the gun loaded? Did the red dot mean the safety was off or on? He couldn't remember. Couldn't think. Sheer panic blotted higher thought, leaving only opposing base instincts: *fight or flight*.

Easy answer.

He only wished he hadn't paused to grab some ammo first. No sooner did his hand close over the crisp, waxy new box of shells on the corner shelf than both the outer doors and their frames exploded inward, driving him against the far wall, strafing him with broken glass, twisted aluminum, and jagged splinters of broken lumber. A piece of something banged off his forehead, setting off sparks in his brain, creating a hot numb place above his right eye. Which now had blood running into it.

He wiped with his forearm and kicked with his boots and plowed mindlessly through the debris, bolting up the four steps leading into the kitchen, perhaps two steps ahead of what sounded like a thrashing Clydesdale trapped in a coat closet behind him. He made the kitchen level just as an even louder crack of wood splintered directly over his shoulder, prickling his skin from the base of his spine to the top of his scalp. He spun toward what was coming, unable to help himself . . .

. . . just in time to witness the creaky old steps collapsing beneath the weight of Wasserman's creature.

Ben found himself looking down into the thing's grim blank of a face – close enough to see fragments of twigs and flecks of leaves embedded in the clay. Those false, eerie green eyes never wavered from their target even as the creature plunged out of sight, dragged by its own mass down through the short box of stairs into the cellar below.

Ben's legs tingled. His knees loosened. *Holy shit, what a break*, he thought, even as a more forceful voice in his head screamed: *Move, dummy!*

He raced to the sink, dumping the box of shells in with the dirty coffee mugs. Shaking with fear and adrenaline, he fumbled a shell at a time into the pump gun's magazine tube, shoving them home with his thumb, one after another. The shells he dropped all hit the kitchen floor and rolled in the same direction, following the almost-imperceptible kilter of the old house.

The next moment brought an ear-splitting, mind-erasing clap of thunder as the kitchen floor . . . erupted. Up came the creature in a cloud of dust and grit like a warhead from an underground silo, pinpointing the general region of the floor the rolling shells had crossed as they piled up against the far baseboard.

Water sprayed. Chairs overturned. The solid oak kitchen table slid toward him like an oversized shuffleboard puck on stilts, slamming Ben back against the counter behind him. He stood frozen, pinned just below the hips, disoriented by sensory overload. Again the voice in his head shouted at him to move.

But he could only watch, paralyzed, as the creature pulled itself the rest of the way up through the jagged hole in the floor. *What rough beast*, Ben thought crazily, snippets of some long-forgotten high school poetry assignment sparking through his short-circuiting mind, *its hour come round at last*. Broken floor joists poked up and out of the hole like fractured ribs. Severed piping spouted water in an arterial gush. Even amidst the destruction, the creature's unearthly green eyes achieved target lock once again.

And now it stood, drawing itself up to its massive full height, facing Ben across the kitchen table. The ambient temperature in the kitchen seemed to drop ten degrees. The smell of rotting sewage smeared away the lingering aroma of freshly brewed coffee.

The creature moved its arm. Ben heard an airy whickering sound followed by a hollow, quivering *thonk* an inch from his head.

An arrow – an *arrow?* – had lodged itself in the cupboard door so close to his face that the clay-caked fletching tickled his ear.

He racked the twelve-gauge (*this thing has* arrows?) and fired from the hip (*does it have any more??*), blowing a divot the size of a soccer ball in the thing's midsection. The creature looked down at itself.

Ben pumped and fired again, pumped and fired again, the roar of the shotgun deafening in the close quarters of the kitchen. Each direct hit dug a new chunk from the creature, lacing the air with the sharp tang of burnt powder.

But the cumulative effect seemed negligible. It was like shooting a riverbank: visible damage, easily absorbed. And with each blast, the creature's eyes seemed to illuminate, pulsing a bright, eldritch green. The divots filled in and smoothed themselves over almost as fast as Ben could make new ones.

It's fixing itself, he thought, snugging the buttstock against his shoulder, pumping and firing until the trigger went *click*. He went for the head. For those *eyes*.

On the last round he managed to fire before the shotgun went dead in his hands, the creature spun away as if slapped. When it turned back to face him again, the eyes were gone.

Ben's spirits soared with triumph. *Yes!* The thing's blank face was now a ragged crater. A punch-hole in a mud pie. *Gotcha, you reeking freak*. Still pinned against the counter, he suppressed the urge to blow across the barrel of the Mossberg like a movie cowboy as he waited for the creature to fall. *You don't mess with First Floor IT*.

But the creature remained standing. While Ben watched, this last gaping wound filled itself in like all the others. The blank face resumed its shape. A pair of slits opened in the reforming clay like new wounds. The green eyes resurfaced . . .

. . . and found him again.

You gotta be kidding, Ben thought, adrenaline giving way to uprising doom as the creature moved its arm once more, this time in a whip-like gesture – a man flicking water from his fingertips. Ben ducked and covered instinctively, feeling the peppery sting of number four buckshot pellets puncturing the tough canvas of his work jacket, burrowing like red-hot insects through soft flannel and into the skin of his arm, his shoulder, his upper back and neck.

Feeling trickles of new blood down his ribs, he ditched the twelve-gauge and dropped down low and shoved the massive old table toward the creature like a battering shield. The creature raised one blocky arm and pulverized the table to kindling, but Ben was already in full retreat, pounding out through the same door he and Anabeth had used not ten minutes prior to this. He felt a jaw-rattling thud as a splintered table leg sank into the door frame beside him like a heavy spear.

Cats scattered in all directions. as he bolted across the porch
and down the steps. Behind him, Wasserman's creature made yet
another crashing hole in his house. The creature broke through
the porch and sank again, mired to the waist in more jagged
lumber. This time the creature simply plowed forward, shredding
its way through the old peeling floorboards as if wading against
a low tide.

Ben thought: *Now what?* The creature kicked through the poured-
concrete porch steps with approximately as much visible effort
as a bully wrecking a sandcastle at the beach. Unsure where else
to turn, Ben sprinted toward the barn, no idea what he'd do if he
managed to get there.

Just then, in the distance, came an uplifting sound: vigorous
honking. Ben veered toward the sound even as Gordon Frerking's
A-Team van came barreling into view, jouncing and bouncing
down the old, overgrown machinery lane, sunlight flashing off the
windshield like a rescue beacon.

I love it when a plan comes together, he thought, just as he
stepped in a low place in the ground, tripped over his own boots,
and skidded belly-first down the sloping, dew-drenched lawn.

The ground thundered behind him.

Ben scrambled to his feet and poured on all the speed available
to his banged-up, long-out-of-shape system, racing across the rocky
lane and veering again, this time in the direction of the oncoming
van. He strained to ramp himself up to speed.

The van still passed him easily, slowing as it did, the side-panel
door sliding open on its track. Jeremy leaned out, shouting, '*Get In!
Get in! Get in!*'

Ben stretched his legs and pumped his arms and willed himself
faster, as the ground beneath his feet abruptly stopped rumbling.
The sensation was alarmingly familiar. A cold stone of dread sank
to the bottom of his stomach. *It's airborne again*, he thought.

Ben tried the same tactic himself, launching himself through the
open door of the van, barking his shins painfully on the running
boards, screaming:

'*Floor it, Gordon!*'

ELEVEN

Reuben Wasserman regained consciousness in the dim back seat of a Lincoln Town Car at highway traveling speed. He calculated, based on the sunrise now in progress, that it was early morning. Travel direction: west, according to the angle of the shadows beginning to creep out from under the car and on to the blacktop ahead of them. The tinted window glass to Reuben's left was smudged with face prints and smears of drying slobber. His head felt like a rotten melon filled with broken teacups.

'Ah,' said Malcom Frost, turning in the front passenger seat. 'Welcome back. How are you feeling?'

Reuben tried to look at him and winced. His neck was kinked and painfully stiff. He tried to speak but could not. His tongue felt swollen, mouth lined with wool. His throat was a dry leather tube.

Frost nodded to the be-suited, sunglassed goon wedged into the back seat an arm's reach from Reuben. The goon handed Reuben a juice box, like the kind soccer moms purchased for their grade-schoolers. The little plastic straw was already inserted and bent to sipping angle, ready for action.

Apple.

Glorious.

Reuben sipped harder, squeezing the juice box in one hand, rubbing his neck with the other. In no time he'd sucked the juice down to a few gurgles in the bottom of the box. The goon extended his palm. Reuben handed over the empty.

Frost smiled. 'How about now?'

'What's happening?' The words came out in a croak.

'We're preparing to breach the eastern limits of Des Moines, Iowa,' Frost said. 'Feel free to speak up if you need a restroom.'

Reuben looked out his window at the autumn cornfields scrolling past on the far side of the interstate, brown and desiccated and waiting for harvest. Towering wind turbines dotted the land-scape like bone-white alien artifacts, stretching rank and file to the horizon, their enormous blades turning lazily in the elevated breeze.

A gauzy curtain of confusion hung between himself and the view beyond the window. Somewhere in the wings there lurked a sense of dark urgency he could not interpret.

'How did I get here?'

'Under the circumstances, I felt that it would be best to give you a little something to help you travel.'

'What circumstances? Travel where?' Reuben massaged his temples gingerly. He'd never had such a headache in his life. 'You *drugged* me?'

'Let's call it a discretionary sedative. For your own protection, assuredly, but it does pack a bit of a wallop. I can't say I envy you right now.' Frost checked his wristwatch. 'How much do you remember?'

In rubbing his neck, Reuben had discovered a bruised area the size of a silver dollar beneath his fingertips. The sensation put him in mind of the flu shots he and Claire had gone in for last month, and he thought: *injection site?* He couldn't remember the jab itself.

'She told me to come home,' he said, trailing off. 'I . . .'

'Don't try to force it. You'll only feel worse.'

'Claire cooked dinner. You were . . .' Reuben could not, for the life of him, seem to collect his thoughts. It was as if the lobes of his brain had separated and floated apart from one another, like helium balloons trapped in opposite corners of his skull. 'Did Claire invite you?'

Frost nodded in a way that seemed meant to convey sympathy more than affirmation. 'The serum has that effect.' He tugged his sleeve, covering his watch and, thankfully, the pale, blue-veined, vaguely obscene-looking knobs of his skeletal wrist. 'But you appear to be assembling phonemes into words, so I'd say we're officially in best-case-scenario territory.'

'But I . . .' Reuben tried and gave up. But he what? What did he want to say? He looked to the goon beside him for help.

The goon abandoned him, turning his gaze out the opposite window.

To the living cadaver in the passenger seat, Reuben said, 'Your name is Martin.'

'Malcom.'

'Malcom Snow.'

'Frost,' the man corrected, 'but you're within the general weather pattern. Another good sign! I think you're going to be fine.'

'You came to ask me something about the creature.'

Frost touched his finger to the tip of his nose: *bingo*. 'Excellent. I was hoping we wouldn't be starting entirely from scratch.'

'Who *are* you?'

'A thorny existential question for all of us, but let me attempt to summarize.' Frost arranged himself in the seat to speak toward the back more comfortably. 'Until somewhat recently, I served as a consulting operative to the Order of Dingir. Ever heard of us?' When Reuben only stared at him, Frost nodded. 'You're right. Silly question.'

'The Order of who now?'

'How to put this simply.' Frost adopted the tone of a middle school history teacher in lecture mode. 'The Order is an interfaith consortium. Founded in secret by clerics and scholars half a millennium ago. Under the auspices – you'll find this quaint – of the Sumerian name for God. All for the purpose of keeping the mortal realm safe from . . . well. Let's just say *supernatural* dangers.'

'Supernatural dangers?'

'That more or less covers the bases.' Frost shrugged. 'Most major governments have a branch for this now. If you want my opinion – and I realize you're not asking – the Order these days is approximately as relevant as a stone tablet. But you've got to hand it to the dusty old fossils: they take a licking and keep on ticking.'

'What are you *talking* about?'

'Routine exorcisms, mostly, at least during my tenure. Your occasional rogue imp, minor daemon, what have you.'

'Golem assassins.'

Frost chuckled. 'Actually, this one's a first for me. In fact, I very nearly missed out on the fun entirely.'

I'd like to go home now, please, Reuben thought.

'I can tell you that Ba'al Zəbûb gave us a run for our money in '68, but we managed to keep a lid on things in the end. Arguably.'

'OK.'

'2016 was almost another story. Although, personally, I believe the jury may still be out on that one as well. Lucius? Aberdeen?'

'Still out on that one, sir,' the driving goon agreed.

Lucius?

Aberdeen?

At hearing those names, a faint bell seemed to ring somewhere deep in the fogbound moors of Reuben's mind. Almost too faintly to hear. He sat up in his seat, rode out an agonizing cramp behind his right knee, and said, 'What about now?'

'Pardon?'

'This club of yours. The Order of Whatever. You said "until recently."'

'Now I'm in business for myself.' Frost nodded serenely. 'We can leave it at that.'

'What do you want with me?' An invisible ice pick pierced his brain just then. Reuben closed his eyes involuntarily. 'Where's Claire?'

'You should rest. We'll be arriving at our destination in just a couple more hours, and there's much work to be done. Assuming we're not already too late.'

Reuben realized that the faintly sour odor he'd noticed seemed to be coming from him. Specifically: from his pants. The distant bell in his mind chimed louder.

'Did you . . .' Reuben paused. He tried to make himself remember. It hurt too much, and the chipped shards of thought he did manage to excavate from the sand clogging his synapses didn't seem to fit together properly. 'I had a dream you ate my bird.'

A pair of sunglasses appeared in the rearview mirror. The driving goon was watching him.

Reuben glanced at the goon keeping him company in the back. He was watching, too.

Reuben checked his pockets. His phone wasn't in any of them. The chiming bell in his head began to sound like an alarm. He could feel his heart rate speeding up. Face flushing. For some reason he began to tremble like a wet kitten. 'Where's Claire?'

'Oh my.' Frost sighed. He looked to the goon in the back seat. 'Perhaps not yet, then.'

Reuben followed Frost's glance. The goon had discarded the crumpled juice box. In its place was a gun. The gun was pointed at Reuben.

'Hey, no,' Reuben said weakly. 'Wait.'

The goon pulled the trigger.

Reuben felt a sudden sharp bite near his breastbone. The sensation seemed confusingly anticlimactic. He looked down and saw a feathery orange puff sticking out of him. Again the thought flashed in his mind – *injection* – this time followed dimly by another:

Did that guy in the sunglasses just shoot me with a tranquilizer dart?

Because that was sure what it looked like to Reuben. Just like what those khaki-wearing TV zookeepers used on the Discovery Chann . . .

Each and every quarter, Ajeet Mallipudi occupied the number one slot on Corby McLaren's stack chart. He was a toothy, bird-boned force of good cheer who smiled through everything, overpowered workaday drudgery with gratitude, and conveyed bright-eyed optimism in the face of dystopian corporate indifference. Jeeter could take a support call from one user while repairing account permissions for another while analyzing network traffic on a separate monitor, all without committing suicide. He also happened to be Ben's favorite colleague in First Floor IT.

So of course he'd be the first to suffer in Ben's place.

'Hang in there, sweetie,' Abe said, stroking Jeeter's brow as Gordon careened along the county gravel toward Highway 6, his eyes flicking back and forth between the rearview mirror and the road ahead.

The interior of his prized restoration was – predictably – a rolling nerd cave, complete with leather captain's chairs, Marvel Comics-branded carpet tiles, low-level strip lighting, and an in-vehicle WiFi transceiver. Ben saw various gaming consoles in padded retaining brackets, all connected to a flat-screen television, which was itself attached to the windowless side wall panel on rubber shock mounts.

They'd gotten Ajeet loaded into the rear of the van, laying him out on a leather-upholstered bench seat that folded out into a small cot. The elastic strap of his goggles was the only thing keeping the halves of his ruptured helmet on his head. He was breathing, but he'd been unconscious nearly a quarter of an hour by now.

Abe crouched beside him, doing her best to hold his head steady as the van shimmied and swayed. She looked toward Ben. 'Where's the nearest hospital?'

'There's a fire and rescue station in Ashland. Somebody call 911 and tell them that's where we're headed.' Eyes fixed on the view behind them, Ben saw that Wasserman's creature had lost significant ground. The thing had not given up its loping, lumbering pursuit, but it had fallen back at least a quarter-mile now, still receding amidst the swirling rock dust, a dun-colored smudge against the horizon line.

Jeremy crowded in beside him. 'What the hell *is* that thing?'

'It's a golem.' He glanced at Jeremy. 'I know how it sounds.'

'You mean, like, from *Dungeons & Dragons*?'

'As opposed to *Lord of the Rings*, that's what I'm told.'

'This isn't happening,' Devon said, raising his phone to his ear. 'This *can't* be happening.'

Ben crouched down next to Anabeth. 'How is he?'

'If you're asking for my medical opinion, not swell,' Abe said. 'But all I really know is that he needs a doctor. The only thing I've ever nursed is a hangover.'

'So,' Jeremy went on, tapping Ben repeatedly on the shoulder as Devon chattered to the emergency operator in the background. 'About this golem.'

'Please don't ask me to explain right now.'

'I was just wondering if anybody could tell me why we haven't run over it with a four-ton conversion van yet.'

'I can tell you that I shot it four times in the chest and once in the head with a twelve-gauge pump gun.'

'And?'

Ben referred him to the portal windows.

'Ow!' Devon said, lowering his phone and rubbing his arm. 'What the hell?'

'Just making sure I'm not dreaming,' Jeremy said.

'You're supposed to pinch yourself, dickburger.'

Ben ignored them, touching Ajeet's cheek with the backs of his fingers. The kid's skin felt like warm cheese. He couldn't help thinking of Corby McLaren's words: *Life hasn't kicked any of them in the balls, yet. Not really.* Poor Jeeter.

'Am I misreading the situation,' Abe asked him quietly, 'or did that thing seem to come after you specifically?'

'To the best of my understanding, it seems to be functioning as designed, yeah.'

Jeremy said, 'Please don't tell me you've been sleeping with Mrs Golem.'

'Wait a minute,' Devon said. 'Are you saying you *knew* about that thing? And you let us *sleep* out there?'

'Look, somebody told me this might happen, but I didn't believe it.' Ben looked up. 'Would *you* have believed it?'

'I don't believe it now,' Jeremy said.

Ben checked Jeeter's pulse again. Devon's censure may have been misplaced, he thought miserably, but the guy still had a point. If Ben had an ounce of decency to spare, he'd tell the others to dump him here on the road to fend for himself and get Ajeet to the rescue station as fast as the Vandura could carry them.

But he also needed to get to Charley, and he had no wheels. No phone. He didn't even have his wallet. Nothing but the clothes on his bleeding back.

'What's it doing now?' Devon asked.

'Around fifteen miles per hour, top foot speed,' Gordon called from the driver's seat. 'Jump range: call it one hundred feet at . . . hang on . . . approximately twenty-four feet per second. Ballpark.'

Ben said, 'Are you high right now?'

'I wish.' Gordon reached through the steering wheel to tap the dashboard gauge window with his index finger. 'Been clocking on the speedo since the tree line. Me being you, I'd want data.'

It was, Ben conceded, an extraordinarily even-minded outlook under the circumstances. *Let's get some numbers on this thing.* He made his way up to the front of the van and climbed into the shotgun seat. 'Gordon, what did McLaren rank you this quarter?'

'A four, right above you. But only because I threw you under the bus on that voicemail outage last month.' Gordon glanced over. 'Sorry. Dick move.'

Ben nodded. 'Figure out how fast you need to make this van go, and we'll call it square.'

RATTLED BONES AND RUBBER BANDS

TWELVE

They were received just after seven forty that Saturday morning at the volunteer fire station in small-town Ashland. Awaiting their arrival was a middle-aged couple – Tiff and Tom – holding lidded foam coffee cups from the nearby filling station. Tiff appeared to be dressed for a morning of autumn yard work; her husband, a uniformed county sheriff's deputy bearing the name 'Curnow' on his pocket plate, was dressed for patrol. Tiff handed Deputy Tom her coffee, grabbed her med pack, and climbed into the Vandura to check Ajeet's vitals, asking over her shoulder, 'Dispatch said he fell out of a tree?'

'We were camping,' Devon explained.

Deputy Curnow asked, 'What was he doing up a tree?'

'That's what we'd all like to know,' Jeremy said.

Curnow looked to Ben, as if experience dictated that he was most likely to find coherent elaboration in the eldest member of the group. But Ben could only shrug. 'I was in the house.'

'The house?'

'I'd just gotten up.'

'I thought you said you were camping?'

'*They* were camping,' Ben said. 'I'm only the landowner.'

'I see.' The deputy narrowed his eyes at Ben's abraded face and neck, his shredded coat sleeve. 'Did you fall out of a tree, too?'

Tiff poked her head out of the van just then. 'Hon, I need a hand. Right now.'

The calm firmness of her tone gave Ben a chill. Deputy Curnow handed him both cups of coffee and sprang into action.

Nineteen minutes after that, First Floor IT's fallen member was airbound via medevac chopper to the University of Nebraska Medical Center in central Omaha, thirty miles away.

'Fall in behind me!' Deputy Curnow shouted to them over the *whop-whop-whop* of the UNMC medevac's rotor blades. The helicopter lifted off the cracked asphalt of the fire station parking lot, taking Tiff and Jeeter away with it. 'I'll lead you there in the cruiser.'

And I have more questions, his eyes seemed to say.

By the time they pulled into the UNMC visitor's entrance, Ben had given Anabeth and the others his quickest possible version of events surrounding one Reuben Wasserman, water carrier. He'd also called Charley thirteen times using Jeremy's phone. No answer. Nor could he raise Christine.

'Take her,' Gordon Frerking said, handing over the keys to the Vandura while Jeremy and Devon followed Deputy Curnow into the building. 'Please be gentle.'

Ben's panic had reached desperation level by now, and Gordon's unsolicited goodwill nearly overwhelmed him. 'Are you sure?'

'I'd give you a lift myself, but Jeeter's my boy,' Gordon said. 'I should hang here. Besides, his crazy hot sister will be arriving any minute. She's going to need comforting.'

Anabeth smirked. 'How sweet.'

'Anyway. Me being you, I'd vamoose before Deputy Dawg comes back out here to ask why you're bleeding through a canvas shop coat. I'll tell him you had a family thing.'

Ben didn't know what to say. 'Gordon. Thank you. I'll—'

'Need wheels,' Gordon finished, waggling his phone. 'Just leave her parked when you're safe, I can track her on this. Speaking of, there's a prepaid in the glove box. Use that until you get your own phone back.'

Anabeth eyed him sideways. 'Gordon, why on earth would you need to keep a drop phone in your glove compartment?'

'Emergencies and Craigslist,' Gordon said. 'Why?'

'I owe you,' Ben said seriously. 'More than you know.'

'Go get your kid. I'll keep you updated on the prepaid.'

'I'll go with him,' Anabeth said, giving Gordon a quick hug that seemed to catch him pleasantly off-guard. 'Tell Jeeter I'll be back just as soon as I can. Don't you three leave this hospital.'

'How could we? You're our ride.'

Ben shook his head. 'Look, this isn't—'

'You're in no state to drive,' she said. 'And clearly you need first aid.'

'Thank you, really, but I'm fi—'

'I've been fine before. I'd recognize it if I saw it.' She grabbed the keys out of his hand. 'Step one, find Charley. Step two, tweezers and Bactine. We'll figure out step three from there. Sound good? Good.'

Before Ben could speak, she'd already climbed in behind the wheel of the Vandura. She looked back as if to ask, *Are you coming or not?*

He stood there with Gordon on the sidewalk in front of the medical center, blinking his eyes in the October sunlight as strangers passed him on their way in and out, heading to and from their own private triumphs and tragedies.

Gordon patted him on the shoulder. 'No offense, bro, but I kinda would feel better if Abe did the driving.'

THIRTEEN

Although Ben had never bothered to spend even a moment actually getting to know the man, Antonio Montecito had always struck him as the kind of guy who would keep his spare house key in one of those fake landscaping stones from Hammacher Schlemmer. Possibly this was an unfair evaluation on Ben's part, rooted in humiliation and hurt feelings. Also, possibly, it was because of the time he'd watched Charley stoop into the flowerbed to retrieve the spare house key from one of those fake landscaping stones from Hammacher Schlemmer.

He rang the bell and pounded on the door for five minutes before resorting to the same stone in the same flowerbed, only to find a nine-button combination panel tucked into the stone's under-belly. He took the man-made rock down to the curb, placed it beneath the front tire of the Vandura, and asked Anabeth to please drive over it.

Abe looked dubiously up and down the quiet, sun-dappled street. 'Are you sure this is a good idea?'

'It's a completely terrible idea,' Ben said. 'But Christine's the last person I know who still keeps a calendar on the fridge, and I need to see what's written on the today square before my mind flies apart. Open to suggestions.'

Crunch.

As soon as Anabeth saw him giving her the thumbs-up signal, she pulled a cautious three-point turn in the street and headed back to the Walgreen's on Pacific for first-aid supplies. Meanwhile, Ben stooped and fished the house key from the pile of thermoplastic shards near the curb. Three women in tennis caps and ponytails jogged past him, gave him a skeptical once-over, and carried on their way without breaking stride. None of them was Christine.

Her mobile phone, on the other hand, was inside the empty house.

This was the first thing Ben discovered upon illegally entering. He found the device abandoned on the marble breakfast bar next to a forgotten pair of sunglasses and deduced that she'd run out somewhere and left these items behind – a point he would be sure to bring up, after all this was over, the next time she gave him a hard time about mislaying his own phone. Her lock screen showed twenty-four missed calls, all of them from him.

The second thing he discovered was that the house wasn't empty after all.

'*Aaaah!*' cried a shrill voice behind him, startling Ben half out of his skin.

He spun on a heel to find a panting, wide-eyed Francesca Montecito standing frozen in place, one hand to her mouth, the other clutching a set of car keys over her heart. She was dressed in sneakers, hip-huggers, and a Huskers sweatshirt cut to show off her navel ring. Her cheeks were flushed, her still-damp hair pulled back under a military cap.

'Geez, kiddo,' he said. 'You almost gave me a heart attack.'

'*I* scared *you?*'

'Sorry about that.' Ben waggled his fingers. 'Hi.'

'Dude, what are you *doing* here?'

'I need Charley. Nobody's answering their phones, and I didn't think anybody was home.'

'So you just came in?'

'I rang the bell first,' he said. 'A lot.'

She rolled her eyes and plucked the telephone receiver from the wall nearby. 'I was in the shower.' In a moment, she spoke to somebody on the other end of the line, recited a long number, and hung up again. Ben understood that he must have tripped a silent house alarm when he came in.

'Sorry about that, too,' he said. 'Thanks.'

'Save it.' She showed him the black plastic canister attached to her key ring. 'You're lucky you didn't get pepper-sprayed. I almost peed myself.'

'I'm glad neither of those things happened.'

'Seriously, man.' She looked closer. 'What happened to you, anyway?'

'Look, Frankie, I really am sorry – I didn't mean to freak you out. I just need Charley. Are you the only one here?'

'Dad's out of town. Christine's gone for the day with friends. Don't remember where.'

Ben struggled to remain patient. 'And Charley?'

'Still sleeping, as far as I know.'

He shouldn't have been surprised. It was a Saturday, and it wasn't noon yet. Of course Charley was still sleeping. 'Could you do me a favor and tell him I'm here?'

'Sorry, no go.' She raised her palms. 'That room is radioactive.'

'Then can you show *me* where to find it?'

'I don't really think you're supposed to be here. My dad would shit a brick.'

'I won't tell him if you don't?'

Francesca shifted her weight, finally rolled her eyes. 'Down the hall, left, down the stairs, left again. You'll see the *Sticky Fingers* poster.'

'Thanks, Frankie. We'll be gone in ten minutes, I promise.'

'I'll be gone in five.' Francesca popped in earbuds as she headed on through the kitchen. 'Lock the door, put the key back where it goes, and if anybody finds out I let you stay in here alone, I'll tell 'em you tried to touch me in my swimsuit area.'

'Fair enough.' Ben nodded. 'You're all right, Francesca. I owe you one.'

'Uh huh.'

They went their separate ways, then, as if they'd bumped into each other on a public sidewalk instead of inside her home – Francesca toward the garage, Ben ever-deeper into the cavernous, magazine-quality Montecito household.

He found Charley snoring in his basement bedroom, just where his new stepsister said he'd be, his unanswered phone on the pillow beside his head. Ben shook him gently, then harder, raising his voice until he was practically shouting in Charley's sleeping face. At last, the kid's eyes cracked open: '*Unmm.*'

'Morning, sunshine. Roll out. I've got a surprise for you.'

'That's not spaghetti.'

'Charley.' Ben patted him lightly on the cheek. 'Wake up. Here we go.'

Gasp of breath . . . open stare . . . gradual uptick in consciousness level. Finally: 'Dad?'

'Shake a tailfeather, gorgeous. Jack White is putting on a VIP clinic at Ground Floor Guitars. Buddy of mine got us tickets.'

'What?' Charley sat ramrod straight at the edge of the bed, eyes ablink, sheets still tangled around his legs. His shaggy, jaw-length hair looked like a rabbit's nest dug up by a crazed badger. 'No, he isn't.'

'Fine, stay here, then,' Ben said, thinking: *Other than mangling his childhood, this is the cruelest thing I've ever done to him.* 'I'll text you pics from there. This whole room smells like feet, by the way.'

Charley looked at him. 'Dad. Are you being serious right now?'

Not for the first time, Ben noted how much his son was changing, and how fast; cheekbones emerging, chest and shoulders firming up, voice gaining depth and resonance. His nose and forehead thrived with ripe red acne. It pierced Ben's heart every time he saw the kid – not just watching his guileless little boy disappearing before his eyes, but seeing it in such clear, striking, time-lapsed increments. *That's just how it is when you don't see him every day*, Christine had told him recently, intending no malice, or at least not much. Malicious or not, she'd been 100 percent right, and the truth of it had been depressing him ever since.

'Actually, I was being kind,' he said. 'It smells worse than feet. Also, I'd brush my teeth if I were y . . .'

But he was now talking to an empty bed. Charley had leapt up so quickly, disappearing into his own personal bathroom with such miraculous haste, that it was almost as if he'd never been sitting there at all.

They pulled up beneath an oak tree at the curb in front of the big brick house just as the garage door opened. Out rolled a teenage girl driving a late-model Subaru, bopping her head to music only she could hear.

Lucius glanced over. 'Boss?'

'Let her go,' Frost said, watching the car turn out of the driveway and tool away down the street. 'I admire her sense of timing.'

'What if she comes back?'

'Then her timing will no longer be fortunate.' He looked at Lucius. 'It's impossible to admire the unfortunate, don't you find?'

'Yeah, boss.'

'Speaking of which, Aberdeen? How is our charge?'

From the backseat: 'Still out.'

Frost glanced over his left shoulder toward the young man once again drooling liberally upon the Town Car's window glass. He shook his head. 'I do hope we haven't incinerated this poor young man's mind completely.'

'No disrespect, boss, but would it matter?'

Frost sighed. 'Not overmuch, I suppose.' He looked at the house. He looked up and down the quiet, tree-lined street. It really was a lovely neighborhood, if you liked newer things.

Malcom Frost preferred older things.

They waited for several minutes, listening to the tick of the cooling engine beneath the Town Car's hood. Otherwise, the street remained quiet. Frost finally nodded. 'Aberdeen, be a good fellow and take the back. Lucius—'

'Front. Got it.'

'Please ring the bell first. We'll begin courteously and proceed from there.'

Just as Lucius unfastened his seatbelt, an acorn fell from the overhead oak, striking the roof of the Town Car with a sharp, hollow *ploink*. Lucius moved so quickly for a large man that Frost never failed to be impressed by the display. Even with one arm still half-tangled in the seatbelt strap, Lucius had his gun out of its holster and pointed above their heads in perhaps the same amount of time it would have taken most men to break wind.

Frost chuckled, patting his driver soothingly on one seam-straining forearm. 'Upon reconsideration, *boychik*, maybe you go around back instead.'

While Charley was getting ready, Ben flew around the room, stuffing as many piles of dirty clothes as he could into the drawstring gym bag he found hanging on the closet door.

He ran out of space before he ran out of time, but not by much. Charley emerged from the bathroom in cuffed jeans, hand-painted Chuck Taylors, and a Western-cut flannel shirt with pearl snaps. His eyes were bright. He was practically vibrating with excitement, wearing the first unselfconscious grin Ben had seen on his handsome, zit-ravaged face in ages. It appeared that he'd even smoothed his hair with tap water – an out-of-character extra step that made Ben feel even worse for lying to him than he felt already.

'Record time,' Ben told him. 'I like the shoes.'

'Mom did 'em.'

'She's still got it.' He hooked an arm around Charley's neck and pulled him close, smelling freshly-applied Speed Stick. 'Come on, we're already late.'

Charley craned back. 'Why are you all bloody?'

'Tripped coming up the front steps. No big deal.'

'Don't you want to . . . is that my bag?'

'You're at my place tonight. I grabbed what I could see.'

'That's next weekend.'

'Boy's day out. Already cleared it with the boss.'

'For real?'

'For really real. But we gotta pick up the pace, here.'

'I thought I was grounded.'

Good grief, Ben thought. *Again, or still?* 'We're temporarily lifting your sentence. Consider yourself lucky. Can we pretty please go now?'

Charley pumped his fist. 'This is gonna be sick!'

Somebody's gonna be, Ben thought, and steered Charley down the carpeted hall toward the stairs. Up on the main level, on their way through the foyer, he said, 'Hang on a sec,' and veered back toward the kitchen. He scribbled out a hasty note on a piece of scratch paper:

I have him. Will call you. –B

He wrote Christine's name on the other side, tented the paper, and left the note sitting beside her cell phone and sunglasses on the breakfast counter. While he was doing all that, Charley rooted around in a cupboard, emerging with a prepackaged granola bar. 'Where is everybody?'

'Search me,' Ben said. He remembered his original intention and checked the calendar on the fridge. The entry scribbled on the today square read *AppleJack Festival – Neb City – Heather yes, LaDonna yes, Angie maybe*. 'Francesca let me in on her way out.'

Something passed across the kid's face: quick, subtle, uninterpretable. Gone in a flash.

'What's the matter?'

'Huh? Nothing.' Charley waggled the granola bar. 'You want one?'

Ben almost said no, then realized he was starving. 'Got any bacon and eggs in there?'

'Ha, ha.'

Ben held up his hand. 'Hit me with the rabbit food, then.'

Charley tossed him a second bar and they headed toward the front door together. Ben had been hoping that Abe would be back by now, and his heart sank when he opened the door to a bare, sunny driveway. There was a demolished combination rock still visibly littering the street out front. He hoped Charley wouldn't notice. How to explain?

Anyway, the empty driveway and the busted keyholder weren't what bothered him most. What bothered Ben most was the giant slab of beef in a suit and sunglasses coming up the front walk.

Charley said, 'Who's that guy?'

Ben didn't know. Maybe the universe had finally decided to rule in his favor for once and put Tony Montecito under federal investigation for something?

But the big man in the black suit addressed him specifically: 'Ben Middleton?'

Shit. Ben shielded his eyes with the back of one hand. 'Who's asking?'

'That's what I thought.' The man continued up the sidewalk. 'Isn't this lucky?'

Down the street, beneath the same oak tree where he'd first confronted Reuben Wasserman, now sat an anonymous-looking black Lincoln, its windshield blanked by sun glare.

Charley sighed. His tone was disappointed, but not surprised. 'Dad, what's going on?'

'I don't know,' Ben answered honestly. He held the front door open and stood to one side. 'Why don't you go back in the house while I figure it out?'

That was when they saw a second slab of beef in a matching suit and sunglasses entering the Montecito foyer.

From inside the house.

Coming toward them.

With a gun.

FOURTEEN

Ben slammed the door closed, heart suddenly racing. He stepped in front of Charley and turned back toward the first man, thinking, *This definitely isn't about Jeeter*. How could it be? They'd left the hospital less than an hour ago. Besides: something about these two didn't look local. *Or* official. Suits or no suits.

The man coming up the sidewalk was still twenty feet away. Ben didn't like the way the guy looked both ways as he approached the front steps . . . then both ways again. He didn't like the way the guy held up his gloved hands in what appeared to be a calming gesture, like an overdressed ranch hand approaching a pair of spooked horses.

Ben dug the spare key from his pocket and quickly locked the front door, sealing the second man inside the house. *There. All safe.* Ridiculous. He looked around in a panic. What was he looking for? He didn't even know. He only knew they couldn't go back in the house. Couldn't go down the front steps.

'*Dad?*' Frightened, now.

The doorknob rattled behind them, then stopped. Ben heard the *clunk* of the deadbolt turning from inside. He looked at the granola bar in his hand and, on idiotic impulse, chucked it at the guy on the sidewalk. The guy took half a step to one side and watched the granola bar helicopter past him. Then he cocked his head, fists on hips.

'Come on down now, Mr Middleton.' His voice sounded like half a gallon of pure testosterone swirling down a drainpipe. 'We'll all behave like mature human beings.'

The house door opened behind them. Ben felt Charley jump and squeeze in close. He thought of the time he and Christine had taken him to his first big-person haunted house. Charley had surprised them both by being legitimately, sincerely terrified to tears. They'd felt horrible all the way out the side exit. Unqualified to be parents.

Side exit. Ben glanced toward the far side of the portico.

'Easy does it,' the second man said on his way through the door.

He joined them outside, effectively blocking any hope of the quick escape scenario forming in Ben's mind. He held his gun on them casually, at hip level, cleverly concealed from street view.

So Ben retreated instead, shoving Charley into the corner behind him, where the brick knee wall joined the house. He patted his pockets, desperately searching for Gordon's prepaid phone, realizing he'd left it in the van with Anabeth.

But he wasn't entirely empty-handed. He plunged one hand into the deep front pocket of his coat, finding the last thing he'd have expected to need on his ex-wife's front porch at eight thirty on a Saturday morning, or any other time of any other day:

A forgotten quarter-inch Narex bench chisel from his shop in the barn.

Ben closed his fingers around the handle. His heart pounded so hard that it blurred his vision. He blinked his eyes, feeling suddenly lightheaded.

The man with the gun sighed heavily as he thumbed back the hammer. 'Come on, man. Don't make me sound like a TV show.'

'That's the last thing I'd want to do,' Ben said.

Still, almost anybody would have conceded it: what happened next seemed exactly like a television show.

All at once, Ben heard honking. Then the roar of a big engine. He heard the bark and whine of oncoming tires, the clank and rattle of a heavy-duty suspension system under strain.

So much like a television show was the sudden appearance of Gordon Frerking's own personal *A-Team* van, in fact, that Ben could almost hear a paramilitary fanfare swelling behind it. All attention turned toward the street as the Vandura bounced heroically up over the curb and aimed itself straight toward Sidewalk Guy, tearing parallel lines across Tony Montecito's dormant front lawn.

From there, everything seemed to happen in the same instant. Anabeth Glass stayed on the horn as she crossed the empty driveway, picking up speed. Sidewalk Guy spun around to find a leering grille bearing down on him, its metal teeth glinting in the sunlight like a mouth full of chrome. Gun Guy shouted something unintelligible, springing instantly into a three-point shooting stance. Charley cried, '*Dad!*'

And Ben Middleton – thirty-nine, bankrupt, divorced, thirteen months sober, and suddenly enveloped in an inexplicable pocket of calm amidst the developing bedlam – tightened his grip on the handle of the chisel in his coat pocket, turned to his wide-eyed son, and shouted, '*Run!*'

In the dream Reuben Wasserman was having, it was Sunday morning. He and Claire were strolling along the lakeshore with the tourists, holding hands. It was warm out. The water was calm, and he could smell flowers on the normally fishy breeze. Bright morning sunlight made a blue mirror of the lake, glinting off the ripples and wavelets like an undulating net of jewels.

They stopped to look out at the Harbor Lighthouse for a minute. Reuben kissed Claire on the cheek and said, 'How come we never do this?'

She smiled at him.

Then her eyes flew open. Her mouth dropped wide. She began to blare like a car horn.

Reuben sat up in a bolt of panic, head pounding, his body one big all-over ache.

He was in the back seat of a car.

The car was parked at a curb. In front of a house.

The house looked familiar.

But Reuben understood that he was still dreaming. Dreaming within a dream. There would be no other way to explain why that van from *The A-Team* suddenly flew past his window, caromed up over the curb, and ran over some guy standing in the front yard.

It did explain the horn, though.

Ben had never stabbed anyone before. Up to this point in his life, it simply hadn't made it on to his bucket list. He wasn't very good at it, either, although probably there was something to be said for using the right tool for the job.

As it was, he stood dumbstruck for several beats too long, watching Sidewalk Guy attempt to leap out of the way of the oncoming Vandura . . .

As Abe actually swerved in perfect anticipation, catching him in mid-air with a sickening *thud* and plowing him under, into the turf.

The Vandura bounced and swayed as Sidewalk Guy passed beneath its wheels. The van skidded to a stop in the grass, leaving a pile of bent limbs in a black suit lying jumbled in its wake.

Then the reverse lights came on. Ben thought: *she's gone to the zoo.* For one yawning, sickening moment, he stood in disbelief, certain that Anabeth Glass had not only run down a human stranger in a borrowed vehicle for a person she'd known only two days, but she was going to back over him a second time for good measure.

Instead, she rolled down her window and screamed, '*Come on!*'

Gun Guy fired a round that shattered the van's sideview mirror, along with what little remained of this neighborhood's peace and quiet. Abe ducked her head back inside. Charley, for once in his young teenage life, did exactly as he'd been told, slipping between Ben and Gun Guy in a silent flash of flannel.

He'd almost made it to the front steps when Gun Guy reached out a hand and grabbed him by the back of his collar, yanking him off his feet as easily as picking up a sack of laundry. Charley landed hard on his ass with a blurt of pain and fear, the unmistakable crunch of a smartphone shattering in his back pocket.

Ben lunged with extreme prejudice, raising the slender, tempered-steel chisel high above his head. He pulled down hard with both hands, aiming for the center of Gun Guy's chest. He missed high and right instead, burying the blade somewhere in the thick trapezius muscle running between Gun Guy's bull neck and shoulder.

Gun Guy reared back and bellowed like a wounded rhinoceros, dropping his weapon with a clatter, clawing at his neck.

Moving as if controlled by somebody who knew what they were doing, Ben scooped up the gun with one hand, grabbing Charley's arm with the other. He pulled Charley to his feet, then along down the steps. They took a wide berth around Sidewalk Guy – still lying motionless in a freshly-chewed rut – as they raced toward the passenger side of the van. Ben wished he could screen Charley's view of the poor mangled son of a bitch.

In the background, Gunless Guy wailed in rage. All up and down the street, people had emerged blinking from their houses in various states of dress. Ben heard a car door slam, then saw a familiar figure tumbling out the back of the Lincoln and running away down the street.

Well. Sort of running. Sort of stumbling.

Carrying no damned water at all.

Reuben Wasserman.

You filthy little garbage-sucking rat, Ben thought bitterly. A few minutes from now, he'd be glad he'd forgotten that he was holding Gun Guy's gun in his hand. Because in that moment he might well have shot the fleeing coward in the back. The moment lasted just long enough for Ben to register the pale, strange-looking man sitting in the Lincoln's front passenger seat.

Then he was yanking open the panel door of the Vandura and shoving Charley inside. Ben piled in after him, barking the same shin bruises he'd already made. How many times was he going to have to dive into the back of this van today?

'*Hold tight!*' Abe shouted to them, already reversing as she wrenched the wheel hard to her left, sending them rolling around the back like two walnuts in a bucket.

The van skidded to a stop again. Ben grabbed on to a captain's chair and hauled himself up to his knees. Through the windshield, he saw that they were aimed directly at the Lincoln's broad side. He watched the pale man's odd, scarred-up face screw into a hostile grimace as the man pressed his palms against his window from the inside. He saw Abe clench her jaw as she hunkered down over the wheel.

Then Ben went flying again, backward this time, as Abe mashed on the gas and the Vandura heaved forward.

There wasn't enough room to build appreciable ramming speed, but still they hit the opposing vehicle with enough force to slide Ben and Charley together in a pile. The Vandura shook with a hollow, steel-crumpling *boom* that seemed to fill the interior and echo back on itself. Ben flipped himself over and grabbed Charley's face in both hands, shouting, 'Are you OK?'

Charley's eyes were wide as hubcaps, swimming with confusion, trauma, terror, and . . . excitement? Maybe just the faintest glimmer of a thrill, somewhere deep down in those gold-flecked irises he'd gotten from his mother?

Whatever he was feeling, he nodded his head yes. He was OK.

'Is there insurance on my phone?'

Ben felt a warm wave of relief. Yes: gone was the little boy of nine who'd cried at the haunted house he'd wanted so badly to experience. But Charley was still here.

He was safe.

For now.

Meanwhile, Abe kept hard on the gas, plowing the Vandura forward like a passenger-class bulldozer, scraping the undercarriage loudly over the high curb. Ben heard wrenching metal and popping glass. He heard the bark of rubber as their tires found pavement. He untangled himself from Charley and pushed himself up and made his way unsteadily toward the rear windows, where he saw the Lincoln tipped on to its side in the middle of the street behind them, a rear wheel turning lazily in the air.

Then they were off.

Abe fishtailed, corrected, then drove Gordon's van like she'd stolen it, leaving an upscale residential neighborhood full of bewildered property owners looking on. Ben counted among them the three jogging women he'd previously impressed so little. Still none of them was Christine.

But none of that mattered, now. At the moment, Ben was far more concerned with a) the pale man climbing up through his own sky-facing passenger window like the world's ugliest gopher coming out of its burrow; b) the large man in a suit who may or may not have been dead in Christine's front yard; and, c) the matching large man in a suit stumbling out into the street, still clutching at his neck, arm limp at his side, blood dripping from his fingers.

'Everybody OK back there?' Abe called over her shoulder.

'I'm OK,' Charley called back. 'This van is insane.'

'Thanks. It's a loaner. You must be Charley?'

'That's me.'

'So nice to meet you, Charley. I'm Anabeth – call me Abe. I work with your dad.'

Ben shuffled unsteadily over to his son. Charley had found his way into one of the captain's chairs, looking mildly shell-shocked, but seemingly none the worse for wear. Physically, at least.

'Are you sure you're OK?'

'Dad. I'm fine. Who *were* those guys?'

'Nobody you two want any part of,' Abe answered. 'Believe me.'

Ben checked Charley over one last time. Then he stood and duck-waddled up to the front of the van. He climbed into the passenger seat and stared at Anabeth Glass in profile for a long moment.

Finally, he said, 'And who are *you*?'

FIFTEEN

Reuben cut right at the end of the street and made it almost all the way to the corner of the next block before he had to stop and cool his burning lungs. He'd never been particularly athletic, not like Eli, and rolling around with Claire was probably the most strenuous physical activity he'd engaged in since high school. After sprinting a block and a half his wind was gone, he was seeing spots, and his aching legs had turned to overstretched rubber bands. He would have cut through people's yards, except that almost all these people had privacy fences. Some of the houses looked like they could just as well have had moats.

So there he was, stooped over in the middle of the sidewalk, wheezing, when that crazy van zoomed up and screeched to a halt beside him. Cute girl behind the wheel. Angry-looking dude in the passenger seat. Reuben felt like he'd seen both of them before, but he couldn't think where. He couldn't seem to get himself together. Meanwhile, the angry-looking guy rolled down his window.

'Hi, Reuben,' the girl said, leaning over the steering wheel so that she could see him better. 'Hop in. Quick-quick-fast.'

'Do . . . I . . . know you?' Reuben panted. Somehow, she seemed to know him.

'We met at Small's. Night before last. Don't you remember?'

'I . . . don't know?'

'Hurt a girl's feelings, why don't you. Come on, you can apologize better in here.'

Reuben felt like he was going crazy. He did remember, sort of. But everything seemed fuzzy, not quite real. And he still didn't know what in all God's creation was going on. He felt like he'd woken up with the most prehistoric, godawful punishment of a hangover imaginable, gotten out of bed to take a leak, and walked straight into the Twilight Zone. He had no idea where he was or what he was doing there.

And, holy shit, that *guy*. The one back there in that car he'd woken up in, just minutes before this crazy chick with the nose ring had turned said car into scrap metal; pale as a grubworm, face like an acid-bath survivor. Frost? That was the name that popped into Reuben's head. Which seemed appropriate. Just thinking of him gave Reuben a shiver.

The van's engine revved. The girl said, 'Tick tock, sweetie. We really do need to move.'

'Um, yeah,' Reuben straightened himself gingerly in hopes of relieving the stitch in his side. 'I think I'm OK. Thanks anyway.'

Then the angry-looking guy pointed a gun right out the window at him. 'Get in the van, numbnuts.'

Middleton. That was his name.

Ben wanted answers. But considering the more pressing fact that they were running from a crime scene in a vehicle fit for a comic book convention – garish, conspicuous, instantly recognizable – he found himself in agreement with their rescuer about priority one:

Get somewhere safe.

They further agreed that 'safe' meant putting some distance between them, the bad guys, the creature, and the general population until they could figure out what the hell to do next, preferably without the strictures of incarceration due to homicide.

So they took the long way out of town, sticking to residential neighborhoods and steering clear of major streets as much as they could. If the Vandura didn't draw enough attention already, it had now developed a loud rattle in back, and a caterwauling squeal of metal grating on metal somewhere underneath. But they worked their way successfully north to the interstate spur that looped around the top of the city, then east toward the river, the morning silhouette of the Loess Hills rising up from the horizon line to meet them.

Thirty minutes had passed by the time they crossed the Mormon Bridge into Iowa, fulfilling the sum total of Ben's plan so far: a new law enforcement jurisdiction. Reuben Wasserman sat in one of the rear jump seats with his head in his hands. Aside from the occasional low moan, he hadn't uttered a syllable since he'd climbed in.

Charley, who seemed to take it on faith that questions would be answered by present adults in due course, occupied himself with an audit of Gordon Frerking's movie and video game collection, which he'd found in a set of built-in drawers beneath the rear bench.

Ben marveled at his son's apparent ability to roll with all of this. Part of him wondered if it was healthy.

'Two things,' he said.

Anabeth smiled faintly, keeping her eyes on the road ahead. 'Only two, huh?'

'First: thank you.'

'You're welcome.' She sighed. 'I'm sorry this is happening to you.'

'Yeah, that's the second thing.'

'I can only imagine.'

'And you still haven't answered my question.'

'Did you ask one?'

Ben wasn't in the mood for banter. At long last, the tub of adrenaline he'd been bathing in since just after sunrise had drained empty, leaving him naked and aching all over. He was officially on the lam, and all he'd done was wake up and make coffee. Along the way, he'd once again trashed his adolescent son's life simply by being part of it, and he had no idea how to stop making it worse, let alone how to fix it. And 'Anabeth Glass,' the new girl from marketing, knew damned well what he wanted to know.

'OK,' Abe finally said. 'Explanations are in order. I get it.' She glanced down at the speedometer, backed off a touch on the gas. 'For what it's worth, I've never actually lied to you.'

'How can that possibly be true?'

'My name is Anabeth Glass. My friends call me Abe. You're my friend.' She flashed a quick glance over her shoulder. 'You too, Charley.'

'Cool,' Charley said.

'I remember you now,' came a weak voice from way back in the jump seats.

'I'm so glad, Reuben – I had a feeling we might see each other again. I was just hoping it would be under nicer circumstances. We have a lot of catching up to do, you and I.'

'We do?'

'Up ahead,' Ben said, pointing out the ramp to I-29 North.

Abe took the exit without question, looping around to merge smoothly with northbound traffic, which was predictably light this autumn football Saturday. The nearest big home game would be held in Lincoln, or in Ames, or in Iowa City – in other words, every direction except the one Ben had chosen.

Anabeth checked all her mirrors. Checked her speed. 'So, where are we going?'

'I think we left off with "explanations are in order."'

'You don't actually have a plan in mind, do you?'

'Not really.'

'Teamwork it is, then,' she said. 'We need to get this beast off the road.'

This they accomplished approximately twenty miles later, pulling off the interstate and into the parking lot of a Super 8 motel on the edge of Missouri Valley, Iowa – the first town in their path large enough to support a chain motel at its outskirts.

Instead of checking in, however, Ben looked both ways and led their motley quartet back across Highway 30, on foot, to the cornfield-adjacent River Bend Inn on the other side.

Charley, panting lightly from their traffic-dodging jog, said, 'How come we parked over there?'

'How come you're so out of breath? You're only fourteen.'

'Not for three weeks.'

'That's true.'

'Should we, um . . . like . . . call Mom?'

As if on cue, somebody's cell phone rang. Anabeth pulled hers from the cargo pocket of her paintball pants, holding up a finger as she answered. The four of them stood in a loose group in the empty, trash-littered parking lot near the motel's front office while Abe spoke, nodded, then muffled the phone against her shoulder. 'It's Gordon. Ajeet has a skull fracture.'

'Jesus.'

Charley and Reuben, in unison: 'Who's Ajeet?'

Anabeth: 'He also wants to know what we're doing all the way up in Mo Valley.'

Ben held out his hand for the phone. 'What are they saying? Is Jeeter going to be OK, or what?'

'They're doing scans now.' Abe put the phone back to her ear, nodded. 'There's swelling. Possibly bleeding, possibly surgery.'

'*Brain* surgery?'

'They'll know more when they know more.'

Ben dropped his arm and let it hang. Abe talked some more,

listened some more, then hung up the phone and slipped it back in her pocket. She took one look at Ben and put a hand on his shoulder. 'This isn't your fault. You know that, right?'

Ben glanced at Charley, who was pretending to be fascinated by a piece of trash on the ground.

He looked at Reuben Wasserman, who appeared to be standing in some other parking lot a thousand miles away.

He looked at Abe.

She raised her plastic drugstore sack, which she'd had enough presence of mind to grab from the van. Ben had forgotten all about it. Speaking of things he'd forgotten: Gun Guy's gun in the glove box. He looked past Anabeth, out across the road. Gordon was going to have a stroke when he finally saw his baby again.

'Let's get you cleaned up,' Abe said. 'After that, I'll tell you a story. Then we need to make a few decisions.'

Decisions.

Yes.

Ben patted his pockets. Still no wallet. He pointed at Wasserman. 'You.'

Reuben Wasserman blinked. 'Huh?'

'Got a credit card?'

'Um . . . yeah?'

'Good.' Ben swept his pointer finger toward the motel front office. 'Take it in there and book us a room.'

While men from the Douglas County Coroner's Office loaded the zippered bag containing Aberdeen Llewellyn's disfigured corpse into the back of their transport wagon, Malcom Frost explained to the lead detective what he'd already explained to the dough-faced patrol officer who'd arrived first on the scene: why *had* his dead compatriot been found wearing a shoulder holster stuffed with Jehovah's Witness pamphlets?

'He was one of you,' Frost said. 'Once upon a time. Duly sworn.'

The detective looked up from her notepad. 'Do you mean law enforcement?'

'In a previous life, of course. His experiences in your field ultimately led him along his personal path toward ours.'

'I see.' The detective scribbled in her pad. 'And, so . . . why the holster, again?'

'It served as a reminder, he always claimed. And oddly convenient for our work as well.' Frost sighed. 'The Lord never tires of confronting us with irony.'

'I suppose that's a way to look at it.'

'Between you and me, I rather think he may simply have enjoyed the novelty.'

In truth, Frost kept a stack of the pamphlets in the glove compartment of the Lincoln as a matter of routine. One never knew when a believable cover story might come in handy. None of what he'd said about poor Aberdeen was true, of course, nor was it the most polished lie he'd ever concocted.

But it had been irritatingly short notice. Frost was big enough to admit it: he'd had task enough simply performing the required sleight-of-hand, swapping the pamphlets for Aberdeen's tranquilizer pistol in full view of the gathered crowd. Stripping the very jacket from his cooling body in order to remove the holster beneath had been a trick for an altogether more skillful magician.

'Still, you can understand my curiosity,' the detective went on. 'Considering one of the neighbors claims to have heard gunshots, and the victim . . .'

'Brother Johnson.'

'Is found wearing a speed rig.'

'I wish I could shed more light,' Frost said, Aberdeen's pistol digging uncomfortably into his sacrum all the while. 'I don't remember hearing gunfire. But it was a rather overwhelming experience.'

'Could have been a backfire. Or the neighbor saw the holster after the fact, imagination took over.'

Frost could hardly fail to detect the skepticism lurking behind the detective's flat brown eyes. She was attempting to lull him into saying something foolish, he knew. So he said only, 'Does that happen very often?'

'You'd be surprised what people tell me.'

'I'm sure that's true.'

The detective flipped to the next page in her notebook. 'Either way, we'll have the ME run blowback tests. That's a test that shows . . .'

'Whether or not a person has fired a gun recently.' Frost nodded. 'Brother Johnson used to tell stories from his days on the force.'

'Did he? Which force was that, again?'

'Do you know, I'm not certain I ever asked? His stories were not for the faint-hearted, some of them, I must say.'

'Ah huh.' The detective scribbled something down. 'Well. Given that we haven't recovered a gun, or any casings, or located a stray bullet hole anywhere as of yet, there's no reason to think the results won't support your version of events.'

'My version?'

'Your memory, I mean to say.'

While she was busy writing, Frost slipped a small capsule from his pocket, broke it open with a thumbnail, and passed it beneath her nose.

'I can only presume the results will have no other version to tell,' he said, 'since I've personally never witnessed Brother Johnson carrying a gun of any kind.'

The detective flinched and pulled away, glaring at him. 'What the *fu*—'

Then she interrupted herself with a deep, shoulder-quaking sneeze. Trailed by two quicker, squeakier ones in rapid succession: *achoo-achoo!*

She rocked back on her heels. Frost reached out to help steady her balance. When the detective's eyes finally opened, they looked milder and deeper and ever so much more pliable than they had a moment before. Like twin dollops of warm chocolate.

'I . . .' she said. She looked at him, scratched her nose. 'Sorry about that. I'm not sure what just—'

'A bee,' Frost said.

'Beg your pardon?'

'It flew right between us. For a moment I thought it was going to fly right up your pert little schnoz.' Frost blipped the tip of her nose lightly with his fingertip, smiling as he slipped the spent capsule back into his pocket with his other hand. 'Detective? Are you quite all right?'

'I'm fine, thank you.' She consulted her notepad. 'We were talking—'

'About the man I saw leaving the residence.'

'Right,' she said. 'The man you saw leaving the residence.'

While the detective paged back through her pad, re-finding her place in the world, Frost glanced toward the ambulance parked in the middle of the barricaded street. Within the quarter-hour, the neighborhood had transformed from its sleepy Saturday morning quietude into the tableau of controlled chaos before him now: flashing lights, crackling radios, yellow tape everywhere. Crime scene technicians worked the crime scene. News reporters reported. Bystanders stood by.

In the midst of all this, Lucius Weatherbee sat shirtless and bulging between the open rear doors of the ambulance, receiving preliminary shoulder treatment from the local EMTs. He'd managed to kick his own somewhat more practical clip-on holster down a sewer drain just as the sound of incoming sirens swirled in the air. How an untrained buffoon like Middleton had managed to gain the upper hand on Lucius at all – distractions or no distractions – Malcom Frost would never know. But he'd certainly left them in a pickle.

Or had he?

'OK, here,' said the detective, consulting the previous page of her notes. 'You said the teenager appeared to be with the man against his will?'

'So it appeared to me, yes.'

'How so?'

'The man was pulling the boy by the arm.'

'And was the man himself armed?'

'Not that I could see from the car,' Frost said. 'How wrong we all were.'

The detective nodded. 'The chisel. Right.' *Scribble scribble.* 'Then the van showed up?'

'I believe the van came first, and then the chisel, but yes.'

'And you couldn't see the driver?'

'Oh, I'll be seeing her.'

'Beg your pardon?'

'I'm sorry,' Frost said. 'It all happened so quickly.'

There came a loud chorus of effort as a tow truck operator, a police officer, and three helpful neighborhood men, all working as a unit, tipped the damaged Lincoln back on to four wheels. The investigators had all the photographs, measurements, and paint transfer samples they needed, apparently.

Meanwhile, the object in Frost's other trouser pocket vibrated with increased urgency.

He disregarded it for now.

One thing at a time. 'I hope you don't mind my asking, Detective, but surely it won't be strictly necessary for you to impound our vehicle?'

'Impound? I can't see a reason for that, once the techs are finished.' The detective scribbled something and handed Frost her card. 'As long as the truck's already here, I can have the guys tow you to the closest shop. Otherwise you can have it picked up at our lot. I wrote the address on the back.'

'That's very kind.'

'You'll obviously need repairs and an inspection before we can let you get it back on the road.'

'Certainly. But I'm sure it's fine.'

'Looking at it from here, I'm sure it's fine. We'd like you and Mr . . .' she re-consulted the false information she'd unwittingly transcribed in her notepad even before Frost had dusted her, 'Franklin to remain available for follow-up questions.'

'I'm sure it won't come to that. Several of the neighbors offered matching descriptions of the vehicle and license tag. With a little luck, you'll have the suspects in custody soon enough. It's not as if my associates and I were targeted in some way.'

'Wrong place, wrong time, it looks like to me. I'm not inclined to suspect that you and your companions were specifically targeted. But I'll arrange for an extra patrol at your address for a couple of days, just to be safe.'

Saint Peter in a burning pumpkin patch, Frost thought. Why did people insist on clinging to free will? Didn't it tire them? 'We're from out of town. To review, Brother Johnson has no blood family, so we'll be leaving his body in the care of whatever indigent and unclaimed program your county follows. Brother Franklin and I have business elsewhere, so we'll be moving right along. We're in no need of police protection, and you'll have no further need for us.'

'No,' the detective said, paradoxically nodding *yes*. 'Several of the neighbors offered matching descriptions of the vehicle and license tag.'

Frost glanced toward the bright October sky. 'Meanwhile, I'm afraid this sun has my number.'

'Beg your pardon?'

He gestured an apology, indicating his primary areas of exposed skin: hands, neck, face, scalp. 'I have a sensitivity.'

'Of course, Mr Anderson. I'm sorry to keep you standing out here. We could have done all of this in the shade.' The detective used her notepad to shield her eyes, craning her neck to look up toward Frost's scar-webbed face. 'Would you mind if I asked how *you* were injured?'

Frost smiled down at her from above. 'Any pilgrim who claims to you that holy fire can't harm righteous flesh has never experienced the Lord's flame first-hand.'

The detective nodded slowly. 'Holy fire . . .'

She didn't write it down in her notepad.

Frost's trouser pocket buzzed again.

'Please,' the detective said, pointing with her pen. 'Feel free to get that.'

Clearly, she'd mistaken the buzzing sound for a mobile phone with a silenced ringer, presuming, quite reasonably, that somebody was trying to contact him, rather than the other way around.

He slipped his hand into his pocket, closing his fingers around the seamless metal cube waiting for him there.

'That's quite all right,' he assured the detective. 'They'll wait.'

SIXTEEN

I t took Anabeth Glass the better part of the morning to dig the shot pellets out of Ben's back, shoulder, and neck with a pair of drugstore tweezers, dropping the pellets one at a time into a flimsy motel water cup with the faint *tick* of bloody lead on plastic. She refused to speak at length while working, communicating only as strictly necessary to the task at hand, swabbing and reswabbing each wound with antiseptic as she went.

Which was, for the time being, grudgingly acceptable to Ben. He had trouble enough keeping a square thought in his head through the teeth-grinding torment, unless that thought was, *How much of the creature is in my bloodstream right now?* By the time Anabeth was finished, his iodine-stained back burned as if she'd lit it on fire and doused the flames with battery acid. The pellet cup could have doubled as a paperweight.

'I think that's the best I can do on my own,' she said, dropping the forceps on to the bedside table. She stripped one blood-smeared latex glove, rubbing at a kink in her neck as she straightened her spine. 'You still have a couple of deep ones in there. And one stinker that keeps sliding back and forth under the skin.'

'I'm sure they'll heal over.' Ben sat up on the edge of the bed and stayed there until his head stopped spinning. He felt low on everything. 'I thought you said you weren't a nurse?'

'As if you couldn't tell.'

'Felt pretty sure-handed to me.'

'Thank you.'

'Maybe now would be a good time to review a few other things you've said since we met.'

Abe ignored this, turning instead to Reuben Wasserman, who sat on the floor in the corner with his head against the wall. She'd sent Charley to the vending machine for a small bag of peanuts and a bottle of Gatorade, which Wasserman had consumed greedily. 'Reuben? How are you feeling?'

No response.

She went to him, touched his sweaty-looking forehead with the backs of her fingers. 'Can you speak?'

'No.' Wasserman didn't open his eyes.

Ben said, 'What the hell's the matter with him?'

'You know, Benjamin,' she said, 'as much as I understand how you must be feeling, you really ought to try cutting others a little slack sometimes. Reuben didn't ask to be part of this, either.'

'That's for sure,' Reuben said.

Ben sighed and tried closing his own eyes. When he opened them, the room hadn't changed: same thin, faded carpet underfoot; same water-stained ceiling over their heads; same outdated drapes and furniture all around – right down to the rabbit-eared television on the cheap particle-board dresser. The dresser's simulated wood grain had long scuffed away at the corners.

'But seriously,' he said. 'What's wrong with him?'

'I'm pretty sure he's been blotted.'

'Huh?'

'Mal always has loved his serums.'

Wasserman said, 'What did that psycho put in me?'

'His own concoction,' Anabeth said. 'Basically a weaponized sedative. But the cognitive impairment can be unpredictable.'

'What does that mean?'

'If he used it on you, it means one of two things: either your memories aren't important to him, or . . . well.'

Wasserman's eyes popped open. 'What do you mean, "Or, well?"'

She leaned in close, stealing the opportunity to examine his exposed eyeballs. 'I don't think he dosed you past the "It'll still wear off" stage.'

'You mean there's a chance it won't?'

'The important thing is, you're looking better already.'

Wasserman closed his eyes again. 'I don't see how that could be.'

Ben said, 'Who's Mal?'

'The pale man in the car. Malcom Frost.'

'And you know him how?'

'We used to work together.'

'And now he's following you?'

'Not exactly.'

'Then how did he end up at Christine's?'

Instead of answering, she dug a twenty-dollar bill from her pocket and turned to Charley. 'Handsome, do you think you could run to the machines again? Bring another Gatorade and all the bottled water you can buy with this. We need to do everything we can to flush this gunk out of his system.'

Charley remained fixated on Gordon's prepaid phone, having crushed the life out of his own back at the house. Ben had handed over the loaner almost by rote, the way they used to hand over the family iPad on long car trips. Still, as the morning had worn on here in Room 103 of the River Bend Inn, Charley's teenage imperviousness had disappeared like the cheap old dresser's stick-on veneer. He was down to bare wood now like the rest of them.

'Kiddo,' Ben prompted. 'You with us?'

'Mom's still not answering,' Charley said. 'You don't think—'

'No. I do not.'

'You didn't even hear what I was going to say.'

'I just mean there's no reason to worry about Mom.' Ben pulled his tattered shirt back up over his bandaged shoulders. 'She's all the way down in Nebraska City. Hey. Look at me.'

Charley looked away instead, scraping the backs of his hands roughly across his overfilling eyes, clearly angry with himself for leaking.

'I promise. Mom's fine.'

'How would *you* know?'

'Because this has nothing to do with her.'

'Then why isn't she answering?'

'Because she doesn't have her phone,' he said. 'That's all. You saw it on the counter before we left, right?'

'No.'

Ben pointed to the prepaid in Charley's hand. 'Between us we've done a pretty good job of staking out her call list. The minute she sees this number, we won't be able to shake her. Trust me.'

'But who were those guys? Why are they after you?' Charley glanced toward Wasserman in the corner as he plucked the twenty-dollar bill from Abe's hand. 'Who's *he*?'

What had Ben thought? That he could hand the kid a phone and he'd be a five-year-old with no questions? But how on earth to explain?

Really.

How?

It was early afternoon by the time Lucius emerged from the Bergen Mercy Medical Center with a foot of gauze stuffed into the bloody hole in his shoulder, prescriptions for antibiotics and hydrocodone, wound-care instructions, a follow-up schedule, and repeated congratu-lations on his good fortune. Each doctor, nurse, and attending police official seemed to have their own anecdotal example of how much worse his injury might have been, had one thing been one way or another been another. Malcom Frost would have been surprised if any of them had observed a statistically significant number of chisel stabbings in their careers, but he couldn't object to the general sentiment, being perhaps the best possible medicine for a soldier as prideful as Lucius Weatherbee: the indignity of repeated comparison to the common idiot.

Frost assumed charge of ground logistics himself, arranging a car service to transport them to the Omaha PD towing lot. There – with a little help from the same pollen-based hypnotic Frost had used to guide the detective through their interview back at the Middleton child's house – the manager on duty released to them a heavily battered Lincoln Town Car with one working door, a well-cracked windshield, and industrial trash bags for passenger windows.

Fortunately, the vehicle's satellite system remained intact.

Frost called one of the car's various special features into service before leaving the lot, pressing a hidden button installed in the back of the steering wheel. Digital servo motors whined faintly, opening a concealed console. Frost dropped the buzzing cube from his pocket into its custom docking station; the system paired itself to the device without malfunction, illuminating the car's factory display screen with a GPS map of the region.

'Your bug's still alive,' Lucius observed sourly, referring to the cube's unusual inhabitant. The big man looked miserable, slumped there in the passenger seat in his Bergen Mercy t-shirt and shoulder sling. 'I guess that's something.'

'Alive and hungry,' Frost said. 'Though it's not a bug, as I know you're aware, which tempts one to interpret your tone as mockery. I'm willing to chalk that up to frustration on your part – possibly compounded by the commercial opioid you've chosen to ingest in favor of the cleaner, more effective, and generally superior tincture I personally offered to administer.'

'Worm, I mean.'

'Indeed.' *Olgoi-khorkhoi*, to be precise. Commonly referred to by folklorists – along with those modern cryptozoologists who maintained hope of one day substantiating its existence once and for all – as the Mongolian Death Worm. 'It woke up sometime during the night. Little squirmer's been at it for hours now.'

'Neat.'

'There, Lucius, do you see? That's an excellent example of the tone I was talking about.'

'I just don't see how a maggot in a paperweight helps us, that's all.'

Frost kept one eye on the map display as he pulled cautiously into eastbound traffic. It was beneath decorum to be proceeding in the wobbling wreck the Lincoln had become. On the other hand, driving himself anywhere, in anything, had been beneath Frost's personal station for years. Now was no time to stand on appearances.

'First, a maggot is a larva,' he said. 'Larvae transform into entirely new physical beings. The Death Worm merely becomes a much bigger Death Worm.'

'Like a twenty-pound kielbasa, I know. You told us already.'

'Then you know it has to eat.' The hatchling currently in Frost's possession was no more than half an inch long, perhaps the girth of a pipe cleaner. Not so unlike a maggot after all, he supposed. It had been dormant inside the cube since the summer of 2007, hibernating peacefully in approximately two ounces of its native Gobi Desert sand. 'To eat, it must find food. That's how it helps us.'

'I still don't get it.'

'We both know that's untrue, Lucius. You just don't believe a word of it. There's a difference.'

'Is there?'

Frost reached over to pat his surviving operative on the knee. 'I can only encourage you to have faith.'

According to legend, the elusive Death Worm had earned its name by its ability to kill from a distance – either by electrocuting its victim through the ground, or by spitting a concentrated venom so overwhelmingly toxic that even grazing the outer flesh of a fully mature specimen could bring a large man to his swift, excruciating demise.

The legends were all true enough, of course, though trivial to Frost's purpose at the moment. Instead, Frost relied on another well-known Death Worm characteristic – namely, its ability to locate its preferred food source: *cynomorium songaricum,* the Goyo plant.

It was the Goyo plant's unique enzymatic profile which enabled a growing Death Worm to synthesize its powerful venom. The precursor toxins found in Goyo buds offered non-fatal uses as well, factoring prominently in Frost's own blotting serum. Meanwhile, a hungry juvenile Death Worm possessed the remarkable sensory capacity to locate even the faintest trace of Goyo resin within a hundred-mile radius – even when the only available plant matter had already been ingested by another organism (such as, for example, a nebbishy twenty-something MBA student).

'We still have juice left,' Lucius pointed out. 'Maybe it's trying to find *us.*'

'The vials are thoroughly hermetic,' Frost said. 'As are the darts.'

'So's the cube.'

'Not precisely.'

In fact, the cube was perforated by an average 127 micropores per square centimeter, allowing sufficient air exchange to keep the organism inside alive – not that Lucius seemed particularly interested to know such facts. Nor was he likely to care about the cube's unique alloy, which maintained long-term resistance to the worm-let's corrosive secretions. Or the interior sensor panels that converted the animal's natural bioelectric charge into binary signals. When paired with the predictive mapping software installed on the Lincoln's on-board computer system, these signals extrapolated the worm's movements into a kind of rough, inverted breadcrumb trail an experienced tracker could follow.

Of course, in human history to date, there existed only one experienced Khorkhoi Cubist: the inventor of the device, Malcom Frost himself. Maybe, after witnessing a successful tracking operation first-hand, Lucius might become a promising apprentice one day?

'Hard pass,' Lucius muttered.

'Think about it,' Frost said. 'In the meantime, patience will show us the path.'

Lucius raised his Vicodin bottle and shook it like a baby rattle. 'Few more of these and I'll be patient as a mofo.'

'Suit yourself,' Frost sighed. 'But do keep your wits about you. There's no telling what other woodworking tools a man like Middleton may be carrying by the time we catch up with him again.'

'Hilarious. I am gonna murder that dude so hard.'

'Lucius.'

'For real.'

'We mustn't kill our bait. You know that.'

'Bet that mud monster of yours can smell him just as good dead as alive.'

For mercy's sake. 'Let's just wait and see how it all plays out then, would that be fair?' Frost glanced at the map and put on his blinker; left-hand turn at the next traffic light. Northeast appeared to be their general bearing, according to the extrapolated vectors continually refreshing themselves across the display screen. 'In the meantime, we still need the water carrier.'

'Speaking of things I don't get.'

'Fortunately, I remain in command of the larger picture.'

'And if the cops get to Middleton while we're busy chasing Wasserman around?'

'Then they'll have done the heavy lifting for us.' Frost ignored the looks the Lincoln drew from his fellow motorists, which ranged from mild amusement to outright scorn. 'Although it's my prediction that we still have the inside track.'

Lucius snorted. 'If I was Wasserman, I'd be more than a hundred miles away by now, I can tell you that much.'

'But you aren't, and he isn't.' Frost tapped the map display with a finger. 'The little squirmer doesn't lie.'

Lucius rested his head and closed his eyes. 'I'm gonna laugh my ass off when we end up at a botanical garden.'

'Perhaps you'll feel better after a nap.'

The trash bags duct-taped over the passenger windows flapped and billowed loudly next to Lucius's head. 'Damn sure hope so.'

I do, too, Frost thought. A little controlled insubordination may have been good for an injured man's soul, but everything had its limits, including Frost's patience. He'd already lost one good man today. It would be an undeniable shame to see the other one swallow an antibiotic capsule with a Death Worm hatchling hidden inside.

They were exceedingly difficult to come by, the worms.

After the docs rolled the unconscious kid back to where they kept all the machines, Saunders County Sheriff's Deputy Tom Curnow interviewed the injured party's three remaining friends, then asked them one at a time to visit the hospital cafeteria, where he took individual statements from each. He also took down a number where he could follow up with Middleton, their curiously missing compatriot, and the vaguely exotic-looking gal with the distinguished profile. Glass.

Afterward, Tom checked in with Carla at dispatch. Then he gave his high school sweetheart a lift home in the cruiser.

They were twelve-odd miles from town when the call came over the radio: a regional Be On the Lookout alert for a 1980s-model GMC passenger van with unusually specific distinguishing features.

'You gotta be kidding me,' he said, immediately reaching for the handset.

Tiff turned in the shotgun seat, where she rode alongside the actual shotgun. She had yet to touch a clipper to her mums today, as she'd been planning all week to do. 'Did they just describe—'

'Those paintball idiots, yeah.' Tom shook his head. 'Fell out of a tree. Sure. And Middleton. Just got out of bed, he tells me. Just got out of bed and, what, ran into a weed whacker?'

'His appearance was curious,' Tiff agreed.

'Those little shits lied to my face.'

'You already knew they were lying, Tom. That's why you rolled all the way to Douglas County just to talk with them.'

'Family thing my fat hick ass.'

Tiff scowled at him. 'Your hick ass is proportionate.'

Then her cell phone rang. Almost simultaneously, Carla from dispatch came over the radio. 'Car Two, are you receiving? Tom?'

He keyed the squawker. 'Car Two copy. Go ahead.'

'What's your location?'

'Southwest on 6, crossing the river in ten. Dispatch, that black and gray GMC—'

'Forget about the GMC. Is Tiff with you? Please tell me she's with you. Or still in Omaha.'

Tom didn't like this. The department's new 'clear language' radio policy aside, he couldn't remember a time in the past ten years he'd ever heard Carla use anybody's first name over the air. 'We're together.'

'Oh, thank god.'

'En route to the firehouse.'

'Good luck finding it.'

'Say again?' Tom glanced at his wife, who suddenly looked as stricken as Carla sounded. Tiff pointed to her phone and mouthed the name *Roy*. Referring to Roy Webber, with whom she split her on-call weekends.

'Get there hot, Tom. State Patrol on scene. Silver Street barricaded at Twenty-fifth and Twenty-third. Adam Street barricaded at Twenty-fourth. And, um, be advised, Car Two?'

'Go ahead.'

'I wasn't kidding. It isn't there anymore.'

'Say again?'

'The fire and rescue office. It's a pile of bricks now. Break.'

Tom looked at the squawker in his hand. If he hadn't known Carla Malvern since grade school, he'd have wondered if this was supposed to be some kind of a gag. Tiff was still on her phone, her eyes widening by the moment. 'Roy, that just doesn't make sense.'

Then Carla came crackling back: 'Car Two, disregard last info. 10-34 ongoing at middle school football field. Multiple injuries reported, medical en route. Caller reports unidentified subject still on site, large build, probable male, possibly under the influence. God, Tom, that's the Pee Wee football game . . .'

Charley stared at the carpet for a long time without speaking. Anabeth stepped over and put a hand on his shoulder. Still no response.

'I know this all sounds like a joke,' Ben said. 'But I promise it isn't.'

More silence. Then: 'Like you promised Jack White was in town?'

'I'm really sorry, kid, I know that was low. But I . . .'

'Like you promised to come last Thanksgiving?'

'Charley, I—'

'Like you promised Mom you were gonna quit drinking?'

Ben felt a quick, sharp flash of indignation, followed immediately by shame-tingles all over. He sensed Anabeth watching him. Wasserman, too.

'No,' he said, almost wishing that Wasserman's creature had finished him off back at the house. 'Not like that, either.'

Charley stood abruptly, tossed Gordon's prepaid phone on to the bed next to Ben, and stalked toward the door.

'Hey.' Ben rose with him, quickly buttoning his shirt. 'Where are you going?'

'Back to the van.'

'Charley. Stop.'

Charley didn't even pause. He unfastened the security chain and grabbed the doorknob.

'I said *stop*. I know you're pissed off, and I wouldn't believe me, either. But—'

'You said those guys were doing paintball at your place, didn't you?'

'Yeah, but . . .'

Charley turned to face him, pulling the door open with him. 'They were wearing helmet cams. I saw 'em in the back of the van still.'

For a moment, Ben could only stand and stare at his growing son. The cameras! Somehow this, too, had failed to cross his mind.

The cameras. If even one of the guys had been running video at the campsite this morning, they'd have caught Wasserman's creature on film. Ben began to smile.

'You,' he said, 'are a straight-up genius.'

'Guess I got Mom's brain, then.'

'Uh oh,' said Abe.

Ben had been so focused on this new idea about the forgotten GoPros in the back of the van – along with maybe grabbing Gun Guy's gun while he was out there, just in case – that he hadn't even noticed her moving close enough to stand beside him. Her hair and clothes still smelled like campfire smoke. He glanced at her.

Abe was staring past Charley, out the open door. Charley turned to follow her gaze, opening up Ben's view as he did.

From where the three of them stood inside the room, they could see beyond the River Bend parking lot, across the highway, all the way to the Super 8 on the other side.

Which was now crawling with cops.

Red and blue lights flashed as figures in uniform trooped around the competing motel grounds. A small handful of them stood around the Vandura. One appeared to be working on the driver's-side door with a slim jim.

'Holy shit,' Charley said.

Yep, Ben thought.

That about covered it.

SEVENTEEN

Councilman Glenn 'Big Glenn' Rademacher genuinely loved his neighbors, and he considered just about everyone a neighbor. Big-boned, big-hearted, big on your basic community ideals, he was the type of good-natured loudmouth you can find with his hand on a lever – or perhaps caught in the gears – somewhere in the workings of almost any Middle American small town.

Sure, he had his opinions. Along with a tendency toward minding other people's business that had become, over the years, as well-developed as it was well-known. He probably spent more time telling half-true stories at the tavern than Shirley, his wife of forty-odd years, might have liked.

But he almost always laughed at himself before he laughed at others. Opinions aside, he dealt his cards from the top of the deck. He'd never been on the wrong end of Deputy Tom Curnow's handcuffs, tavern or no tavern. And if you were looking for someone to pull you out of a ditch, Big Glenn Rademacher was your man.

In the end, whatever else you wanted to think or say about Glenn, one thing struck Tom as incontrovertible: the guy hadn't deserved to be dead at sixty-two, fatally impaled on a football goalpost like a hog in a windbreaker on a blood-painted spit.

But that – inexplicably – was where they found him, midday Saturday, on the other side of Carla's radio dispatch.

At first, Tom couldn't make sense of what he was seeing; the upheaval all around him looked more like a public square in Kandahar after a good shelling than his own little town here at home. His immediate thought, in spite of the bright blue autumn sky: *Tornado.*

Second thought: *In October?*

'Sweet Christmas,' Tiff said, shouldering open her door almost before Tom pulled the cruiser to a full stop. 'What is *happening* around here today?'

He had no ideas worth sharing.

They hustled in together, past weeping friends and wailing neighbors, past hustling paramedics and disoriented-looking coaches and shell-shocked kids in pint-sized shoulder pads, finally parting each other's company just inside the chain link gate: Tiff veering off toward Roy Webber's makeshift medical station and a crowd of additional wounded; Tom toward his boss, Sheriff Dale Prescott, whom he spotted with the mayor; a middle-aged State Patrol sergeant; and a photographer in a hazmat suit just this side of the thirty-yard line.

Injured, he amended in his mind as he hurried toward them. *Not wounded. Tornado victims get* injured.

Because, seriously, what else could have happened here? The entire west corner of the new bleachers had been demolished. Galvanized steel piping poked this way and that, twisted and tangled like a fistful of pipe cleaners. The visitor's goalpost – already cut off at the base and lowered to the ground – rested askew on its cross-brace. The uprights jutted from the turf at a low angle, like the horns of a bull preparing to charge.

Somehow, Big Glenn had been gored tip to tail on the heavy-gauge steel.

It was, without question, the most gruesome thing Tom Curnow had ever seen, and that included six months in combat – not to mention the ten years he'd spent since that time responding to motor vehicle accidents up and down Highway 6.

Law enforcement personnel from town, county, and state were gathered around the spot, along with EMTs from nearby Gretna. Tom saw his fellow county deputy Martina York and a young state trooper struggling with a polyvinyl tarp, doing their best to drape the skewered corpse from view. Meanwhile, Mel Frazee from town maintenance crouched amidst their ankles, working on the upright with a cutting torch.

Sheriff Prescott saw Tom coming. The State Patrol man nodded a greeting and moved along at a stride. Mayor Bobby Ford – starting center on Tom's own high school football team before going straight into the grain-storage business, then local politics – looked like he'd swallowed something foul. The shooter in the hazmat suit snapped pictures of the ground behind them.

Either the photographer had overdressed for the occasion, or the sheriff and the mayor were flying in the face of advisable precaution, Tom had no way of knowing which. They were standing near a rimmed hole in the field, possibly four feet across, cordoned off with stake posts and police tape. The hole looked to Tom like nothing so much as an impact crater.

Then he got close enough to see inside.

'Holy Jesus God,' he said, staring. 'What . . . *is* that?'

'Ref,' Mayor Bobby said, stifling a gulp with the back of his hand.

'What's left of him.' Sheriff Prescott shook his head. 'Some league kid down from Omaha. Just makin' an extra buck on the weekend. Now look.'

'But what *happened* to him?' Tom looked around. 'What happened to everybody? Carla wasn't making any sense.'

'That's for damn sure going around,' Bobby agreed.

'Something about a—'

'We figure the subject came in through the far gates there,' Sheriff Prescott said, pointing. 'Nobody saw him 'til he was halfway across the field. Just walkin' right on across like nobody's business, according to Jim Watson. Huge bastard. Flying high on something, musta been, least that's what everybody thought at first.'

'Carla said he was all covered in . . .'

'Some kinda mud. Or . . . something. You heard that part right.'

'Kids all say he smelled like a walking turd. Bunch of 'em are claiming—'

'Can we give all that a rest, Bobby? One thing at a time.'

'He had these weird eyes,' Mayor Bobby went on. 'Bright green, they said. Glowing, like.'

Tom stared at them. 'Glowing green eyes.'

'They all scattered like cats, thank Christ.'

'Apparently that's when the ref stepped in.' The sheriff gestured toward the grisly crater in the ground three feet from where they stood. Then toward the near end zone, thirty yards downfield. 'Subject stomped a mudhole in the poor sonofabitch before proceeding roughly thataway.'

'Biglun was helping run the chains,' Mayor Bobby said, lapsing briefly into townspeak for Big Glenn. His voice carried a sprinkling of community pride before it hitched and broke. He cleared his throat. 'Caught up with the mud-caked motherhumper around the one-yard line.'

Tom's head was spinning. Reluctantly, he peered once more into the hole. If not for a visible hand still clutching a flattened referee's whistle, you'd have been hard-pressed to say with certainty that the pile of guts and bone in a pond of blood at the bottom of the crater had once been a human being. He saw scraps of striped fabric and an old joke crossed his overloaded mind: *What's black and white and red all over?* He couldn't even remember the actual punch line.

Tom looked between the sheriff and Bobby Ford. Looked back toward the goal post. 'But how in God's name . . .'

'General consensus,' Sheriff Prescott said, 'seems to be that the subject picked his ass up and threw him in the air. What you're looking at is how he came down.'

'Dale.'

'Just telling you what Jim Watson told me. *Flung*, was I believe the word he used.'

'All 300 pounds of him,' Mayor Bobby confirmed. 'Check Marge Holman's cell phone if you don't believe it.'

'Anyway,' Prescott went on, shooting Bobby a grimace. 'Everybody with a concealed-carry card opened fire from the damn stands after that.' He gestured vaguely toward the nice new bleachers, which the town had voted in only just last spring. 'Goddamn miracle nobody hit one of the kids. That's when all that mess over there happened.'

In direct disregard for accepted forensic protocol – perhaps including basic common sense – Tom stooped and reached across the crime scene tape toward the hole in the field. He ran his bare finger through a globby smear of unusual-looking clay he'd spotted amidst the upturned turf.

'Um, please don't do that,' said the photographer, voice muffled behind his filter mask.

Almost instantly, Tom's finger went cold. He sniffed it reflexively – one of the dumber reflexes wired into the male of the species, it occurred to him – and nearly gagged at the odor: somewhere between a bucket full of pond water and a dead animal bloating in the sun.

And then his mind started playing tricks on him. Standing there, looking at his finger, Tom almost would have sworn that he felt the clay . . . *squeezing* him. He flicked his hand hard, quickly wiped his finger on his duty trousers. Shock and general confusion gave way to anger. 'Do we have him?'

'Have who?'

'The doer,' Tom said, brandishing his befouled index finger. 'The turd-smelling shithead. Where is he now? Tell me we have him.'

'Have *it*, I think is more like,' Mayor Bobby said.

'Bobby. Please, goddammit.'

'Look around, Dale! Are you really going to stand there telling me you think a *man* did all this?' He pointed to the soupy remains in the crater. 'Did *that*? *One* man?'

'Let's at least try and keep ourselves sounding halfway like a couple prof—'

'Fifty feet in the air, Dale. That's how high Big Glenn went up.' Mayor Bobby scrubbed a shaky hand through his hair. 'Go back and look at Marge Holman's cell phone one more time if you don't believe it.'

Before Sheriff Prescott could answer, Tom heard the distant *whop-whop-whop* of a helicopter rotor and looked up to see his second chopper of the morning, this one from the Civil Air Patrol base north of town. Although, given the current state of things around him, something told Tom that the UNMC medevac would likely be making a return trip as well. Possibly a couple of them.

'Anyway,' the sheriff said, acknowledging the search-and-rescue bird as it banked slowly over their heads. 'Workin' on that now.'

Tom shielded his eyes from the sun, watching the chopper carve a widening circle in the sky over their town. He lowered his gaze and caught sight of Tiff near the concession stands, crouched down low to the pavement, pumping up a compression brace around the suddenly famous Marge Holman's elevated right knee.

He took one last look at Big Glenn Rademacher. The man had been a friend – the same guy who'd sponsored Tom's bid for the Junior Law Cadet Academy down in Lincoln, the summer between his junior and senior years of high school. The same guy who'd forked over for fundraiser popcorn, year in and year out, from just about every Cub Scout in town. Girl Scout cookies, too. He'd probably needed one of Mayor Bobby's old grain elevators just to store the stuff. Now he was an unrecognizable mass cocooned in a neon-blue tarp, a fountain of sparks from Mel's torch melting pockmarks in his garish shroud.

The sound of chopper blades slowly faded as the circle widened.

Tom said, 'I'll radio Douglas County.'

Then he turned and stalked back in the direction he'd come.

Sheriff Prescott said, 'Where you running off to now?'

'Speaking of shitheads,' Tom called over his shoulder, 'I can think of at least three more we need to see.'

'Gentlemen.' Anabeth reached between them and pulled the motel room door closed. 'I believe our timetable has accelerated.'

Charley backed up into the room, looking more amazed than alarmed.

Ben felt just the opposite. But part of him wasn't even completely sure why. 'Well, that was fast.'

'As getaway vehicles go, that one's not ideal,' Abe said. 'Somebody was bound to call it in.'

'That, or our good friend Deputy Curnow got Frerking to cough up his tracker app.'

'Hmm.' Abe looked skeptical. 'Maybe.'

Ben nodded. Somehow, he didn't think so, either.

One way to find out. He took Gordon's prepaid from his pocket, pulled up the recent calls menu, and dialed the first number on the list.

Gordon answered on the first ring. 'If this is a cop, the party you're trying to reach is no longer . . .'

'It's me,' Ben said. 'What's the word on Ajeet?'

'Still in surgery,' Gordon said. 'Dude. Where are you? And what the hell did you do to my van?'

'What do you mean?'

'Please do not give me that shit. The front end is *clearly* jacked up. Plus I can see a bunch of chimps with badges failing to break into it even as we speak.'

'Never mind where am I,' Ben said. 'Where are *you*?'

'Still at the hospital. Where else would I be?'

'Then how—'

'Son, I got fiber-optic cameras mounted in the roof lights, the side mirrors, the rear spoi—'

'Never mind,' Ben said. 'Of course you do.'

'I'm watching on my laptop right now. I swear, if that cream-filled flatfoot breaks out my window I'll file a—'

'So it wasn't you, then.'

'Wasn't me what?'

'Who told them where to find us.'

There came a long pause. 'OK, I won't lie. That hurts.'

'Just checking,' Ben said. 'Listen, I'm sorry about the van. I promise I'll pay for everyth—'

'Especially considering you're, like, all over the news right now.'

'Gordon, I really am sorry, OK? It was completely unavoi . . .' Ben stopped. 'All over what news?'

Gordon dropped his voice to a lower tone. 'You've been popping up on my alerts for an hour. All the local stations.'

'I guess that makes sense. Saying what, exactly?'

'You,' Gordon informed him, 'are to be considered armed and dangerous. Oh, also, your kid's officially an Amber Alert.'

'Please tell me you're kidding.'

'Sorry, man. They're running your picture and everything. It's the one from your work badge, I think. They're calling you disgruntled.'

Ben closed his eyes. What had he expected? OK, yeah, technically he'd entered his ex-wife's home without permission. And, given certain legally binding custody agreements, today probably didn't quite fall under the 'reasonable visitation' heading where he and Charley were concerned. But through all of this, it had never once entered Ben's mind that anyone might think to accuse him of kidnapping his own son. He'd left a note!

'By the way, you never said you owned a guitar company,' Gordon added. 'How could it be that for two boring-ass years in Cubelandia you failed to inform us there was something sorta arguably cool about you?'

'Listen, Gordon. Can you do me another favor?'

'Oh, shit.' On the other end of the line, Gordon's voice dropped further, gaining a note of urgency. 'Sorry, gotta go. Deputy Dawg just showed up back here again. With Omaha PD. And . . . yeah. He looks super pissed.'

'Gordon . . .'

'Good luck, man. They won't hear shit from me. Keep it in the wind and check in next time you can. Frerking out.'

The line went dead in his ear. Ben put the phone back in his pocket.

'Well?' Abe asked.

'Yeah,' Ben said. 'It wasn't him.'

'What a relief,' Reuben Wasserman muttered from the corner. He hadn't moved a muscle this whole time. Ben had almost forgotten he was still here.

'OK,' said Abe. 'However they found us, it's only a matter of time before they figure out we're not over there. And it won't be long after that before one of them looks across the highway, gets a bright idea, and thinks to check over here. So.' She clapped her hands and rubbed them together. 'Our need for a plan cannot be overstated.'

Ben looked at her. Something nagged at him – a vague feeling of pieces out of place, of mistakes being made – but he couldn't quite pin the feeling down. 'What sort of plan did you have in mind, exactly?'

'A lightning-fast one, preferably.' She snapped her fingers and pulled out her own phone. 'How many Uber drivers do you think they'd have on a Saturday in a town this size?'

Charley looked confused. 'Um, Dad?'

'Yep?'

'Are we running from the cops, too?'

Ben looked at his son.

Bingo, he thought.

That was it exactly.

EIGHTEEN

'OK, back up,' Anabeth said. 'What am I missing?'

'I'm just saying. Charley's right.'

'Right about what? You're going to have to—'

'Why *are* we running from the cops?'

'Honestly, Ben, I guess I thought we've been on more or less the same page this whole time.'

'I wasn't thinking clearly before,' Ben said. 'Maybe I'm starting to now.'

While Abe had been digging bits of lead from his shoulder, he'd found himself with ample time for thinking. He'd squandered the bulk of that time on a useless recurring question: *Why me?*

But now he was beginning to see the same question from a different angle. These past few years, Ben had become so accustomed to identifying himself as the principal architect of his own misfortunes that his prevailing blamelessness in this situation was disorienting. But setting aside a little admittedly unauthorized dad time, had he even broken a law today?

Even Anabeth seemed stumped for an answer. 'I'm still not sure I understand what you're asking me.'

'I haven't done anything wrong.'

'How is that relevant?'

'Between the three of us, the water boy, the guys, and whatever corroborating evidence we find in the First Floor IT GoPro archive, shouldn't we be running *to* the police?'

Abe tilted her head. 'I can't tell if that's a serious suggestion.'

'Look, obviously they're not going to believe some crazy story about a mud monster from out of the past,' he said. 'But Gordon strung up hidden security cameras all the way around that van. Twenty bucks says there's a hard drive rigged up somewhere in there with ten different angles on what happened back at Christine's. And I *know* those guys were recording this morning – nobody under twenty-five thinks they did anything if they don't put it on YouTube.'

'Hey, Charley,' Abe said. 'You're younger than twenty-five, right?'

'I'll be fourteen in three weeks.'

'Ah! Happy Birthday.' She reached out and gave his arm a friendly squeeze. 'So if you went on YouTube and found a video of a mud monster from out of the past attacking people in the woods, what would you think about that?'

Charley shrugged. 'I'd think it was fake.'

Abe raised her eyebrows at Ben.

'Yeah, sure,' Ben said. 'Fine. But they'll see *something*. The time code will put us at my place. Emergency logs will show what time we got to Ashland. I'd have needed a rocket launcher to do that kind of damage to my own house in that amount of time. Then there's Dr Blotto over there.' He jerked a thumb back toward Wasserman in the corner. 'Him and his psycho-stalker scrapbook.'

'Now you've gone back to being unkind.'

'No good deed goes unpunished,' Wasserman mumbled.

'And don't forget poor Jeeter.' A horrible thought popped into Ben's head: *If he pulls through.* He cursed himself for thinking it, even involuntarily. Then he felt angry for being placed in a position to think it in the first place. 'As soon as he wakes up, he'll tell the same story we do. And it happens to be the truth. What else is there?'

'Well, let's ponder,' Abe said. 'I can think of at least one thing.'

'Which is?'

She smiled at Charley. 'Blue eyes, do you think you could hang tight in here and keep Reuben company for me?' A nod toward the bathroom. 'I'd like to speak to your dad in private a minute.'

'We can talk out here. They're both part of this.' Ben looked at Charley. 'If you want.'

Charley didn't seem to know how to answer. 'I guess?'

Ben turned back to Anabeth. 'So what are *we* missing?'

She folded her arms as if she'd tired of waiting for him to arrive at the obvious on his own. 'You've encountered the creature in person, you tell me. Will the police be able to protect you?'

'The police have more guns than I do. Thicker walls, too.'

'And you're willing to bet your life that they're thick enough?' She tilted her head toward Charley. 'You're willing to bet his?'

Ben felt another flash of anger, but he swallowed it. Because they were finally getting somewhere.

Of *course* he didn't think the cops would be able to protect them. Not even if they did listen to a word he had to say. Ben had already speculated about how a stranger might see him if all they had to go on was Reuben Wasserman's incomplete scrapbook. What if all they had to go on were snapshots from the last two days? They'd see a broke, divorced, mid-life self-destructive type who had a) learned that he was about to lose his job; b) learned that he was about to lose regular visits with his son; and c) finally lost his marbles. That's what they'd see. Each wrong move he made from this point on could only serve to dig him in deeper. Which only put Charley in more danger than he was already.

Besides, he'd already seen Wasserman's creature walk through cinderblock as if it were cardboard. He'd watched the thing absorb a load of buckshot with its face, then throw it back at him. It was – somehow, against everything Ben thought he'd learned about the world through four decades of walking around on it – an actual, legitimate supernatural being. Did the cops have a gun for that?

'Because the creature won't stop,' Abe went on. She sidled a little closer to Charley, draping an arm around his shoulders. Ben marveled at Charley's seeming acceptance of this gesture from a complete stranger. If he or Christine tried to touch him these days, he squirmed away like he was part eel, but somehow Anabeth had tamed him as effortlessly as she had the feral tomcat on the porch. 'It'll just keep . . . coming.'

'I might be moving away,' Charley said. 'If it matters.'

Ben looked at him. 'You know about that?'

'Overheard Mom and Tony fighting about it.'

Abe rested her head briefly against Charley's. 'Sweetheart, I'm so sorry. But it doesn't.'

Fighting about it? Ben thought, then wiped the thought from his head. What the hell was the matter with him? 'Maybe I'll move, too,' he said. 'That thing wasn't built when the world had cars.'

'Move to the other side of the planet every few years, if that's how you want to live your life.' She tousled Charley's hair. 'Hope against hope that this dreamy devil here never gives you a grandchild to worry about. Forget about all the collateral damage you'll be trailing behind you everywhere you go. Not your problem!'

'Look, you can spare me the—'

'But the creature will keep coming,' she finished. 'Forever. Until it's done the job it was made to do.'

'OK,' Ben said. 'The creature keeps coming. Fine. Why do *you* care?'

Abe looked sincerely hurt by the question. 'What do you mean?'

'I mean, what's it to you if I turn us in to the cops, or this mud monster gets us, or I jump off a cliff? Until the day before yesterday, you and I had never spoken. We don't even know each other.'

'Ahhh.' She nodded slowly. 'Now I get it.'

'That makes one of us.'

'You're being incredibly childish right now, you know.'

'Am not.'

Anabeth sighed. 'I know I've been withholding, and I'm sorry for that. My story is long, and it needs to be told properly. Once we've reached a place where I can truly do that, you'll understand everything. I promise.'

Ben made a show of looking around the room. 'Seems like as good a place as any to me.'

'Ow,' Charley said.

Abe seemed to notice that the hand she'd flopped across his shoulder had turned itself into a claw. Her slim knuckles had gone white from squeezing.

'Oops.' She retracted her stiff grip and gave him a quick, almost motherly smooch on his head. 'Sorry about that, doll.'

'It's OK. He brings it out of people.'

'I believe you.'

'Maybe *you're* the one who's running from the cops,' Ben suggested.

'Oh, criminy, Ben. Those cops out there are the least of anyone's problems.' She pointed her finger toward the cheap hollow door currently standing between them and those cops out there. 'Forget about the cops a minute. Actually, you know what? Forget about the creature, too.'

'What creature?'

'Aren't you hilarious.' Abe dropped her pointer finger and looked him in the eye. 'But know this: Malcom Frost is on his way. If the cops are here, he may well be here already.' Her expression darkened. 'We are not ready for Malcom Frost. Please trust me on that.'

'I do,' Wasserman said from the corner.

Ben couldn't help noticing the fresh new worry flickering across Charley's face at the mention of the sinister albino-looking dude she called Frost, last seen snarling at them from behind steam-fogged glass.

He was completely out of his depth. And then there was Abe's comment about collateral damage. How much of that had he caused already? In wasting any more time here, Ben could be making the worst mistake of his life, and there were plenty to choose from.

Then again, maybe all that was exactly how Anabeth Glass – whoever she was – needed him to feel. For all he knew, her goal might be to deliver them to somebody even scarier than this Frost character. How was he supposed to make the right decision if she wouldn't play fair?

So instead of doing something smarter, he said, 'Malcom Frost. Who's that again?'

Charley's eyes widened. He looked back and forth between them, waiting to see what would happen next.

Ben waited, too. Abe looked at Charley as if to ask: *Can I get a little help, here?*

Charley dropped his gaze to the floor. Sheepishly, he said, 'You did sort of promise.'

Anabeth merely hung her head. Her slim shoulders rose slowly, then fell.

'Have it your way,' she finally said.

After nearly two hours of looping and backtracking – essentially meandering their way unproductively through the hardwood bluffs running up and down the Missouri River valley like some cosmic corn farmer's idea of a proper mountain range – Frost finally conceded to a temporary stoppage in order to regroup.

He pulled into the rock-topped strip that passed for a parking lot at the Twisted Tail Steakhouse & Saloon – a shake-roofed structure that looked to Frost like a Pony Express depot with Harley-Davidsons instead of horses. They'd passed by the same establishment twice now, it being the most prominently visible operation at this otherwise unremarkable crossing of roads that called itself Beebeetown, Iowa. The town itself did not appear on Frost's map.

In fairness, that might not have been the town's fault. He switched off the ignition.

'We home already?' Lucius asked from the passenger seat.

'Oh, good,' Frost said. 'You're awake. How's the shoulder?'

Lucius creaked one eye open, used it to scan his immediate surroundings, then closed it again. He never moved his head from the seat rest. 'Feel better after a steak, I bet. Big ole bloody one.'

'Perhaps later in the day.' Frost switched the key on again. The Lincoln's engine gave an uncharacteristic cough, then turned over and purred back to life. 'Right now, I'm afraid the satellite system needs a swift rebooting.'

Something had been haywire ever since they'd crossed the river, although it had taken Frost nearly thirty miles' travel in the wrong direction before piecing that together with certainty.

Or had it been the correct direction after all? The way the GPS software now insisted on lagging, freezing, and redrawing itself in unexpected new vectors made it impossible to know for sure.

Now, as the car went through its digital start-up routine and the system gradually came back online, the screen seemed to have fritzed entirely. Frost could see their reflections strobing in the glass of the flickering display module.

He sighed. Best case scenario: some kind of temporary solar interference playing havoc with the satellite signal. Worst case: the Glass tramp had damaged something in the car's electronics when she'd rammed them after all.

'Looks like we'll have to do this the old-fashioned way,' he said, removing the Khorkhoi Cube from its dock. 'Hold this, please.'

'Um, no thanks.'

'It's perfectly safe.'

'If you say so.'

'I simply need you to translate,' Frost explained. 'The cube has six sides, each with an indicator. Let's name the sides up, down, north, south, east, and west. When the squirmer touches a side, the corresponding cube face vibrates, and the indicator illuminates. A corner-touch activates two sides at once.'

As if by way of example, the panel under Frost's thumb gave a quick sizzle, and its integrated micro-LED glowed to life. West.

Frost turned the active panel toward Lucius and pointed. 'Like so. Do you see?'

Lucius finally opened his eyes and sat up. 'You go ahead and hang on to it. I'll point you to Wasserman myself.'

'Wouldn't that be impressive?' Almost as soon as Frost had rotated the cube, the indicator had extinguished. Now the cube vibrated again on its opposite side. 'Lucius, you know how much I value your skill set. But let's not let adversity and store-bought narcotics make us ornery.'

'Didn't I ever tell you? I got my own little squirmer. Right up here.' Lucius raised a hand to his forehead. 'It's waking up now. It's saying . . . hang on . . . it's saying . . . get back on 66 and take it straight west out of town.'

'That's already the plan. Do you know why?'

'I give up.'

'Because the device I'm holding cost nearly a million dollars to perfect, three lives to properly stock, and it's telling me to go west.' He tapped the corresponding cube face with his index finger. 'See?'

'Where's it tell you to go after that?'

'That's why I need you to navigate.'

'That's what I'm doing.' Lucius tapped his forehead with a finger. 'Boss, you ever hear the story of John Henry and the steam drill?'

'I have.' Frost could feel his patience expiring. 'The protagonist died, if memory serves.'

'Tell you what. I find our boy before the bug does, you buy me a steak.'

'Worm,' Frost corrected. '*Olgoi-khor—*'

'Porterhouse,' Lucius said. 'Rare as hell. And a baked potato.'

A shadow fell over them, followed by a knock upon Frost's window. Frost looked up to see a large man with a long, braided gray beard. The man wore a POW-MIA bandana on his head and several rings on each hand, most of them shaped like either lightning bolts or skulls. The gap between his grease-stained t-shirt and his grimy, sagging jeans showcased ample tufts of belly hair. He offered a neighborly smile, leaning down as Frost lowered his window.

'You boys need directions?' The man recoiled involuntarily as Frost turned up his face in greeting. 'Sweet Jesus. I mean . . . aw, hell. Sorry about that, fella. I get rude when I'm startled sometimes.'

'That's quite all right,' Frost said. 'And so are we. But you're a true modern-day Samaritan.'

'Actually, partner, tell me,' Lucius interjected. 'Good riding up in these bluffs, I bet?'

'You bet right.'

'This road here. That the best way up to Missouri Valley, or should we head back to the interstate?'

'Interstate could be faster, but thisaway's prettier.'

'That's what I figured. Thanks. Keep the shiny side up, now, hear?'

'I'd tell you the same,' the old biker said, scanning the exterior of the Lincoln. 'But it looks like you boys already flipped the cage.'

'Good thing it's a rental.' Frost raised the window. 'Thanks again.'

As the old biker ambled his way along to the building, hauled open the door, and disappeared inside, Lucius said, 'Whatcha think, boss? Faster or prettier?'

Frost turned to face him. 'Missouri Valley?'

'Dumb shits are holed up there in a Super 8,' Lucius said. 'All three of 'em.'

'And how do you know that?'

Lucius reached up to his right ear, previously concealed from Frost's view, and removed an audio bud. He fished out his mobile phone and showed Frost the screen. 'Police scanner app,' he said. '$4.99. Took about thirty-five seconds to download.'

Frost sat in silence for a moment, pondering Lucius Weatherbee. He pondered the cube in his fingertips. He focused on his breathing. Finally, he said: 'Faster, then, I suppose.'

Lucius leaned his head back and closed his eyes again. 'You're the boss.'

Frost put the car in gear and got them back on the road.

'You'll have to settle for the Reader's Digest Condensed Version,' Abe said, sitting down on the bed. 'But if this is the only way to get you cooperating, I'll start with a confession.'

Charley said, 'The *what* version?'

'Never mind,' Ben told him. He took a seat on the air-conditioning unit and motioned Charley back to his chair. 'Confess away.'

'I just remembered that I did lie to you.'

'Which time?'

'The day we met. I told you I was thirty. That's not strictly true.'

Ben copied what he'd seen Catholic priests do in the movies and crossed the air in front of him: *you're forgiven.* 'Is this important to the story?'

'Kind of.'

'Then I'm still listening.'

'I also told you I was married, and I was. I told you it ended, and it did. But I let you believe that my marriage had broken up. That's not strictly true, either.'

'If it matters, what's the strictly truth?'

She folded her hands in her lap. 'My husband died.'

'I'm very sorry.'

Anabeth shrugged. 'I've had time to accept it. We had a happy life, all things considered, and I was with him when it ended.'

Charley asked, 'Was he sick?'

She smiled and shook her head. 'Natural causes.'

Ben said, 'I'm confused.'

'And I turned 162 this past May,' Anabeth Glass replied.

THE WATER CARRIER'S WIFE

iv. Cow Town, USA
Kansas City

Silas Wasserman, the water carrier, carried on.

It was true, especially during those first lonesome years, that he missed home to the point of soul-sickness at times. On the brighter side, Silas imagined that there must have been far duller places to be moored for the rest of one's natural life than Kansas City, Missouri, between 1857 and the dawn of the twentieth century.

It was a time of great change. Upheaval, yes. Unrest, inevitably. But also unparalleled growth and prosperity.

When he'd first arrived, the whole of the town could fit within a single square mile; fewer than 3,000 souls called the newly minted City of Kansas home. By the end of the Civil War, they had a railroad. Half a decade beyond the Battle of Westport, they'd gained 30,000 people and 100,000 steers. When the century finally turned, the stockyards had grown to rival even Chicago's.

It was, in a sense both figurative and literal, like having front-row tickets at the Theater of Manifest Destiny. From his meager little clapboard hovel, tucked away in a gritty, cobbled corner of the boisterous West Bottoms, Silas Wasserman watched a thriving American city climb up out of the ground and tack itself together around his ears.

Of course, none of it would have seemed to amount to much, had he not – by his own outrageous good fortune, and at such long last! – found a harmonious soul to take in the show with him.

And what an extraordinary soul he'd found.

Or had she found him? Silas would spend the rest of his life wondering how such an undeserved gift had come to be his. She had a smile like sunrise and eyes like the smoky dusk; to lowly, dutiful Silas Wasserman, she may as well have *been* the rising and setting sun. Inexplicably, she loved him. And oh, how very deeply he loved her.

Her name was Anabet Glacz.

'Filthy Gyppo whore,' the man snarled in her face. 'I'll melt a snowbank with yer guts.'

Anabet clawed at his face, trying for his rheumy black eyes, her screams making white plumes in the cold. He was a big, stinking ox of a man, with fur-lined boots and pelts on his back and breath reeking of whiskey and tallow. He'd taken her for Romani, which she was, and therefore a thief, which she was not. But such men rarely bothered themselves with distinctions. And every settlement along this river had such men.

This one had torn off her *diklo*, taken her by the hair, and shoved her into the alley between the blacksmith's and the livery. Not to punish her for thieving (although that, surely, would have been his claim, had Anabet made the wiser mistake of crossing his path in a place where the constables came around). No. Merely because he'd considered it his warrant to do with her as he pleased.

Their relationship had soured after Anabet's knee found him square in his overripe plums. Now a filthy hand clamped over her mouth, stifling her breath and making her gag; she heard the wicked steel of his Bowie knife scraping free of its scabbard. Saw the enormous blade winking at her in the silvery moonlight.

Anabet only fought harder; she thrashed against his grip, squirming beneath his crushing weight as he pressed her flat against a plank of rough pine.

'Let . . . me . . . *go!*'

'Get ready now, girlie,' he panted, his foul breath hot in her ear. 'Here it comes.'

Just then, a young Jew wandered past. He saw them and stopped in his tracks at the mouth of the alley: short of stature, slight of build, his flat-brimmed hat and long, corkscrew sidecurls making a distinctive silhouette in the wintry gloom.

'Excuse me,' he said. 'Is everything all right?'

'Keep movin', boy.'

Anabet wrenched her head back and screamed, 'I took nothing! He means to kill me dead!'

At once the greasy, calloused hand clamped over her mouth again, mashing her lips against her teeth. Her head banged against the wall of the storage shack behind her. She saw flashing stars. Tasted coppery blood along the edges of her tongue.

'Now see here,' the young Jew said, taking his first timid step into the alley. Then another. 'By all means, unhand that young lady.'

'I said shove, half-pecker. 'Less you want it whittled down to a nub.'

'See here!' The man with the curls gave the drunken trader three firm whaps across his broad back with the flat of his palm. 'Please leave that young lady be.'

The trader made a sound deep in his chest like a bear waking early in its cave. He turned slowly.

The young man saw the knife and raised his gloved hands. 'Sir. I assure you that I am unarmed.'

Quick as lightning, the trader thrust out his free hand, grabbing this newcomer by the throat until the much smaller man balanced precariously on the toes of his ragged boots.

'I tell you what,' the trader said, 'they mighta clipped the tip, but they musta left every bit of them balls. 'Cause ya got yerself a pair on you, boy. Aintcha?'

The young Jew's hat tumbled to the snow as he pawed at the man's stout arm. His eyes bulged. Spittle flew from his lips as he attempted to make words.

'Eh? Speak up! I got me an infected ear.'

'*You're . . . choking . . . me.*'

'Right observant fella, too.' The trader flicked the big blade of his skinning knife, deftly separating the young Jew's curlicue *payes* from the left side of his head. He flicked the knife again, bringing symmetry to the arrangement. Then he released his grip.

The young Jew collapsed to his hands and knees, hatless and defiled. He collected the limp strands of his *payes* as he struggled to his feet, gasping for breath, eyes streaming with tears. 'Now . . . see . . . here,' he wheezed, stepping bravely forward again, brandishing his severed locks like an accusation.

The trader's low, malignant chuckle sounded like a bucket of corn slop dumped in a trough. He pounded the center of the young Jew's forehead with the butt of his knife as though hammering a handbill to a tree. The young man's chin snapped up, and his eyes rolled back; he wobbled in place for a moment, arms flung out wide.

Blood streamed from the gashed purple knot already rising from his bare, freshly shorn head.

'Back on yer knees, boy,' the trader growled, ramming a ham-sized fist into the defenseless man's midsection. 'Lemme hear ya pray Jesus.'

The young Jew dropped into a bent-limbed pile like a marionette snipped from its strings. The burly trader had stomped the poor dazed man nearly half to death by the time Anabet spied the flat-bladed coal shovel leaning up against the side of the blacksmith's shed. The shovel made a sound like a muffled church bell as she brought it down with all the force she could muster atop the drunken trader's skull.

Her cold hands went instantly numb at the vibration of the impact, which seemed to travel from the shovel's smooth handle all the way up her arms and into her teeth. The trader grunted once, stumbled forward, then pitched over sideways, sprawling on the dirty snowpack like an overturned feed wagon.

By this time, both the smith and the stable owner had charged into the alley, followed at some remove by a tentative scattering of bystanders.

'What in all holy hell's goin' on out here?' the blacksmith hollered. He was short and thick-bodied, with scorch marks decorating his leather apron and steam rising up from his hard, bare arms.

The livery man stood a head taller but narrower by perhaps two stone, even in his heavy barn coat. He took one look at the uncon-scious men on the ground, then at Anabet.

'I know you,' he said. 'You're with them bunch camped out by Brush Creek.'

Anabet dropped the shovel to the frozen ground with a clang. 'The big one was attacking the little one,' she said, pointing to her attacker and her savior in turn.

'So you figured you might oughta hit the both of 'em with yonder shovel?'

'Only him,' she said, pointing again. 'He had a knife. The little one had nothing.'

'Well, hell,' the blacksmith said. 'That's Jacques Degarmo. Shoulda hit the sumbitch harder. And with the short edge.'

The taller one said, 'That other one's my stable boy.'

'He'll be late for work, I 'spect.'

'Tarnation. Didn't even hardly recognize him without his lop-ears.'

'That boy's mother wouldn't recognize him. Either one of 'em alive?'

As if in answer, the stable boy released a low, plaintive moan.

'Fair enough,' said the smith, turning a skeptical eye toward Anabet. 'I thought I heard a woman screamin'. Sure that wasn't you, young miss?'

Anabet spat blood and shook her head quickly, pointing at the stable boy. 'I only heard him.'

'Then why you bleedin'?'

'I think I bit my tongue.'

'The hell you doin' back here in the alley, anyhow?'

'Just cutting through.'

'Never mind how she got here,' the stable owner said. 'We best get these two the hell somewhere's else before big hoss wakes up.'

'Soon as young miss here figures out how she's gonna pay me for damages,' said the smith, stooping to retrieve his shovel. He raised the implement to inspect its noticeably misshapen blade. 'That was my good scoop.'

'Oh, pipe down, Guthrie. You can pound the durn thing back into shape if you like it so much. What am I supposed to do?' The livery man nudged the blood-covered fellow with one manure-caked boot. 'That's my good stable boy.'

'My grandmother does our doctoring,' Anabet said. 'I'll take responsibility for his care.'

The blacksmith smirked at the stable owner. 'That right?' he said. 'And how ya plannin' on that, young miss? Figure on carryin' him out to Brush Creek on your back?'

The stable owner sighed. 'I got a wagon. My sister's boy's inside. He'll take you.'

Anabet lowered her eyes. 'I thank you for your kindness, sir. I'll return with payment for both of you.'

'You just bring Silas back in one piece, and sooner the better,' the stable owner said. 'My sister's boy ain't worth a fart in a high wind.'

The smith *harrumphed* and returned to his shop, bent shovel on his shoulder. The stable man planted his fists on his hips and surveyed the job on the ground at his feet.

Silas.

That was the young Jew's name.

* * *

He awoke three days later, during a snowfall, in the tent Anabet
shared with her grandmother near the south bank of the frozen
creek.

They'd settled here for winter, her small clan, in a community
of humble bender tents arranged around the *vurdon*, their living
wagon. Beneath the low-hanging promise of a hard gray sky, the
camp prepared for the coming storm. Women and children gathered
water and firewood. A party of able-bodied men had gone afield to
check the rabbit snares, while others set about repairing and rein-
forcing the shelters to withstand the weight of a heavy snow. The
younger boys fed and bedded the three aging mules. Anabet stayed
behind, in the warmth of the tent, where she attended to the mending
while she watched and learned.

Never did she tire of watching her grandmother's crooked, long-
practiced hands doing their business. The old woman prepared a
bolus of yarrow and meadowsweet for the fevered young Jew called
Silas, who continued to surprise all in the camp by not dying. Finally,
on this morning, he surprised his two caregivers further still,
suddenly coughing, then groaning, then sitting bolt upright upon
the straw mat that had served these past days as his bed.

'The stone,' he mumbled, feebly patting at his pockets like a
drunken man searching for his money clip. 'My stone . . .'

Anabet set down her stitching and came to Silas's side. From her
pocket she retrieved the unusual object for which she knew, at once,
he must be searching – a totem of some kind, she'd surmised.

But not quite a stone, as he'd called it. Rather, something like
a stone, shaped from some manner of clay. The clay appeared to
have been smoothed by hand and hardened by sun or by fire. It was
flat like a river stone, slightly larger than the cup of her palm, with
a surprising heft for its size. It smelled vaguely unpleasant to her
nose, even in the cold. It had been engraved with what appeared to
be a single word in his given Hebrew, which Anabet recognized,
but could not translate:

א מ ת

She pressed the stone into his clammy palm as she stroked his
sweat-slick brow. 'I found it in your pocket,' she whispered. 'It
didn't look comfortable to sleep on.'

'My stone.'

'Yours again.'

She smiled at him, but the young Jew called Silas didn't seem to notice. He closed his eyes and sagged back to the mat, clutching the stone to his breast.

'He spoke,' she said, patting the back of his hand. 'He must be gaining.'

Her grandmother clucked her displeasure as she worked her bolus into a finger-shaped lozenge. She disapproved of a *gaje* in her tent. Or in the camp. Or, indeed, anywhere within range of her failing sight, let alone her granddaughter's caring hand. But for his actions in the alley, as Anabet had described them (and Anabet had described them just as they'd occurred, despite the bitter tongue-lashing she'd be bound to receive for venturing about alone in the town – doubly for venturing about alone in the town after sunset), she owed this particular outsider a debt.

So she peeled the young Jew's upper lip away from his teeth and tucked the medicinal wad into the pocket between lip and gum, just above his prominent eye-tooth.

'The stone,' Anabet mused, wringing a cloth and dabbing Silas's brow. 'What must it mean?'

The old woman clucked again.

'*Mamio*? Have you no idea?'

The old woman grumbled a short phrase before she brushed her hands together over the brave young man – a brief gesture of riddance as she turned away.

She spoke no English, of course. Unlike Anabet, the old woman had no desire to learn. But if she *had* spoken the tongue of this new country, Anabet knew what she would have said instead:

This one is cursed.

v. The Witch

All through that winter, Silas spent as much time in the Gypsy camp as in his own meager home, which seemed somehow colder and emptier to him now than it had before.

His intentions, of course, were transparent even to the children. But little by little, his devotion earned Silas a modest yet rarified esteem in the camp. The wages he didn't lose to the men and their good-natured *bujo* – the beguiling riddles and clever tricks and impossibly crafty games of chance that had given them their misinformed (yet not *entirely* undue) reputation amongst Silas's fellow *gajo* – he spent on the food, supplies, and trinkets for the youngsters he brought with him on his regular visits. They placed great value in a name, these Roma, and seemed to appreciate Silas's pride in his own. So whenever he shared their company, Silas Wasserman always made a special point of making at least one trip down to the frozen creek with two of their odd, square-shaped wooden pails in each hand. To carry their water.

Anabet – already regarded as practically a spinster amongst her own kind, even at her glowing twenty-two years – had a word for his standing among them: *pash-ta-pash*. The word meant *Gypsy friend*, she explained. It applied to any trusted outsider and entitled him to the hospitality of the camp. It did not, Silas was gratified to learn, apply easily, or often.

Nor was it – to his abiding chagrin – a sentiment shared by the old woman who had restored him to health.

More than once, Silas questioned the wisdom in his attempts to win her favor, which only seemed to make matters worse. In fact, the old woman seemed to despise him more the harder he tried. Long ago, she had renounced her *nav gajikano* – the name all Roma used for themselves in their interactions with outsiders. Silas had learned the imprudence in attempting to pronounce (or, indeed, to utter) her *nav romano*. And he dared not follow Anabet's manner in addressing her as *Mamio*. So he had no way of thinking of her except as 'the old woman' – a stooped assemblage of wrinkles and sinew, with eyes as dark and watchful as a hawk on the wing.

'*Mamio* is of the old world,' Anabet reassured him, always with the same playful grin – that grin which caused her eyes to twinkle and Silas's heart to stutter in his chest. 'But I am of the new.'

Ironically, the old woman reminded him, in so many ways, of Rabbi Loew, who remained the closest thing to family that poor, orphaned Silas Wasserman could claim. Especially when he learned the other word the children in camp used for her:

Choxani.

That one meant *witch*.

*   *   *

As fascinated as her sweet, silly Silas seemed to be with the Rom and their ways, Anabet was every bit as curious to know all he could tell her about his world. But nothing intrigued her more than the one thing he seemed so reluctant to explain.

He called it his Shepherd Stone, and he claimed it meant nothing. But Anabet could see that the strange-smelling stone with the even stranger markings was never further than his pocket (or, during those times when his pockets were elsewhere, an arm's reach from his hand).

One day, he brought snowshoes with him from town. Using them, in the days and weeks that followed, he and Anabet were able to take even longer walks amidst the winter-bare trees. Eventually, they discovered a spot of their own, at the base of a limestone bluff, an hour's travel upcreek: a natural dugout in the rock that gave shelter from the wind and warmed nicely with a fire.

It was here that Anabet, those long months in the prairie cold, came to know Silas as a wife knows her husband. It was here that she pleaded with him to travel on with them after the thaw. And it was here, finally, that Silas unburdened to her his soul.

'The body of the creature,' he said, once he'd finished telling her his incredible tale, holding the Shepherd Stone between them in the dancing light of the fire. He showed her the thin scar tracing the lifeline of his palm. 'The blood of the shepherd. That's me.' He turned the stone over. '*Emet.*'

Anabet traced the stone's inscription with her finger, softly repeating back the name of each character as Silas spoke them aloud: *aleph, mem, tav*. 'What does it mean?'

'It means *truth*,' he said, holding her finger to each letter in turn. 'Breath of God: *aleph*. Water: *mem*. And faith: *tav*. First letter, middle letter, and last letter of our alphabet. All things, beginning to end.'

Anabet took the stone from his hand. It felt cold. '*Emet*,' she whispered.

'And so you see why I cannot go with you,' Silas told her, openly weeping by then. 'Should the creature awaken, my duty is here.'

It was the shepherd's job, he explained, to prevent the mindless creature from wreaking unintended havoc on the people and places in its path. And only the shepherd, armed with the stone, held the power to terminate the mission if things went irretrievably awry.

It seemed that nobody had imagined a shipwreck on the prairie placing the creature out of reach entirely.

'We'll find this man Wolcott ourselves, then,' Anabet said. 'Before the thaw. I'll hit him with a shovel.'

He choked on his own sweet laugh. 'Rabbi Loew's magic could not account for the possibility that Wolcott might be slain by another hand. Or by illness. Or by any other means.' He sighed. 'It was among the reasons he needed a shepherd in the first place. If I'd arrived to discover Wolcott already dead, I was to use the stone to send the creature back to the earth.'

Anabet felt confounded by the foolishness of the idea. 'And what if *you* had died while traveling? What if the creature had arrived with no shepherd at all?'

To this, Silas had no answer.

She pressed him further. 'And if Wolcott had passed his blood to another? If he'd sired children?'

Again, Silas could offer no response.

It seemed there were many things that Beecher and Loew, in their righteous wisdom, had not bothered to consider.

'And if you die tomorrow? Before the creature wakes?'

She'd never seen such sadness in his eyes. 'Then my failure will be complete.'

His failure!

Anabet could not understand, no matter how he tried to explain. Had Silas Wasserman destroyed a steamboat? Had Silas created the monster that slept in this river even now? If this preacher and this rabbi stopped making monsters and went back to sending rifles instead, would it be Silas Wasserman's duty to catch every stray bullet before innocents could be harmed?

Shepherd. Water carrier. Duty. Anabet saw none of these things before her now.

She saw only Silas. *Her* Silas.

And so she finally took him by the hands, meaning only to comfort him, to make him see her in return. But she recoiled with a gasp. 'Silas!' For it was not, she discovered, merely his eyes that wept.

Somehow, as they sat together in the last of the warmth from their dwindling fire, the scar on his palm – long sealed and faded – had begun to ooze droplets of blood.

'Oh dear,' he said, staring at his own hand as if it belonged to somebody else. 'I . . . I must have . . . how very strange.'

Without hesitation, Anabet followed an impulse. She retrieved a thin shard of limestone from the ground, drawing its edge along her own lifeline. When she saw red fill the shallow new channel in her freshly separated flesh, she pressed their palms together and said, 'If you must stay, then let your duty be my duty. Let your burdens be mine. Let us stay here by your river and fail together.'

It was only then that they discovered – as Silas held her gaze with a yearning so pure that it warmed Anabet more deeply than the fire – that they were no longer alone.

'Anabet,' a voice behind her croaked.

Anabet spun her head to find her grandmother's silhouette at the mouth of their hideaway, stark against the snow glare outside. It was almost as if a gnarled, stunted tree had quietly grown there as they'd whiled away their afternoon.

'*Mamio!*' she cried, scrambling to her knees. 'What are you doing? How have you come so far in the cold?'

'*Te avel angla tute.*' The old woman spat on the ground, slashing a line through the air in front of her with the long, yellowed fingernails of one knobby hand.

Then she hissed out an incantation that made Anabet's blood run cold.

Silas yelped like a puppy and dropped the Shepherd Stone, which now glowed, mysteriously, like a coal from the fire. The old *choxani* pulled up her headscarf like an executioner's hood, retreating from view so quickly that she might not have been there at all.

Anabet's heart raced. She knew she should follow.

But she couldn't seem to move. A dizziness overtook her. Her limbs felt spent of all strength.

Silas spoke with a trembling voice. 'I fear I haven't the courage to ask you what she spoke just then.'

'*It is so,*' she whispered.

And when they looked down at their hands and saw that they'd healed, she knew in her heart that it was.

The thaw came. The Roma broke camp and moved on. Anabet stayed, and the world became green again.

Once again, Silas had ruined everything.

But Anabet, somehow, convinced the poor bumbling wretch she'd married – for that was how they saw themselves, as husband and wife, even though they'd conducted no further ceremony beyond that late-winter day in the cave – that despite their extraordinary tribulations, they truly had been blessed.

She taught him lessons without teaching: in her manner, in her presence, in her faithful, abiding love. In her seemingly unquenchable wonder at life all around them. She harbored a particular affinity for the abolitionists, his Anabet, and a special empathy for the American Negro. This she owed to over the centuries of enslavement her own people still endured, back in her homeland, even as the plantations here thrived. To understand her sentiments, Silas had only to think of the Israelites in Egypt before Moses returned.

Together they followed, with great interest, the Reverend Henry Ward Beecher's adultery trial back in New York. It was a sensational case that seemed to enrapture the country's attention even as it tore the gun-running preacher's own family asunder. Letters from Rabbi Loew, of course, had stopped coming long before this time. Silas knew, though no word ever reached him, that the old rabbi – his caretaker, his mentor, his own *choxani* – lived no more.

Silas wept.

And carried on.

The old woman's curse had, among other things, left Anabet barren. Or so they'd come to believe. And then came a spring that showed them differently. In late September of that year – on the same day the notorious James brothers robbed the ticket office at Kansas City's booming Industrial Exposition of $978 and a few odd coins – she bore him a son.

She would have been well into her thirty-sixth year by then. But years had already ceased to mean the same to Anabet as they meant to others, including Silas himself. They named the boy Abraham. After Silas's true father, the father of the Jews; after the assassinated American President, whom Anabet so admired.

They called him Abe.

And they watched him grow. They watched him grow like the new Union Depot, near the stockyards – the largest building west of New York, which always made Silas think fondly of home. They watched him grow like the railroads that replaced the great paddle steamers that had, once upon a time, brought Silas here. They watched him grow like the trees along the muddy river, no longer harvested as boiler fuel. They watched him grow into a man fit to carry more water than his foolish, doddering father ever could.

If only, as Silas wished often – often, and until his last breath – he and his darling Anabet could have grown old together.

Let your duty be my duty. Let your burdens be mine.

The old woman had been known for her faith in all manner of wards and spells. Blessings for every occasion. Retributions as varied as life itself. The new world called them superstitions; the old world knew better than to tempt fate with disbelief. For Anabet, they were, simply, her *mamio* – as much a part of the old woman who'd raised her as wrinkled skin and crooked bones. But to the extent of her knowledge, the old woman had never before issued the curse she considered direst among them all:

Immortality.

Let your duty be my duty. Let your burdens be mine.

Anabet's own words to Silas, pressing their wounds together that day in the cave.

And her *mamio*'s unthinkable words in return: *It is so.*

And so it happened that the moment Silas passed, his blood forever fused with Anabet's own.

She'd been at his bedside, holding the stone against his weakening hand, when the light finally left his sunken, wrinkle-bound eyes. Where for decades the rabbi's unhallowed clay remained cold to Anabet's touch, even through the heat of the sultriest Missouri summer, now the stone became like a part of her flesh, as warm as the skin of her own palm. Its markings glowed briefly, like flaring embers. Just as they had on that day in the cave, so many long years before. The peculiar smell of it lingered no more in her nose.

Let your duty be my duty. Let your burdens be mine.

And Anabet, at last, truly understood.

An old man's foolish magic had bound the water carrier to the Shepherd Stone; an old woman's vengeful magic had bound Anabet to the water carrier. Even in that moment, she somehow felt the deeper truth of this in her soul: the curse would remain hers until the duty she'd sworn to this detested outsider had been fulfilled.

And then her Silas was gone.

It happened again, just two cruelly brief years later, when their beautiful son Abraham died – cut down by racking, wasting consumption even as he entered his prime. Anabet was not permitted at his bedside; still, her crippled heart knew exactly the moment her only child passed. She knew because the markings on the stone once again flared like embers. Then, as quickly as they'd illuminated, they faded back to crude scratchings. In a false rock commissioned by arrogant men. Now forever warm in her hand.

So faded the last of Anabet's joy.

Without it, she marveled at how inescapably bitter the irony of it all now seemed.

For the outlaw marauder William Wolcott hadn't *needed* a soulless assassin from the East after all; the West had taken care of that unsavory matter for all parties concerned. Indeed, the man they'd called Bloody Bill had been dead since the very spring her *familiya* had traveled on. Shot through the liver at a poker game in Atchison, Kansas. By a fur trader named Jacques Degarmo.

And what did it matter, anyway? An entirely new William, this one named Quantrill, had already taken Wolcott's place by then. The newspapers had given away his repugnant *nav gajikano* to Bloody Bill Anderson, yet the next William in line. Together, this pair – along with the James brothers and the rest of Quantrill's so-called Raiders – spilled more Jayhawker blood on their way to Kentucky than Bloody Bill Wolcott had dreamed in his bloodiest dream.

Her Silas was gone. Her Abraham was gone. Reverend Beecher, Rabbi Loew: gone and gone. Even the river itself had abandoned its prior course. Their creature, their precious golem, was lost to the ages.

But Anabet lived on.

vi. Dingir

They gave her boy to the ground on a windy day in late November, after the leaves had fallen, but before the first winter snow. Abraham's young wife, Ilsa, stood silent behind her veil, a protective arm hooked around Levi, their heartbroken nine-year-old son. Anabet's grandson.

Anabet, who had not aged a day in the past forty years, did not approach them. She resisted the urge of her straining heart to pull little Levi into her embrace. Ilsa – who detested Anabet every bit as deeply as the old *choxani* woman had feared a *gaje* in her tent – had forbidden her from their home after Abraham took ill.

But now there *was* no Abraham. Only a box near a hole in the earth. A new rabbi, just in on the train, who'd never met the body the box contained. A group of people standing in the cold like black crows in a field, waiting to eat hardboiled eggs and lentil stew.

And Anabet. Still younger in body than the one they'd all gathered here to mourn.

Ilsa did not acknowledge her presence. Nor did she release Levi from her side. The boy's mother would never, Anabet understood that day, knowingly allow him to accept the stone that was his birthright. Ilsa Wasserman rejected and dismissed the exasperating superstitions of her family-by-marriage.

Paradoxically, she clung to superstitions of her own. It was Ilsa's belief that Anabet – this aberrant Gypsy interloper among them – represented a *dybbuk*, or an agent of the *shedim*, or some other manner of devil in human form. She resented the Roma blood that flowed in her Levi, just as she abhorred the peculiar teachings of duty and station that Silas and Abraham had already begun passing along to the boy – already preparing him to accept the understanding that one day this river would unleash hell. Sooner or later, a crate would disintegrate. An unholy creature would drag itself ashore, hunting for blood. And only a water carrier would be able to stop it.

But if they'd succeeded in planting the seed in Levi, it would not be sprouting today, or any day soon to come. Nor did such teachings tell the complete story anymore. The Shepherd Stone had warmed for another, after all. So Anabet left their adjacent graves the same way she'd arrived: alone.

Until a voice at her elbow said, 'Such a pity.'

She looked to see the rabbi from the ceremony matching her step. He wasn't a young man, nor yet was he old; his voice carried no particular dialect Anabet could discern. He wore a fur hat with his four-cornered shawl that made him look silly, if warm.

'Oh?' she said, unable to temper herself. 'Were you acquainted with the deceased?'

'Alas,' the rabbi said. 'Rabbi Mandelbaum would have preferred to officiate the ceremony as planned, of course. I tried to do my best in his place.'

Anabet sighed. 'Thank you. You did just fine.'

'That's kind of you to say.'

'Where is your temple?'

The rabbi chuckled and waved a hand. 'Oh, I'm not particularly religious. Though I *am* a believer.'

Anabet stopped. 'What is your name?'

'You can call me a friend.'

'Where were you ordained, Rabbi Friend?'

'I suppose that depends what you mean by *ordained*.'

She felt a hot bite in her chest, then. All at once, the day seemed to become too bright for her eyes. Her fingers began to tremble inside her gloves.

'What is the meaning of this?' she demanded. 'Who are you?'

'So many questions. How did *you* know our good Abraham, if I may ask one in return?'

Anabet stood mute. She disregarded the curious looks from the other mourners as they passed. Anger and confusion tied her tongue. After a long moment, she said, 'He was family.'

'I see. Then it must not be true.'

'What mustn't?'

'What they say about grief.'

'And what do they say of it?'

'That it ages a person.' The rabbi who was not a rabbi gave a sly wink. 'You must tell me your secret, Anabet.'

Harrow.

That was what the man called himself. He didn't reveal where he'd come from, nor the destination to which he'd return. He shared no first name. Only Harrow.

'What does it mean?'

'What does what mean?'

'Your name.'

He seemed amused by the question. 'I have no earthly idea. Why do you ask?'

Anabet went with him to the Hotel Savoy, near the depot, where he'd arranged a room for the duration of his stay. Though she and Silas had delighted in observing the construction of such a marvelous establishment so near their humble home, something about its opulence, on the day of her son's funeral, offended her.

But she joined Harrow there just the same. They shared a table in the new west wing, which now featured a grill and dining room. She and this man from nowhere who didn't even know his own name.

'The Order of . . .'

'Dingir,' Harrow said. '*That* name I can tell you about.'

And tell her he did, uninvited, carrying on around impolite mouthfuls of his dinner. He spoke of a dubious-sounding faction in which he and Silas's mentor, the old rabbi back East, had once shared a fraternity. He explained his Order's mission as stewards of the mortal realm, a kind of self-appointed vanguard against otherworldly harm.

'Silas never spoke of you.'

'Don't take it as a betrayal. The water carrier was unaware. Rabbi Loew kept his own counsel, it must be acknowledged. Even after he was banished, the rebellious old fool.'

'Why?'

'We wouldn't be a very good secret order if we went around talking about ourselves, now, would we?'

'I mean, why was Loew banished?'

'We drive the monsters out, my dear. We don't invite them in. Rabbi Loew abandoned an extraordinarily sacred oath when he elected to meddle with the infinite.' Harrow sawed himself another piece of bloody meat. 'Are you sure I can't order you a plate? They do know how to fix a steer in this town of yours, let's give credit where it's due.'

Even if she could have eaten a bite, Anabet wouldn't have broken bread with this riddling Sphinx across the table from her. And she'd lost what little patience she'd brought along. 'Why are you talking to me now?'

'Given the unfortunate circumstance of Abraham's passing,' Harrow said as he chewed, 'and the relative youth of his successor, the Order felt a limited measure of exposure would be . . . judicious. Hence, an emissary.' He raised his linen, dabbing the glistening juices from the edges of his beard. 'That would be me. Given what I observed of Ilsa and the boy during the service, I'd say it's a good job I'm here. Wouldn't you agree?'

'The benefit escapes me.'

He produced a folded handbill and offered it over. The bulletin announced a date that coming December, when Buffalo Bill Cody and his traveling Wild West Show would be returning to town. She and Silas themselves had attended in '86 – long after Anabet had resigned herself to posing in public as a daughter instead of a wife – to witness Annie Oakley, the sharpshooter, plying her trade on stage.

'As you peruse the new featured attractions,' Harrow said, 'does anything catch your eye?'

AND INTRODUCING HENRIETTA MIDDLETON! this latest flyer proclaimed. *The World's Most Dangerous Grandmother with Kitchen Cutlery in Her Hand – Observe Her Thrilling Feats of Deadly Derring-Do!*

Anabet shoved the handbill back across the table. 'No.'

'Poor old dear,' Harrow observed on her behalf. 'Born in a brothel. A prostitute for a mother, a murderer for a father . . . is it any wonder?'

'Is what any wonder?'

'That she'd end splitting apples in a glorified sideshow. And at her age! It borders on undignified, don't you think?'

'Am I to know who you're talking about?'

'Henrietta Middleton,' Harrow said, tapping the flyer with a finger. 'William Wolcott's only known child. Illegitimate, of course. It's all part of her stage patter. But we've confirmed her extraction.'

'You mean her blood.'

Harrow seemed pleased with her. 'Precisely so.'

Anabet didn't know how else this man expected her to respond to this news. She didn't know how he expected her to feel. Or what she was meant to say. Or why he'd come here to tell her these things.

But of course none of that was true. He expected her to feel grief. She was meant to say nothing. And he'd come here for the stone.

'That's quite a trick,' she told him. 'Perhaps the Order should start its own show.'

'Trick?'

'Naming with any kind of certainty the father of a prostitute's child.'

'The poor thing. After her first paying customer had his way with her, she left the profession.'

'That sounds like a gift, then.'

'As does everlasting life.' Harrow refolded the flyer and returned it to his pocket. 'But enough about the past. Shall we examine the dessert cart while we discuss our future?'

CREATURE

NINETEEN

When she'd finished speaking, Anabeth sat quietly, looking from Ben to Charley to Wasserman and back.

'It's a lot to take in. I know.'

Ben didn't know what to think, let alone say. She'd been right, obviously: on any normal day, he'd have discounted every word of her outlandish story. But after squaring off against an impervious animated mudball with glowing green eyes and superterrestrial strength, disbelief was beginning to seem like a waste of time.

'So you work for the Order.'

'I like to think of it as more of a partnership, but yes,' she said. 'The Order has resources. They've helped me in ways I wouldn't have been able to help myself, over the years. They've helped my family in ways I could not. Secretly, yes. But they've lived up to the recruitment posters, so to speak.' A shrug. 'When called upon, I've helped them in return. Being death-proof turns out to be something of an asset in this line of work.'

Charley said, 'You really can't die?'

'Not until the creature does.' Her smile seemed to come from somewhere distant. 'And people say life is short.'

'How do you know?'

'How do I know what?'

'That you'll . . . you know. After.'

'You mean die? Preferably at home, in bed, during a comfortable sleep? After finally experiencing for myself what old age is actually supposed to feel like?'

Charley blushed, dropped his eyes.

'I'm not sure I'd be able to explain.' Abe tapped her heart. Then her stomach. 'It's a down-here kind of knowing, if you know what I mean.' She tapped her noggin. 'Not so much up here.'

'Do you feel old now?'

'Physically, no. But I'll be honest with you, Charley: I do feel tired.'

'Yeah, but . . . I mean . . . it must still be kind of awesome, right?'

'In the sense of inducing awe, I suppose it is,' Abe said. 'But take it from me, handsome. Being young is a young person's game.'

It was probably some form of textbook narcissism that caused Ben to apply Anabeth's observation to himself, but having been accused of being a textbook narcissist, maybe he couldn't help it. It just seemed so unbearably *silly* now to think that up until two days ago, he'd been hung up on turning forty soon. Feeling stuck. Embarrassed with himself. Like he'd fouled up his best days, and now they were behind him forever. Often, the thought had occurred to him that he should be working on a time machine instead of the world's ten-millionth new overdrive pedal; part of him would do anything for the chance to go back and do a few things differently. Now he remembered something she'd said this morning – *It was me who couldn't grow up* – and he wondered: what would Anabeth Glass give for the chance to move forward?

'So let me see if I have this straight,' Wasserman said from his spot in the corner. He was sitting up a little straighter at last. He still looked like day two of a heroin detox, but his eyes now seemed comparatively alert. 'You're claiming to be my grandmother.'

This gave Anabeth a chuckle, which she seemed to need. 'Well. Great-great-great-great-grandmother, technically. But yes.'

'And I'm supposed to believe that.'

'Why not?'

'Because it's impossible.'

'You're here, aren't you?'

'What does that mean?'

'That some part of you must believe the impossible already.' She looked at Wasserman with such genuine warmth and affection that Ben almost envied the guy a little. 'Circumstances aside, it's the delight of a very long lifetime to share your company, Reuben. How I wish I could have met Eli, too.'

Wasserman sat quietly, staring straight ahead.

'You've done him proud, you know.'

Now Wasserman pushed himself up against the wall, swaying unsteadily on his feet. Without a word, he shambled around the bed and into the bathroom, closing the door behind him.

Field Agent Constance West stood amidst the gritty rubble of brick, glass, framing lumber, and corrugated steel siding that had, up until this morning, comprised the administrative office and two perfectly good vehicle bays of a small-town volunteer fire station.

Ten feet away, her partner, Field Agent Simon Battis, plugged one ear with a knuckle while he spoke into his mobile phone. When he was finished, he pocketed the phone and said, 'That was Washington. We're on with the Joint Chiefs in forty minutes.'

'So I gathered.' West extended her hand. 'Smell my finger.'

Battis grimaced as he approached. 'Thanks, but no thanks.'

West stripped her gloves and tossed him the evidence pouch. It seemed like an unnecessary formality, at this point; she didn't need a molecular analysis to know that the sample she'd just recovered matched the ones they'd taken down in Kansas, then a timber stand in Brownville, then a cow pasture in Peru. Anyone with a nose could have made that call.

Battis glanced at the pouch, equally unimpressed. He didn't even remove his shades. 'Where?'

'Severed electrical conduit.' She pointed. 'Right there. Took a nice little plug out of him.'

'Him? What makes you think of it as a *him* all of a sudden?'

'Big, smelly, likes to smash things . . . gosh, I dunno.'

'Sexist.'

'Fair point,' she said. 'Took a nice little plug out of *it*.'

'We could just go home,' Battis said. 'This thing keeps leaving pieces of itself behind, at this rate it oughta be whittled down to nothing in, what? Five, six more decades?'

'Unless it grows back as it goes.'

Battis sighed. He looked to the north, then to the south. Local law enforcement at this latest site had dwindled to crowd control and the last of the tech teams. Meanwhile, beyond the cordon, in the parking lot of the Food 4 Less down the street, the crowd of townsfolk and media crews had only grown.

West balled up her gloves and sealed them in a biohazard pouch. 'I say we keep working backward from here. Run down the initial dispatch.'

Battis jerked a thumb over his shoulder, opposite her suggestion. 'It's traveling that way. Apparently.'

'Suppose we catch up with it. Then what?'

'You just wrote my pitch to the Joint Chiefs.'

'Perfect,' she said, thinking instead of the one and only Anabeth

Glass. She was around here somewhere. West would have bet her pension on it. *Leave it to the boys to run straight for the guns when all they needed was to find the right girl.* 'That makes it your turn to drive, then.'

The first annual Tops-Optional Sandbar Volleyball Invitational had just gotten underway when it started raining fish from the sky.

In sunny daylight, no less. Barely a wisp of a cloud overhead.

It was completely bizarre. One minute the guys from Theta Delta were serving 0–5 to the girls from Alpha Sigma Phi (all of whom, disappointingly, had chosen the 'tops-on' option for tournament play, most of them even going so far as long-sleeved Under Armour against the crisp October afternoon). The next minute, river carp the size of lapdogs were hitting the sandbar all around them: flopping, twisting, gills flaring, mouths gawping for air.

'What the . . .?' Tyler Crabtree yelped, just as a fat one hit him between the shoulder blades with a wet, fleshy smack, driving him to his knees.

'The coolers!' somebody shouted. 'Use the coolers!'

Then it was chaos, everybody shouting, screaming, squealing, running in circles, tripping over themselves and each other, kicking up sand. The calmer heads among the group began pairing up as if trained for this very scenario, dumping the coolers, raising them over their heads like portable shelters and then huddling underneath, two to an Igloo.

Meanwhile, the fish kept falling: thudding into the sandbar, splashing back into the river, thonking off the empty coolers, tangling in the volleyball net. Jordy DeFord stood agape, feet plugged into the cold sand up to his ankles, thinking: *Somebody needs to be Tweeting this.*

About that same time, Jordy recognized that the fish weren't actually falling after all. Rather, they appeared to be voluntarily hurling themselves out of the Platte River like wriggling, silvery torpedoes. He'd actually heard of this: some invasive species of Asian carp flinging themselves into fishermen's boats up and down the nearby Missouri River, where the Platte eventually emptied. But he'd always thought they were just . . . well. Fish stories.

But now he was seeing it first-hand, with his own two eyes: an approaching wave of kamikaze jumpers that split off in a flapping V around this wide, undulating sandbar in the middle of the wide, shallow Platte, where the Theta Delts and the Alpha Sigs had gathered for one last off-campus fling before the weather turned. It was almost as if these crazy fish were performing some kind of synchronized routine.

Or running away from something, Jordy thought.

Then he saw it.

Something.

Something coming up. Up from out of the deeper water. Now breaking the surface, following the river bottom like a man climbing a long flight of stairs.

No, Jordy thought. Not a man.

More like some hulking, primordial, sludge-born prototype of a man. Now trudging up on to the far end of their sandbar, shedding river water as it lumbered forth.

And that's when Jordy DeFord stopped believing his eyes and started shrieking.

TWENTY

They proceeded in silence, west and then north, for twelve short miles. The hatchling hadn't been *so* far off, Frost thought petulantly, even hampered by the mechanical shortcomings of a base model Lincoln Continental with $75k in high-tech modifications. But he was forced – reluctantly – to acknowledge Lucius's point:

When mining the ancient magic of the cosmos, one mustn't mistake tunnel vision for a tunnel.

From I-29, he saw the motel sign in the distance on their left. Frost took the upcoming exit, which fed them on to US-30 amidst the westbound minivans carrying families, the gleaming new SUVs and rust-eaten rattletraps carrying citizens of all ages and incomes, the semi-trailer trucks carrying doomed livestock to its unceremonious, unimportant end. All of them struck Frost as versions of the same basic vehicle.

They saw police flashers as they approached the Super 8. Within the next half-block, Frost could see a handful of men in uniform all gaggled around a familiar charcoal van with a red stripe and a crunched front end.

Lucius said, 'Looks like the place.'

Gone, Frost noted with gratitude, was the belligerent, self-sorry tone in the injured man's voice. Lucius Weatherbee might not have been his old self quite yet. But it was work time, now, and he was back on point. In fact, it was Lucius who first looked right while Frost was still looking left.

'Boss?' he said.

Across the highway, opposite the law enforcement convention currently in progress, sat a shabbier establishment: the River Bend Inn and Suites, according to the sun-faded sign in the empty parking lot. Across the same parking lot trudged a lone figure.

Lucius came to attention in the passenger seat. 'Isn't that . . .'

'Reuben Wasserman,' Frost finished for him. 'In the flesh.'

Wasserman – eyes downcast, shoulders slumped – appeared to be shambling toward the embankment leading up to the roadway itself.

'The hell's he doing?'

An excellent question indeed.

Anabeth gazed toward the closed bathroom door and sighed. 'Poor thing,' she said. 'He's had a rough twenty-four hours.'

Ben, who could claim better days himself, found himself somewhat less than concerned with Reuben Wasserman's. He sort of blamed the kid for all this, he recognized. Yeah, OK: that wasn't fair. Don't shoot the messenger, et cetera. But he felt entitled to be mad at somebody.

'Frost,' he said. 'Who is he?'

'My trainee, once upon a time. He believes that I betrayed him. That the Order betrayed him. But that's sort of just Malcom being Malcom. And it's a whole other story.'

'What I mean is, how does he fit in?'

'Malcom believes he can harness the creature.'

'To do what?'

'We'd have to ask Malcom, but here's what I can tell you for sure: since his dismissal from the Order, he's been freelancing underground as a . . . a sort of supernatural arms dealer, I suppose you might say.'

'Supernatural arms dealer.' Ben nodded along, thinking: *Sure, why not?* 'And that's a thing?'

'Malcom's always fancied himself an innovator.' She checked her phone. 'Fortunately, he's been occupying himself somewhere on other side of the world since the *Arcadia* dig began, so he's been a step behind the times until now. To be honest, many in the Order believed he might finally be dead.'

'I guess they were mistaken.'

'It wouldn't be the first time. Knowing Mal, he probably has bidders already lined up from here to Crimea to the Levant.'

'Bidders for what? I thought you said the creature was made for only one thing.'

'That's why he needs us,' she said. 'You to draw the creature out, and me to control it. It doesn't take a military mind to imagine the weapon it might make.'

Ben waved a hand dismissively toward the bathroom. 'Then what does that make him?'

Abe looked at him. The depth in her eyes just then seemed unfathomable to Ben, and he instantly regretted his tone. There were those, he imagined, who might have construed it as callous. Perhaps indirectly bordering on textbook narcissism.

'A lowly emissary,' she finally said. 'With limited power to affect change on his own.'

Ben nodded. 'Sorry. It's been a long day.'

'Which makes him stronger than he realizes,' she went on. 'Upholding tradition. Keeping the memory of my Silas alive. Remembering his example. Passing it on. That's the water carrier's job, now.' Abe shrugged. 'Finishing his work is mine.'

'That's why Frost grabbed him up first. Reuben.'

She nodded. 'Reuben is Malcom Frost's way of drawing *me* out. And letting me know the stakes of the game.'

'Do what he wants or he kills the water carrier.'

'With Malcom, "kill" is a pedestrian concept, but yes. But it's not just Reuben in danger, I'm afraid. It's every living Wasserman. *My* bloodline. Which includes an infant, soon.' Her eyes gained a wistful twinkle. 'Reuben's sister Sara and her husband are about to have their first. He's soon to be an uncle.'

'I see.'

'I swear I can't stay off their Facebook page.'

'He's your creature,' Ben said. 'Frost.'

Anabeth tilted her head. 'I hadn't thought of it that way. But in a sense I suppose so. One of them, anyway.'

'And he didn't follow us to Christine's.'

'No.'

'We beat him there.'

Another nod. 'Right to the end of Bloody Bill's line.'

Ben glanced at Charley. Charley stared at the floor.

'And all the more leverage for Malcom,' she added. 'Just in case.'

'In case what?'

'In case you turned out to be a stubborn, uncooperative, mule-headed so-and-so, I suppose.' She smiled. 'Thank goodness we don't need to worry about that.'

Ben adjusted his position on the uncomfortable air unit and sat with that a moment. He decided that Anabeth, intentionally or not, had lied to him again; she'd told him her story, and he *still* didn't understand everything. In fact, he had just as many questions now as before. They were just different questions, that was all.

Starting with basic logistics:

'If the goal was to correct a hundred and fifty year-old mistake, why finagle a job at my company just to babysit me for part of every workday?' Ben asked her. 'Why not hang around the *Arcadia* dig site until the creature woke up, then nip all this right in the bud?' He thought about it a moment. 'Actually, why wait for somebody else to dig the thing up in the first place? And where is this Order of yours, anyway? They can't be bothered to send a little backup?'

'These are all intelligent, reasonable questions,' she said, checking her phone again, 'and they show me you've really been listening. But right now I'm begging you: can we *please* turn our focus back to how we're going to get . . .'

'This rock of yours.'

'The Shepherd Stone?'

'This Shepherd Stone,' Ben said. 'That turns the thing off?'

'There are rules involved,' Abe answered, 'but basically yes.'

'That sounds like basically maybe.'

'To put it in terms of your computer analogy, think of it like an override code. If entered correctly, I should be able to take control of the system.'

'But that also overrides your . . . situation.'

She grinned. 'It's OK. You can call it a Gypsy curse.'

Whatever they called it, here at last was the one thing Ben felt he truly did understand: in looking out for them, Anabeth Glass wasn't just fulfilling a duty.

She was conducting a kind of suicide mission.

'And you'd trade immortality,' he said. 'For us.'

'Try menstruating for a century and a half, then come talk to me.'

'Ugh,' Charley said, looking instantly horrified with himself. His face flared crimson. 'Sorry. I didn't mean to say that.'

Anabeth chuckled. 'Don't give me too much credit, that's all I'm trying to say. I like you both very much, please don't misunderstand. I couldn't bear to see either of you harmed. But I'd dearly love to know what it feels like to break a hip one day.'

'Besides complete and total cooperation from this moment on,' Ben said, 'what do you need from me to help you make that happen? That also came out wrong.'

'I gleaned your meaning. Do you want the honest truth?'

'All the way.'

'I haven't completely figured that out yet,' she said. 'But step one is to retrieve the stone.'

'Retrieve?'

'For starters.'

Ben patted his own thighs, signifying the cargo pockets of Anabeth's paintball pants. 'You mean you don't have it?'

'I did.'

'Where is it now?'

'I'm not sure I quite know the best way to tell you that.'

'Honest truth, remember?'

'You might want to brace yourself.'

'Abe.' He felt himself growing impatient. 'Trust me. After everything we've been through today, whatever it is, I can take it.'

Anabeth took a deep breath. 'Remember that rock I threw this morning?'

'Lucius,' Frost said, extending his right hand as he steered with his left. 'The glove compartment, if you wouldn't mind.'

They crunched across the gritty, littered parking lot of the River Bend Inn and Suites, setting a course to intercept this latest in

a long line of indescribably hapless water carriers. Lucius grunted
in discomfort as he leaned forward in his seat, popping the glove
box as requested. Then Frost felt the cool, pebbled handgrip of
Aberdeen's dart pistol in his palm.

Wasserman had almost reached the embankment by the time Frost
braked the Lincoln to a caterwauling stop directly in his path. The
car's last working window slipped free of its mechanism as he
pressed the button to lower it down, dropping with a thud and a
shatter somewhere inside the door. Wasserman finally looked up.
His eyes registered nothing for a moment, then flew open wide.

'Reuben,' Frost said cheerfully. 'Thank goodness we found you.
You look unwell.'

'Oh, shit,' Wasserman said.

'How on earth did you manage to get all the way up here?'

'Room 103,' he said, pointing over his shoulder. 'OK? They're
all in there. You found 'em.'

'Indeed,' Frost said. 'Shall we go and say hello?'

'Look man, they're all yours. I'll just stay out of your way.'

'Nonsense,' Frost said. 'Hop in. The rear door sticks on this side,
you'll need to really give it a pull.'

But Wasserman raised his hands and took a step back instead.
'Yeah, that's OK. Claire's probably going out of her mind. I
should call.'

Frost raised the dart pistol and aimed it out the window.

Wasserman's eyes widened again; he thrust his hands out in
front of him in a warding gesture, shaking his head vigorously.
'No, no, hey, wait wait wait—'

Frost pulled the trigger. Wasserman flinched, yelped, then turned
his left hand over to look at the tufted dart sticking out of his palm.

'Oh, come on,' he pleaded, already sagging to his knees.

That rock I threw this morning.

Ben had a quick mental flashback: Abe charging the creature
like a kamikaze lunatic; him grabbing her and shoving her to the
ground; a fist-sized rock hitting nothing but breeze as it sailed
away into the timber.

'Please, please, please,' he said, 'tell me you're joking.'

She shook her head. *Nope.*

He put his head in his hands. A faint humming sound seemed to emanate from somewhere in the small, interlocking bones deep within his ears. The sound built in gradual waves until it filled his brain with white noise. Somewhere on the periphery, he felt light, almost feathery pressure: a gentle hand on his shoulder.

'Ben.' The hand gave a squeeze. 'Hey, come on. Say something. Don't check out on me now.'

'You're telling me all this could have been finished.' He pressed the heels of his hands into his eyeballs until he saw fireworks. 'Done and over. At sunrise this morning.'

'Nobody can say that with 100 percent certainty.'

'You had everything under control.'

'I wouldn't go that far, either.'

'Until I stepped in.'

Ben heard Charley mutter something under his breath. Just two little words, barely audible: *That figures.*

'Hey,' Anabeth said sharply. 'That's not fair, Charley.'

'Nothing's fair,' Charley grumbled. 'Ever.'

'Well! Welcome to the human race, sunshine. And you.' She patted Ben briskly on the shoulder. 'Pull yourself together and look at me.'

Ben dropped his hands and sagged back against the wall, shaking his head slowly. 'He's right again. I screwed everything up.'

'How? By instinctively trying to protect me? I'm nearly a complete stranger to you, Ben. You've said so yourself. Repeatedly.'

'I'm a hero, all right.'

'Oh, grow up. Both of you. I swear.' Abe kicked him in the foot with the toe of her combat boot, then Charley, then turned and plopped back down on the bed. 'Who left their post this morning? You? Who decided to stop for coffee and flirting instead of taking care of business?'

'Abe, stop helping,' Ben said. 'Please.'

'I'll tell you something else, just for your information. Part of me cheered when you stepped in front of me the way you did. It told me everything I needed to know about you.'

'That I'm a born idiot?'

'That despite what *you* clearly believe, you're a good man,' Abe said. 'A good father. That the stranger I've been waiting to save all these years turns out to be worth saving.'

Before Ben could think up a response to that bunch of

well-meaning nonsense, there came an authoritative pounding on
the door. He couldn't suppress a gallows chuckle as he looked
at Abe. 'You were saying?'

Pound pound pound.

Anabeth sighed. 'I guess story time's over. Let me handle this.'

Charley jumped up and said, 'I got it.'

He was to the door before Ben could react. Abe lunged from her
spot, calling out, 'Charley! I said let me.'

Charley threw off the chain and opened the door. Ben, to his
utter confusion, did not see a police uniform on the stoop.

He also did not see a pale, hairless, disfigured supernatural
arms dealer.

'Oh,' he heard Anabeth say. 'Well, now. Hello.'

Ben sat with his mouth gaping for several beats before his brain
finally caught up with his eyeballs. '*Frankie?*'

Francesca Montecito stepped into the room and gave Charley
a quick, sisterly hug – waist bent, hips a foot apart – then leaned
back and looked him in the eyes. Ben heard her say, 'You OK?'
Saw Charley shrug, then nod his head.

He stood. 'Francesca, what the hell are you doing here?'

'I texted her,' Charley said.

'You what? When? *Why?*'

'I wanted to go home. But then it turned out we all needed a
ride anyway, so . . .'

'So you sooooo owe me,' Frankie told him, popping a hip as
she looked around the room. 'Like, for the rest of forever. This
place is a dump. Can we stop being here now?'

'That's an excellent idea,' Abe said, raising her voice as she
turned toward the closed bathroom door. 'Reuben? Honey, come
on out. We're leaving. Quick-quick-fast.'

No response.

'Reuben?'

Abe glanced at Ben. He shrugged, following her over. She wiggled
the knob. Locked. She did some pounding of her own. 'Reuben?
Are you OK in there?'

Ben shouted: 'Water boy!'

No response.

'OK, stand back.'

Abe saw Ben's intention. To the door, she said, 'Reuben? If you can hear me, please stand clear. And maybe cover your eyes just in case. We're coming in.' To Ben: 'Be gentle with him, please.'

He took the greatest care possible in splintering the jamb with his boot. The door flew open, banging against the toilet. Abe caught it on the rebound as she slipped into the bathroom. Ben followed her inside.

The bathroom of Room 103 at the River Bend Inn and Suites was remarkable for being the only motel bathroom he'd ever seen – possibly the only residential bathroom he'd seen anywhere in the past thirty years – with a tub but no shower. The window over the tub was open. Aside from the tub, the pedestal sink, and the toilet, Ben saw no other water carriers.

'I don't believe this,' he said.

Abe was already shoving past him, heading back out the way they'd come in. 'It isn't good.'

'Is he OK?' Charley asked.

Francesca said, 'Is who OK?'

Abe had already rushed out of the room, straight through the door Francesca had left standing open behind her. Charley and Frankie looked at each other and followed along.

Before Ben could catch up to them, Gordon's prepaid buzzed in his pocket. He dug it out and answered on the move. 'Gordon. Little busy. What's going on?'

'You're asking me?' Christine's frantic voice shouted in his ear.

TWENTY-ONE

'Christine, thank god.' Ben stopped in his tracks and lowered his voice, reflexively pushing the motel room door closed so Charley wouldn't hear them fighting. Old habits died hard. 'We've been calling you all day.'

'Ben, what have you done now? *Where are you?* What have you done?'

'Honey, listen, Charley's OK. Frankie's OK. We're—'

'Francesca? What do you . . . Ben, goddammit!'

'She's with us. Everybody's OK. Whatever you're hearing is

100 percent wrong, and you'll have a hard time believing me when I explain, but we need your help. This is serious.'

'You're telling me this is *serious*? They took a dead man out of my yard, Ben. And that awful mess down in Ashland. They're saying you—'

'Christine. I know. Please just listen.' Ben stopped. 'Wait. What happened in Ashland?'

But Christine's voice was gone. A new voice came on the line. Still female, but calmer, more official, unfamiliar to Ben. 'Mr Middleton? This is Detective Sergeant Valerie Contreras, Omaha Police. I want you to stay on the line with me now and—'

Shit.

Ben hung up immediately, thinking: *I thought giving up the sauce was supposed to make life get better.* He pulled open the door and hustled outside, into the parking lot. Francesca's Subaru was parked just outside the room. He scanned left, where he saw nothing, then right, where he saw three things at once:

A black Lincoln Town Car that looked like it had come in last place at the county fair dirt track; Anabeth Glass and Francesca Montecito standing with their backs to the parking lot, palms pressed up against the next door over; and an albino-looking beanpole with scar tissue for a face holding the nozzle of a portable jet injector to his son's neck.

The fourth, fifth, and sixth things Ben saw a moment too late: a shoulder sling, a smile, a fist coming at him.

Then what felt like a speeding cinderblock landed in the center of his face. The world exploded in a crunching of nose cartilage and a blooming supernova of light. Somewhere in the far distance – possibly inside his own head – Ben heard a voice say: *Goddamn, I been waiting all day to do that.*

Then the light faded into a cool, engulfing darkness.

'Guys,' said Gordon Frerking, 'I don't know what else to tell you. We're really, truly not jerking you around, here.'

'Gee,' Deputy Tom Curnow said. 'I wonder why I'm having trouble believing that.'

'Look, man, I know we got off on the wrong foot this morning.'

'Deputy Curnow,' Tom said. 'Or Sir, if you like shorter words better. "Look, man" me again and see how far it gets you.'

Frerking sighed. He seemed to be the informal leader of these numbskulls. 'No disrespect intended.'

'Water under the bridge. Now cut the shit and start over from the beginning.'

Devon Miller piped up. 'Deputy, if I may . . .'

'Nerd,' Jeremy Zwart muttered under his breath.

'Eat a dick,' Miller snapped.

'I'm gonna have to,' Zwart said. 'Yours didn't come anywhere close to filling me up.'

'Gentlemen,' Dr Truong interjected. 'Perhaps the condition of the patient may further our understanding.'

They were gathered in an administrative conference room at the hospital: Tom, the paintball idiots, two Omaha PD patrol officers whose names Tom couldn't remember, and Dr Khoa Truong, the surgeon who'd removed a poker chip-sized section of Ajeet Mallipudi's skull to relieve pressure on the young man's brain.

'Couldn't have said it better myself, Doc.' Tom pointed at Frerking. 'You. Go again. Start with finding your buddy on the ground.'

'With all due respect, Deputy, it's gonna sound exactly the same a second time.'

'What it sounds like to me is bullshit.'

'I know! But I'm telling you: we've got it all on video. The cameras are in my van. If we can just look at that footage, you'll see what we're trying to—'

'Actually,' Dr Truong said, 'I was attempting to add something to what these young men have said.'

Tom turned to him, thinking: *Am I doing something wrong, here?* 'By all means, Doc. Feel free to jump in.'

'Yes. Well.' Truong adjusted his eyeglasses. 'In preparing the patient for surgery, my nurses recovered a sample of material.'

'What kind of material?'

'A small amount of residue from beneath the left *corpus unguis* of the patient's third distal—'

'Pretend I'm a dumb cop who couldn't get into medical school.'

'The middle fingernail.' The paintball idiots snickered as Truong demonstrated the fingernail in question. 'I thought nothing of it at first, given the clay-based soil in our region. However—'

'Clay, you said?'

'That was my presumption. But the material exhibited unusual properties. We've transferred the sample to our—'

'These unusual properties, let me guess,' Tom said. 'It was cold. And it smelled like ass.'

The Omaha cops looked at each other. The surgeon looked directly at Tom. 'Yes, actually. And extraordinarily viscous. Forgive me, I mean . . . sticky.'

Frerking pointed urgently at Tom. 'You've seen it too! Haven't you? So you know we're not—'

Then his mobile phone buzzed on the table in front of him, interrupting the flow. As he reached for it, Tom extended his hand instead. 'May I?'

'Got a warrant?' As soon as Frerking said it, he relented, handing the phone over. 'I mean, yeah, sure. Knock yourself out.'

Tom glanced at the screen. Then he turned the phone to show Frerking the incoming text. 'Red Ball One. What's that supposed to mean?'

Frerking glanced at his pals, then back to Tom. 'No idea. Who's it from?'

'Just a number.'

'What's the last text in that thread?'

Tom looked. 'There isn't one. Just "Red Ball One."'

Frerking looked at his pals again. More of a glare this time.

Jeremy Zwart raised his hands, wiggling his fingers. 'They've been on the ends of my arms this whole time.'

'My phone's right there,' Devon Miller said, pointing to the table. 'Anyway, we're in your contacts list.'

'I wonder why sometimes.' Frerking turned back to Tom with a shrug. 'Wrong number, I guess?'

Tom scrutinized him closely.

Then he sighed. He slid the phone back across the table. 'OK, Doc. Tell me more about this sample. You say you sent it where, again?'

Ben's eyes creaked open to painful, piercing light. His throat was dry, and he couldn't breathe through his nose. His head pounded like a subwoofer. The light flared and then receded, slowly resolving into the image of a water-stained ceiling.

'She's clean,' a deep voice said.

A second voice seemed to come from the ceiling itself: 'Betsy. Take this only for what it's worth, but you seem uncharacteristically underprepared for the job at hand, if I may say.'

'Don't worry, it's in a safe place.' Abe's voice. 'And *don't* call me Betsy. You know how much I hate that.'

Wincing, Ben lifted his head to see the man in the shoulder sling – now wearing a Bergen Mercy hospital t-shirt with his suit pants and dress shoes – shove Abe roughly toward the chairs near the air unit. He saw Charley and Francesca already sitting in the chairs. Charley had his knees up, head down on his arms. His shoulders bounced in time with his quiet sobs, which he was trying to hide but couldn't. At least not as easily as his face. It was the classic Charley Middleton breakdown position. Ben hadn't seen it in several years now.

Over them all loomed the tall, knobby carnival mutant now calling the shots in Room 103.

Frost.

'If you're keeping the stone in the same van you used to coldly murder my second-best employee,' he said, 'I'll be very disappointed.'

'Give me *some* credit. Speaking of things that aren't here, where's Reuben?'

'Also in a safe place. Well, that may be putting too positive a spin on it. But for now he's only napping.'

Ben tried to sit up, but the room started spinning. He gulped, sucked in a breath. Pressed his palms into the mattress.

Then he lurched to one side and vomited weakly on to the carpet beside the bed, setting off a small bomb inside his brain and starting his flattened nose gushing again.

'Dad?'

Francesca: 'Gross.'

'Not to worry,' Frost said. 'A mild concussion, I should expect. Entirely survivable. With sufficient group cooperation, of course.'

'Mal,' Abe said, 'just stop. Somewhere, deep down, I know you're better than this.'

'You have a point,' Frost agreed. 'Honestly, I can't help feeling like all of this is really much easier than we've been making it.'

'Easier than taking five people hostage in broad daylight? In full view of a busy highway? Across from a parking lot full of police officials?'

'Still grading my performance, I see.'

'I'm not grading you, Malcom. It never worked anyway.'

'Knowledge acquired under compulsion obtains no hold on the mind. Plato said that.'

'Didn't he fly too close to the sun? Wait, that was another guy.'

While he was hanging over the bed, Ben's eyes came into focus long enough to spot a familiar object beneath the edge of the bed: Gordon Frerking's prepaid phone. He braced himself for the pain and pretended to retch again, hanging off the mattress a few inches farther, scooping up the phone as he did. He had just enough time to tap a few buttons and press Send before his knuckles exploded, his hand went numb to the wrist, and the phone thudded to the threadbare carpet.

'Dad!'

'I'm OK,' he said, gritting his teeth as he shook some feeling back into his fingers.

'Sneaky,' said the man in the shoulder sling, stooping to retrieve the phone he'd pistol-whipped out of Ben's hand. On the subject of pistols, he'd outfitted himself with a new one since Ben had seen him last. This one was fitted with a silencer.

Frost accepted the phone as the man in the shoulder sling handed it over. 'Thank you, Lucius.' Without a glance, he tossed the phone on to the dresser with Abe's and Francesca's, apparently confiscated while Ben's lights had been out. 'Now that everyone's present, allow me a brief moment to run down the program. Then we'll be on our way.'

They were in the elevator, on their way back down to Ajeet's floor, before Jeremy said, 'And what was that bit with your phone, anyway?'

'Wrong number,' Devon told him. 'Try to keep up.'

'It wasn't a wrong number,' Gordon said.

'But you told Curnow—'

'It was the prepaid. I think Ben and Abe need help.'

Jeremy said, 'How do you know that?'

'Red Ball One.' Gordon shook his head. 'Middleton. I swear that guy's sort of turning into my hero.'

'I don't get it.'

'It's a distress code. He knew *I'd* get it.'

'How'd he know that?'

'Season one, episode six.'

The elevator stopped. The bell dinged. The doors opened. Devon said, 'Huh?'

'*The A-Team*,' Gordon said, already moving. 'Try to keep up.'

'One for you,' Frost said, circulating around the room, handing a set of disposable plastic flex cuffs to each person not already wearing a shoulder sling. 'One for you. One for you. Aaand one for you. Everybody put those on. Nice and snug. My associate, Lucius, will be available for those who need special assistance. He'll also be performing final inspections.'

Charley's eyes still looked red and wet, but he'd pulled himself together. He looked at the restraints, then at Ben.

Ben sat at the edge of the bed, breathing through his mouth, trying to will himself back to clarity. His eyes wouldn't stay focused, although that seemed almost academic, given that they'd swollen halfway shut anyway. His right hand – also now swelling to cartoonish proportions – throbbed in syncopation with his shattered, blood-plugged nose.

He nodded to Charley. 'Do what he says.'

'That's excellent parenting,' Frost agreed.

'Get bent,' Ben told him nasally.

Lucius stepped over, casually swinging his good arm, clobbering Ben once more with his pistol. There came another sharp burst of tooth-rattling pain; the room went dark again, then wobbled back into focus. In the meantime, he'd slid off the bed, on to his knees. The back of his scalp burned as if seared by a hot iron. He could feel warmth trickling down the back of his neck.

Ben heard Charley before he saw him – he was wild-eyed, fighting against Anabeth, who'd wrapped him up tightly in her arms, holding him back. She whispered something in his ear, trying to calm him.

'Lucius,' Frost said. 'If you're not careful, you're going to bend your last gun.'

'I got two more in the trunk still.'

'I stand corrected.'

Anabeth helped a still-vibrating Charley into his cuffs. 'Malcom, you can't think we're going to get very far in that heap outside.'

'I was beginning to have my doubts, now that you mention it. Lucky for us, a fresh new vehicle has arrived just in time.'

Francesca said, 'Who, me? My car only seats five.' She held her own cuffs away from her on the end of an index finger, looking at them as if they were Charley's dirty undies.

'No problem,' Lucius said. He pressed the muzzle of his gun to Ben's head. 'Got more people than we need anyway.'

Charley shouted, *'Nopleasedon't!'*

'Lucius.'

'Boss.'

'While I can't fault your logic, we've been over this. Our mission may still benefit from a certain amount of redundancy in personnel.'

Lucius swung the gun up and pointed it at Francesca instead. 'Anything we need her for?'

Now Charley's voice jumped up a register: *'No!!'*

Ben saw the panic in his eyes, saw the way he twisted against the cuffs, and something sparked in his jangled brain – two bare wires accidentally rubbing together. He remembered the strange look that had passed across Charley's face this morning, back in Christine's kitchen, at the mention of Francesca's name. Suddenly, as Ben found himself contemplating Francesca Montecito as if through Charley's eyes, something became perfectly, dismally clear to him. He thought: *Ohhhh, no.*

Forget about guns and handcuffs and lurching mud monsters. Ben tried to imagine what the poor kid must be going through already. He certainly didn't need to try very hard to remember what it felt like to be fourteen. What would *he* have thought of Francesca Montecito at that age?

He'd have been utterly, hopelessly besotted, that was what. Now he tried to imagine the added torture of being forced to live in the same house with her, day in and day out. As instant, circumstantial siblings. Pushed together by forces completely beyond his control. Poor, poor Charley. What had they done to him?

Francesca, for her part, seemed remarkably unfazed by a gun in her face. 'Who else is gonna drive?'

'I bet we can manage.'

'Yeah, OK,' she said. 'Good luck with that.'

'What's that mean?'

'It means my dad hooked up the Sube with fingerprint start. So I wouldn't get carjacked.'

Lucius snorted. 'So all we need's a finger, then.'

Francesca lost her smirk.

Frost chuckled, patting his operative on his non-bandaged shoulder. 'I know it's silly to get attached, but I like her.'

'Yeah,' Lucius agreed. 'It does seem silly.'

Anabeth took Charley's face in her hands, spoke a few quiet words to him, then left him standing alone as she stepped over to crouch next to Ben. She looked him in the eyes as she helped him on with his cuffs, conveying an unspoken version of the same message she'd just given Charley: *I said let me handle this*. Then she did her own cuffs, first using one hand to zip in the other, then the other hand by itself, pulling the strap tight with her teeth.

'We're ready to go,' she said. 'I'll sit on Ben's lap. Reuben will be out for who knows how long – we'll cuff him while he's sleeping and he can curl up behind us in the cargo hatch. Francesca drives, leaving you and Mr Personality free to ride herd. There's no problem here, Malcom. Absolutely none at all.'

'The Subaru people ought to put you in a television commercial,' Frost said. 'Shall we?'

Lucius transferred the gun to his sling hand and grabbed Francesca by the meat of her arm. 'We'll make sure the coast is clear. Get all settled in.'

'I still need the keys,' Francesca said.

'What happened to fingerprint start?'

'It's aftermarket shit. I still need to turn the ignition on for it to work.'

Lucius sighed. He held the gun on her while he dug in his front pocket. 'You make any kinda move I don't like, I'll make you stop making it. Hear?'

'Loud and clear.'

'Good girl.' He tossed her the keys.

Francesca laughed. 'God, you're so easy.'

In one deft motion, she flicked the key ring, flipped the attached pepper spray canister into her palm, and triggered it right in his face.

TWENTY-TWO

For approximately the next seven to ten seconds, Room 103 at the River Bend Inn and Suites became part cage match, part crucible, and part comedy of the absurd. The whole thing seemed to develop in slow motion, yet somehow it was over before Ben fully recognized that he'd participated.

First, the big man who answered to 'Lucius' bellowed and stumbled back, clawing at his eyes with his free hand. Francesca used the opportunity to plant the laces of her sneakers in his crotch. He grunted and stooped, wheezing, still wiping at his face, now glistening with tears and mucus. Ben sat blinking for a moment, first in surprise, then at the first tendrils of pepper fumes as they reached his eyes.

He saw Frost move with unnerving speed and agility. The man's long, gangly limbs seemed to gain extra segments, unfolding and working in disjointed concert as he flew across the room like some great mechanical buzzard. He grabbed Charley with one hand, using the other to backhand Francesca to the floor. Her keys flew, jingling to the thin carpet as she sprawled backward over a chair. She landed in the corner with a yelp and a thud.

In the same moment, Ben launched himself from the floor, going straight for the bigger man's gun hand.

Lucius – even with half his total number of arms out of commission and a face full of capsicum foam – made a firm obstacle. Ben, on the other hand, made something less than an unstoppable force even on a good day, let alone in his current condition. He came out on the short end of the collision he'd engineered, knocking the wind out of himself on impact and bouncing harmlessly away.

But the gun came with him, clutched in his swollen, cuff-bound grip like a priceless artifact. From somewhere he heard a desperate, glottal croaking sound, had a peripheral awareness of Anabeth leaping on Frost's back like a monkey climbing a tree . . . whipping her bound hands over his head . . . choking him from behind with her own cuffs.

Meanwhile, Lucius stripped his sling and tossed it aside and stood over Ben like a grizzly rising up on its hind legs. Riding a surge of adrenaline, Ben forced himself to ignore the bothersome fact that he couldn't breathe. He rolled on to his back, pointed the gun at the center of the big man's chest, and pulled the trigger three times: *splurt-splurt-splurt.*

His first shot gouged a long, splintered hole in the headboard of the bed. The second round shattered the lamp on the far side table. Only the third round found its mark – sort of – clipping Lucius high on his previously injured shoulder, knocking him back a step.

Lucius took one look at the red flower blooming on his hospital t-shirt, then re-zeroed his attention on Ben. His inflamed, snot-slick face twisted into a mask of such pure rage – such undiluted hatred – that Ben definitely would have shot him again, or at least tried his best, had he not been in the process of passing out from lack of oxygen himself. The weight of the gun seemed to double, then triple, then became a fifty-pound dumbbell in his aching hand. He gasped and gulped for air. Tiny lights buzzed in the corners of his vision like gnats.

Then Lucius was on him, roaring. He planted a knee in Ben's chest. Clamped a hand around his throat. Twisted the gun out of his hands by the barrel.

Ben had enough time to think: *This is it.* He had enough time to register the sensation of his ribcage compressing beneath his opponent's bull weight. Enough time to become familiar with the unforgettable taste combination of oil and gunpowder, time to experience the invasive finality of a gun barrel in his mouth. He had time to hear screams in the hazy distance, time to think: *Charley.*

Or maybe it was only in retrospect that he had time to think any of those things. Maybe he'd made all of it up in his mind, retelling the story after the fact.

All Ben could say for sure, in the very last moment before he checked out for good, was that everything changed suddenly, completely, and for no clear reason he could discern.

First, the crushing weight disappeared. The vise around his throat disappeared. Ben drew in a rattling breath; the first sweet sip of oxygen touched his foundering lungs, opening his throat like a shot of epinephrine. With it, his vision cleared.

He looked up to see Lucius sitting back on his heels, slapping at his own neck as if swatting a mosquito. Frost's thug pulled his hand away, looked at the odd tuft of orange pinched between his fingers.

Then he looked down at his left forearm and saw another orange puff stuck to his skin. He brushed it away and winced as he lifted the arm, plucking a third orange puff from his blood-drenched t-shirt, just beneath his armpit.

Then he looked toward the bathroom.

Reuben Wasserman stood in the open doorway, brandishing a strange-looking pistol of his own. Where he'd gotten it, Ben had no idea. Where he'd come from, Ben had no idea. But he'd obviously come back in through the bathroom window, the same way he'd escaped in the first place.

'You stupid motherfu—' Lucius started to say, just as Francesca rose up behind him and smashed the remaining bedside lamp over his skull.

Anabeth disentangled herself and leapt up from the floor, where Frost lolled, belly-up, like a fresh cadaver. Except that Ben could see the son of a bitch still breathing. Instead of finishing the job, Abe rushed to Wasserman's side. 'Reuben!'

Reuben Wasserman staggered past her, into the room. He pointed the pistol down at Frost and pulled the trigger.

Nothing happened.

He tried it again: still nothing. Just empty clicks.

No more darts.

'Huh,' he said. He looked straight down the barrel of the pistol and clicked the trigger three or four more times in his own face. Then his arm fell. The gun hung loosely at his side. He looked around the room. 'What happened just now?'

'Reuben, honey.' Abe helped him over toward the bed. 'Lean on me. That's the way. How do you feel?'

'OK, I guess.' He waggled the pistol. 'I must be getting immune or something. This stuff hardly works now.'

Then he pitched face down on to the bed and started to snore.

'Well,' Anabeth said. 'OK, then.'

Charley hurried over to Francesca. Abe snatched Frost's jet injector, shot him in the neck with it, and hurried over to Ben. They both stopped in their tracks at the unmistakable *shick-clack* of a shotgun slide racking up and back.

'OK, all you assholes get down on the floor with them others,' a new voice said.

'He's not answering,' Jeremy said.

Gordon sat at the lights at Douglas and Tenth, drumming his fingers impatiently, yearning for the bridge just beyond the intersection, waiting to carry them over the river. 'Call Abe.'

'I'm trying her,' Devon said from the back seat. 'She's not answering either.'

The light changed. Gordon stomped the gas and popped the clutch. Jeeter's sister's car, a base-model subcompact, still had no guts to speak of. When they returned it to her, he'd advise her to spring at least for the turbo-charged two-liter next time. Miles per gallon were a crock of shit. This thing was like driving a sewing machine.

But at least it was a set of wheels. 'Try 'em again,' he said.

'Obviously.'

'Don't mind him,' Jeremy muttered, holding the phone to his ear. 'He hasn't had his afternoon feeding.'

'I heard that.'

'I know.'

'You're such an asshole.'

'*Somebody* has a full diaper.'

'Just keep trying,' Gordon said, thinking, *how does McLaren keep ranking these dipshits 2 and 3?*

Ben looked up to see a scrawny guy in a faded River Bend Inn polo shirt splotched with food stains. The guy had a patchy red beard, a wad of chaw plugged into his cheek, and a twelve-gauge plugged against his shoulder.

Anabeth raised her bound hands. 'We're the good guys.'

'Those cops across the way can figure that all out,' the guy said. 'I figure you're the ones they must be looking for anyway. Meantime?' He waggled the gun barrel. 'On the floor like I said.'

Everybody looked to Abe for guidance. Ben was already on the floor. He'd swallowed so much blood in the past ten minutes that he feared he was about to be sick again. Heard a muffled buzzing: somewhere, Gordon's prepaid was ringing again, just like it had been doing every couple minutes since he'd hung up on Christine.

'Wherever that phone is, let it go,' the motel day manager said. 'You three: on the floor. I'm really not gonna say it again.'

Abe nodded. Charley and Francesca got down on their knees, then their bellies. Then, over on the dresser, Abe's phone started vibrating.

'That one, too,' the manager said.

'No problem,' Abe said. She got on her knees next to Frost. Instead of going face down like the teenagers, however, she started digging through Frost's pockets. 'What's your name, Red?'

'None of your business. And whatever the hell you're doing, knock it off.'

'No problem. I just need to show you something.'

Red's voice gained a nervous tremble as he stepped further into the room. 'Look, I don't want to shoot a girl, OK? But I will if you make me.'

'It's important. I promise.'

The phones fell silent. Then Abe's chimed audibly: incoming text.

Red glanced over, then back at Abe. Ben saw him flick off the safety with his thumb. 'I'm gonna count to three, now. Seriously.'

Ben marshaled every last pitiful gram of strength he had left and struggled unsteadily to his feet. Red wheeled on him, eyes going wide, trying to keep track of Abe and Ben at the same time. 'Stop right there!'

Ben raised his hands. 'We're already cuffed. See? You've got us right where you want us.'

Red raised the gun an inch. 'If you don't get back down I'll drop you down. One. Two . . .'

While he was counting, Abe moved quickly, silently, sidling up beside him. She held some kind of capsule in her fingers. Ben watched her break the capsule open with her thumb and pass it beneath Red's nose.

Red flinched, then reared back, seized by a sudden, powerful sneeze. Abe grabbed the shotgun out of his hands before he could accidently pull the trigger. She leaned the gun safely against the bed as Red doubled over, hands on his knees, sneezing again.

'*Gesundheit*,' she said, patting his back.

Red straightened, looking disoriented. He raised his chin, mouth open wide, caught in limbo between the last sneeze and the next.

Then it passed. He blinked at Abe.

'Red, sweetie, I don't know what they're paying you,' she told him, 'but it can't be enough. Listen to me, now.'

TWENTY-THREE

R ed used the folding knife clipped to his belt to cut their cuffs, then thanked them for staying at the River Bend Inn and Suites. Then he wandered back to the front office, seeming to enjoy the lovely autumn weather.

If the River Bend had the privilege of serving any other guests this October weekend, none made themselves present to inquire as to the mid-afternoon ruckus in Room 103. As to Room 103 itself, the rest of them moved quickly, first employing Francesca's unused cuffs to bind Lucius and Frost together by the wrist through the bed frame. Then they gathered all the phones, Francesca's keys, Lucius's gun, Red's gun, and Reuben Wasserman.

Of these items, Anabeth caught Ben with only one of them, a few minutes after he'd left the others arranging Wasserman in the backseat of the Subaru outside.

The honest truth was that he'd come back into the room only long enough to clean himself up. Ben hardly recognized the defeated prizefighter looking back at him in the bathroom mirror. He soaked a towel in warm water and went to work, doing his best to dab the thick, congealed *impasto* of blood and snot and whatever else from his muzzle.

It was so much fun that he'd ended up staying longer.

'We're all ready,' Anabeth eventually called, hustling back into the room. 'Are you coming or . . . Ben?' She stopped. 'What are you doing?'

What he'd been doing was standing over a supernatural arms dealer and a one-armed hitman, pointing the silenced pistol at Malcom Frost's hanging head. Trying to work up the guts to pull the trigger.

'I thought you said we weren't ready for this guy.'

'We caught a few breaks,' she said, approaching him cautiously.

'Besides, I never said he was indestructible. Just ruthless. How about let's put the gun down and get out of here? We don't have all that much daylight left, and we're not going to find my rock in the dark.'

'He's just going to keep coming,' he told her, still pointing the gun. Not all that steadily, really. But generally in the right direction. 'I've already got one freak following us around. I don't need two.'

'That sounds like rationalizing.'

'It's a skill.'

'Ben, listen to me,' she said. 'Malcom is like a jackal. He's ruthless, but he's also an opportunist. Basically a coward at heart. If we remove the opportunity that brought him here, I can almost guarantee you'll never see him again.'

'No offense, but "almost" doesn't do much for me right now. And you already killed one of them, so don't patronize me.'

'That was different.'

'Yeah? How so.'

'He wasn't defenseless, for one thing.'

'That sounds like rationalizing.'

Abe sighed. 'Fine. If you're going to do it, hurry up and do it. Just give me one second first. I'll be right back.'

'Where are you going?'

'To get Charley,' she said. 'Maybe it'll do him some good to see what his dad's willing to do for him.'

Ben finally looked at her.

Abe stopped in the doorway and looked back.

'That's pretty low,' he told her.

She shrugged. 'I'm a bitch. Wanna shoot me, instead? I can *almost* guarantee I'll live through it.'

Ben stared at her so long that he didn't even notice he'd lowered the gun until he felt it resting against his leg. Anabeth cracked a grin.

Ben wasn't in the mood to grin back. 'You're the worst.'

'At least I don't stand around farting at the printer everybody else has to use. Are we finished here, then?'

Outside, she stopped at the ice machine and filled up the plastic liner she'd swiped from the bucket in the room. She twisted the top and shoved the ice bag at Ben. 'Here. You need this. Front seat's all yours.'

They headed toward the car. Anabeth went around to the driver's side and knocked on Francesca's window. Francesca lowered the glass.

'Can I see your lighter?' Abe asked her.

'What lighter?'

'Sweetie, I'm not your parents. I couldn't care less that you obviously smoked at least two cigarettes on the way up here. Stupid habit, by the way.'

'Hey! How did you . . . whatever.' Frankie dug in her purse, handed over a disposable plastic lighter.

Abe took it and hustled over to the Lincoln. For the first time, Ben noticed the tail of what looked like a pillowcase from the room sticking out of the neck of the open gas tank. The cloth was dripping.

And then it was flaming.

Abe came sprinting back to the Subaru, calling, 'OK, here we go – quick-quick-fast!'

Ben held the door while she piled into the back next to Wasserman, who lolled against a squashed-looking Charley, who stared out his window with widening eyes. Ben piled into the front passenger seat after her, Frankie throwing the Sube into reverse gear before he'd closed his door.

'Fast but not too fast,' Abe cautioned. 'No careening. We want all those cops over there to notice the explosion, not the white wagon with Nebraska plates squealing *away* from the explosion like a bat out of hell.'

Frankie white-knuckled the wheel but followed Abe's instructions, proceeding out to the access road, then on to the highway, heading back toward the ramp to I-29 South. Back toward home.

They heard it and felt it when the Lincoln blew: a low, rumbling detonation, followed by the muffled *whump* of blast waves strafing the car. Everybody but Wasserman turned in their seats to see the husk of Malcom Frost's battered transportation in the near distance behind them, now engulfed in orange flames, trailing thick black smoke toward the sky.

'Oh my god,' Charley said, momentarily awestruck, the first non-terrified words Ben had heard from his mouth in half an hour.

'Francesca?' Abe said. 'Eyes on the road, honey.'

'Yeah. OK. Holy balls.'

'You were stupendous back there, by the way.'

Ben couldn't have said it better. 'She's right. I don't know how to thank you.'

'Uh huh.' Francesca's eyes flickered between the rearview mirror and the road ahead. 'My dad is so gonna kill me.'

'Don't worry. I'll explain everything.'

'I just meant he'll be mad at me. He's *actually* gonna kill you.'

'Yeah, probably,' Ben said, nails shooting through his brain as he pressed the ice baggie against his face. 'If he doesn't get tired standing in line.'

Tom Curnow ran lights and sirens down I-80, using his personal mobile to keep the radio clear. 'Say again, Sheriff?'

'Knock it off, Tom, you heard me fine. What's your location?'

'Heading back now, ten minutes out. How can there be no sight of him?'

'I'm comin' around to Mayor Bobby on this one,' Prescott said. 'No sight of *it*, is what I think we gotta be talkin' about. Either that, or maybe they put me in a nuthouse somewhere and this whole damned day's been happening in my head.'

'You're telling me we've got a helicopter, and a subject on foot, and we've got nothing?'

'Nope. I'm telling you we got three helicopters now,' Sheriff Prescott said. 'And a trail that stops at the river. Bunch a deep prints on a sandbar half a mile down, then again a mile later. State's got a SWAT crew in Louisville, but they ain't intercepted jack shit yet. Them three paintballers with you?'

'Left them where I found them,' Tom said. 'Omaha PD agreed to babysit until Frerking's passwords check out on the van cams. The other two didn't have much to add. What they did say made sense.'

'Now there's what I'd call a relative comment.'

'Where do you want me?'

'State's got a scene up and running at the Middleton place. That's where I'm headed. Let Tiff know you're safe and meet me out there.'

Tom nudged the speedometer needle up to 105. 'On my way.'

'And slow the hell down,' Sheriff Prescott said in his ear. 'Last thing I need's a dead deputy to scrape off the road.'

They met up with Gordon, Jeremy, and Devon at a Casey's General Store in Crescent, a few miles north of Council Bluffs, just across

the river from Omaha, still forty minutes from Ben's house in the
Platte Valley hills.

'You look like you fell off a building,' Gordon told him. 'Who's
that guy passed out in the back?'

'Reuben Wasserman,' Ben said. 'The name means *water carrier.*'

'Oh.'

'What's the word on Jeeter?'

'Back in his room. They're keeping him under, but so far, so
good.'

'Speaking of water,' Abe said, 'we should stock up on provisions.
I'm buying. Everybody follow me. Except you, Charley.'

As they headed inside, Ben and Charley lingered at the pumps
in order to a) gas up the Sube; b) keep an eye on Wasserman; and
c) avoid any notice they could succeed in avoiding. Ben doubted
anybody would actually recognize his face, even if they'd been
following the news, but his tattered, bloodstained clothing certainly
might raise a flag. Especially if anyone recognized Charley.

Ben wanted to pull him close and squeeze the daylights out of
him. But Charley stood away, hands shoved in his pockets, eyes
looking at the ground. He seemed unsure what he ought to be doing
with himself. Ben gave him some space, feeling the boy's occasional
worried glance whenever he thought Ben wasn't looking.

'I've been better,' Ben finally said. 'But I'm OK. How are *you?*'

Charley shrugged, looked away. 'I dunno. OK, I guess.'

'You saved our bacon back there, you know. Texting Frankie.'

'Yeah.'

*Got it pretty bad for her, huh pal? Sounds like murder. You
must be going out of your mind.* Ben didn't dare say any of these
things. Only: 'It's all kind of crazy, huh?'

A silent nod from Charley.

'I don't know how you're doing it, kid. But I'm proud of you. I
love you like hell. And I'm sorry this is happening.' Ben thought
hard, tried to come up with something else. Maybe something like,
Don't worry. We're going to be OK. But he couldn't think of
anything. 'I guess I don't know what else to say, really.'

'Yeah.' Charley started walking toward the building. 'I gotta use
the bathroom.'

'Hey, hang on.'

'Can't wait.'

He was just about to call Charley's name when a minivan opened its doors and spilled out a family. Ben bit his tongue and turned away, thinking: *You stubborn little numbskull.* The others emerged just as Charley went in, Abe and Gordon and Francesca all laden with bulging plastic sacks.

'Hey,' Francesca said as they approached. 'Wasn't he supposed to stay out here?'

The pump clicked off. Ben grabbed the nozzle and crammed it back in its cradle. 'Don't get me started.'

Abe took one look at him and said, 'We were the only ones in there. The counter guy is reading a magazine, he barely looked up. I'm sure he'll be OK. Here, make yourself useful and take one of these.'

Ben grabbed a sack. They'd purchased several liter-sized bottles of water, a pile of prepackaged sandwiches and trail mix, more first-aid supplies, and a new burner phone to replace the one Gordon had cracked in half and tossed into the Dumpster alongside the building. Jeremy and Devon, meanwhile, carried a single bottle of Game Fuel and a package of Donut Gems each.

'Help me remember when we get back,' Gordon said.

Devon said, 'Remember what?'

'To get new friends.'

Zwart flashed innocent confusion. 'What do you mean?'

'OK,' Abe said. 'As soon as Charley gets back, we need to keep moving. Can you guys follow us? We could sure use your help.'

'Right behind you, Gold Leader.'

'As long as we don't get pulled over,' Devon said.

'Good point. Let's all keep an eye out for speed traps. That would be . . . inconvenient. To say the least.'

'Nah,' Jeremy said. 'He means our plates.'

Ben barely heard them. He was busy watching a shiny new Ford F-150 pull in. A young farmer got out. Counting the minivan, that made five new customers since they'd arrived.

Devon said: 'Riya's plates, you mean.'

Jeremy looked at Gordon. 'New friends. That's a good idea, count me in.'

'Guys, what are we talking about?' Ben asked.

'We sort of ditched some cops back at the hospital.'

'Oh.'

'Ancient history,' Gordon said. 'We're ready to roll.'

Now Ben's heart flooded with relief as Charley emerged from the building again, hands still shoved in his pockets. He walked with his eyes down, turning his face away instinctively from the young farmer on his way in. They were doing an excellent job, it occurred to him, of preparing the kid for a career in crime one day.

Abe squeezed Ben's arm in reassurance as she nodded to First Floor IT. 'Fellas, I'm going to make this up to you somehow. In the meantime, let's hit it. I'll call you from our car as soon as we have a plan together.'

'This could be stupid,' Ben said, watching Charley all the way back to the car, 'but I might have an idea.'

TWENTY-FOUR

Three hours before sundown, Tom stood on Ben Middleton's front porch with Sheriff Prescott and watched a dark, ominous-looking sedan climb the lane toward the house, trailing streamers of exhaust and rock dust behind it.

Within a few moments, the car crunched to a stop in the increasingly crowded turnaround, parking behind a KETV NewsWatch 7 microwave truck. The car's front doors opened together. Out stepped a man and a woman, both wearing dark suits. The newcomers looked around at the crime scene in progress: the yellow tape strung around the property from shrub to bush to tree; the police photographers inside the tape; the news photographers outside the tape; the forensics personnel scurrying around in filter masks.

Prescott looked at Tom. 'Looks like the Feds are here.'

'That would have been my guess.'

'Never thought I'd say this, but that's just fine with me. Let's go make ourselves acquainted.'

They headed down the steps and across the leaf-strewn grass to meet them. 'Hello the driveway,' the sheriff called out. 'Dale Prescott, sitting sheriff here in Saunders County. This is Tom Curnow, my senior deputy. Can we help you, folks?'

The man stepped forward. 'Sheriff. Field Agent Simon Battis,

Federal Deviative Assessments Bureau. This is my partner, Field
Agent Constance West. Are you in charge of this site?'

'It's the state's site as of one o'clock this afternoon,' Sheriff
Prescott said, perusing the identification Battis offered. 'I'm just
holding down the fort at the moment. Can't say I'm familiar with
your agency.'

'We maintain unofficial attachments to Homeland Security and
the FBI,' Battis said. 'Currently working through the FBI's Omaha
group. But we operate independently.'

'So I see.' Prescott handed back their IDs. 'Still never heard of
you. No offense.'

'None taken. We're not on the org charts.'

'Deviative Assessments?'

'We're a specialty unit,' said Agent West, handing each of them
a card. 'Non-standard jurisdiction. Please feel free to call this number
– Johnson Robetaille, Special Agent in Charge of the FBI field office
here. He'll confirm our credentials.'

'Non-standard jurisdiction, huh?' Prescott put the card in his
pocket without looking at it. 'What's that cover?'

'Paranormal phenomenon.'

'Uh . . . right.'

Tom glanced at Prescott, thinking: *If he's dreaming all this
from the nuthouse, we must be sharing a room.* 'Sorry, did you say
paranormal?'

'That's correct.'

'You mean like *The X-Files*?'

Agent Battis sighed. 'Why does everybody always say that?'

Agent West grinned at Tom. 'The question he should be asking is,
how come they all think *he's* supposed to be Scully?'

'I thought we agreed to retire that joke.'

'Sheriff Prescott, Deputy Curnow, we've been investigating
events in the area that may be connected to what's happening today,'
West continued.

Prescott cocked his head. 'You mean events besides our little
town up the road? The one that looks like it got hit by a tornado
full of jackhammers?'

'Livestock mutilation,' Agent Battis said. 'Seventy miles *down*
the road.'

'When the cattle start turning up headless, we usually get a call,' Agent West explained. 'Agent Battis and I believe this instance may be connected to an unexplained murder farther south, across the border in Kansas. Both of which may be connected, as I said, to your situation. We're not here to push you around, Sheriff. Just to help.'

'Although we do have a mandate.'

'Mandate, huh?'

Agent West shot her partner a look. 'No different to yours, Sheriff. We all just want to figure this out.'

'And stop it,' Battis was quick to add. 'Before anybody else gets hurt.'

Tom stood quietly, listening.

Sheriff Prescott looked at Field Agent West, then Field Agent Battis. He took off his hat, wiped his forehead with the back of his arm. Put his hat back on.

'I guess "paranormal" seems to just about cover it,' he finally said, tipping his head back toward the empty glider chairs on the empty front porch. 'Come on up to the command center and we'll fill you in best we can.'

Ben wasn't much good at remembering numbers, but he remembered email addresses in his dreams. While Francesca drove, he used Abe's phone to log into his webmail, fired off a message containing the new burner number, and hoped against hope that Caleb Warren was still in the habit of doing his yoga routine before sound check. Or at least that he was awake. Either way, if the guy was conscious, he'd have a device within reach. And Ben thought he knew a way to get his attention.

Sure enough, within five miles, the burner rang.

'Benzo!' Caleb's voice shouted in his ear. 'You've made a poor young farm boy very happy. We're in Minneapolis tomorrow, Madison on Tuesday. Pack a bag, son.'

It was so nice to speak to someone who sounded happy to hear from him that for a split second, Ben almost forgot why he'd called. 'Hate to tell you, Cal, but you're not *that* young. Neither am I.'

'Trust me, you'll get younger every day we're on the road. Grab a pen, I'll throw you some deets.'

'Actually, I wasn't thinking quite that fast,' Ben said. 'We can talk it out. But right now I really need a solid.'

'If I can do it, it's done.'

As MiddleTone's first and best customer, Caleb Warren had done Ben plenty of favors already. Founder and front man of Crane, a local band made good, Caleb was now headlining his own mini-tours, occasionally opening for national acts. He'd been after Ben to be his full-time guitar technician ever since MiddleTone Labs went belly-up, mounting an especially pressing campaign after the divorce, but Ben had never given it a moment's serious thought. There was just no way he'd ever consider going out away from Charley for eight months of the year. And now that he was sober, he didn't need the temptation, anyway.

Funny how a couple of days could change a person's perspective. Crane had a following in the South. Ben figured they probably played Atlanta at least two or three times a year. Food for thought.

But that still wasn't why he'd requested the call.

'The Grotto?' Caleb said. 'Ha. Yeah, it's still there. Can't imagine what you'd want with it.'

'Just trying to look like a hero,' Ben lied. Or maybe it was the truth. 'My kid's a fan, he's got a little thing going with some buddies, his birthday's coming up, I just thought . . .'

'Hell, man. If they can take it back from the spiders, they can have it whenever they want. Seriously. I'll text you the combo as soon as we hang up.'

Which happened approximately three minutes later, Ben trying to hurry off the phone gracefully without seeming like a grasping jerk. When he was finished, the car was silent for a moment.

Then Charley said, 'Tell me you weren't talking to Caleb Warren just now.'

Francesca immediately locked on to him. 'You were not either.'

'Frankie. The road.'

'I'm watching, I'm watching. Caleb Warren from Crane, Caleb Warren?'

'He's an old pal. No big deal, guys.'

'No big *deal*? Are you kidding me right now?'

Abe said, 'Whoever he is, he certainly sounds amazing. What's this Grotto, Ben?'

Ben steeled himself, took a deep breath, and tried the ice bag again. 'It's practically right on our way.'

*   *   *

Malcom Frost awoke to the distant rumble of mastodons thundering over the plains. His half-dreaming mind imagined a great, majestic herd of them, somewhere just over the horizon, stamping up clouds of prehistoric dust. Running straight through a plate glass window.

His eyes snapped open, and the room came into focus. One by one, a few things became clear.

First, he couldn't move properly. Next, there was a hot, fumey breeze coming in through the fluttering curtains. Which helped to explain why Malcom was covered in bits of glass.

These things, in turn, explained the sound that had woken him. It had been the sudden combustion of modern petroleum, and not the tramping of shaggy prehistoric beasts. Had his suspended brain attempted to draw a connection between the former and the latter? Either way, the Lincoln was on fire outside.

And Anabeth Glass had dosed him with his own vapodermic, the interminable Gypsy cow.

Calm yourself, Malcom thought, as a secondary explosion buffeted him with waves of heat and the heady stench of burning petrochemicals. *Evaluate.*

He looked around at his predicament, tuning out the distant *pop* and *hiss* of rupturing tires in the background. All things considered, it could have been worse.

The injection he'd absorbed, for example. He'd loaded the jet gun with a simple cloudwater distillation: shrikeweed milk from Melanesia, condensed winter fog from Lake Pleshcheyevo in the Yaroslavl Oblast, a hint of lavender. Useful for hijacking the central nervous system of an American suburbanite, yes . . . but to a person of Frost's hard-earned tolerances, approximately as potent as half a Sominex.

Less tolerable by far was the discovery that he'd been zip-cuffed to an unconscious Lucius Weatherbee.

Frost's disappointment in his longtime operative was immediate and profound. Honestly, what had gotten into the man today? Lucius had seen colleagues perish in the line of duty before. He'd sustained all manner of prior injuries himself. Why choose *today* to become an uneven, lackadaisical, pill-popping grouchbox? Had he become unhappy in his work? Gotten crankier with age? Was it the country air?

Frost supposed it didn't matter. Bottom line: he couldn't work like this.

So he ignored the crackling heat radiating through the vacant window. He contorted himself on the floor, extending his leg as far as he could. He reached until the tip of his left shoe touched a long, scimitar-shaped shard of window glass. He pulled the glass toward him and used it to slice himself free of his restraints.

As the wail of police sirens grew louder, hurrying across the highway from one fool's errand to the next, Frost dug the bothersome Khorkhoi Cube from his pocket. The daffy thing was buzzing and blinking crazily in Lucius's general direction, two feet away.

Useless.

Frost oriented the cube in his fingers, then depressed each micro-LED in order – a nineteen-step combination pattern that caused the top panel to pop free. Almost immediately, the hatchling appeared: pale, wrinkled, glistening with secretions, burrowing its way mindlessly up through its bed of sand.

Frost tipped Lucius Weatherbee's head back, positioned the cube just so, and watched the little squirmer wriggle its way over the edge, up his lip, and into his nasal canal.

'*Bon appétit*,' he sighed to the otherwise empty room.

It seemed like a waste, but perhaps Lucius had been right: maybe it was time, once again, to adapt. What good was an old-fashioned Khorkhoi Cubist in a world full of science fiction made real?

And a triple shot of blotting serum all in one go wasn't about to do the man's cerebral cortex any favors, anyway. Lucius would be extraordinarily lucky if he ever recovered his own name, worm or no worm. Meanwhile, Malcolm Frost had more pressing issues.

So he climbed to his feet. Steadied himself. As he brushed aside the curtains and peeked out through the shimmering heat waves, the scar-thickened skin of his face and scalp seemed to shrink and pull taut, as if triggered by sense memory, an imprinted recollection of flame.

Well played, he thought, surveying his old mentor's handiwork. *Old* being the operative word in more ways than one. And here came the authorities, now.

Until later, then.

Frost boosted himself through the bathroom window just as the sirens arrived, fleeing on foot down a gentle slope into the sprawling brown cornfield behind the motel, a living scarecrow disappearing from view.

TWENTY-FIVE

As a child of the 1980s, Ben Middleton had celebrated his own fourteenth year during the wild and wooly days of the late Cold War. Like many southeastern Nebraska children his age, he'd grown up vaguely terrified that, instead of a new BMX bike with padded bars and handbrakes for his birthday, a nuclear warhead might land on his house.

This fear, cultivated in part by vaguely terrified adults, owed much to the proximity of Offut Air Force Base in Bellevue, tucked just under Omaha's wing. At the time, Offut still served as head-quarters to Strategic Air Command – a fortified underground complex installed by the US Department of Defense to control a full two-thirds of the nation's nuclear strike force from the relative middle of nowhere.

This installation had always gone a long way toward reassuring area residents that they would, in all likelihood, be among the first to be vaporized if the Soviets ever decided to push the button. It also explained a lesser-known feature of the region: namely, the dozens of 1950s-, 60s-, 70s-, and even 80s-era bomb and fallout shelters scattered about the Missouri and Platte River valleys.

Most of these shelters had been built by private citizens, on private land, to wildly varying specifications. Ben had no idea how many were left intact these days, but he'd known of a fair few during his high school and college years. The Wall had come down in Berlin, and the USSR had scattered to the winds, and Reagan and Gorbachev had wandered off into the sunset. But if you had the hook-up, a quality subterranean doomsday bunker still made a great place for country keg parties and garage-band rehearsals.

'I'm not sure I like this,' Abe said, looking skeptically down at the fortified steel hatch nestled amidst the pasture grass at their feet. 'At all.'

The door was roughly the size of a shipping pallet and had squalled like a dying banshee when Gordon, Charley, and Abe helped Ben haul it open. The air coming up from the opening in the ground was cool and musty. Rusty, corrugated iron steps led down to the birthplace of Crane's original line-up, still intact and ready for action on Caleb Warren's parents' farmland.

'Yeah, me either,' Devon scoffed. 'That band is so overrated.'

Jeremy shook his head. *'You're* overrated.'

'I'd be a 2 if McLaren didn't know you kept his browser history on a thumb drive.'

'He only knows that because you told him, idiot. You accidentally blackmailed him for me.'

'Look, I said my plan might be stupid,' Ben reminded them. 'But I'm a little short on better ideas. Anyone else?'

'Maybe we ought to stick together,' Jeremy suggested. 'I mean, it's sort of Monster Movie 101, right? Never split up.'

'We have to find that rock,' Ben said. 'How long will that take? If Charley or I are there, we could lead the creature right to us.'

'I don't know,' Abe said. 'The more hands on deck, the faster we find it.'

'And what if the creature gets there before we do?'

'You'd rather be trapped like rats in a hole if that happens?'

Ben kicked the hatch lid with his foot. The Grotto responded with a hollow *gong* that seemed to echo back to them from somewhere near the center of the Earth. 'This thing's built for brutality. The walls are a foot thick – plate steel and reinforced concrete. It'll hold a hell of a lot longer than a house.'

'You're right,' Gordon said. 'This plan is stupid. Take Riya's car, go park on a back road somewhere. If you hear the creature coming, drive ten miles and wait. Stay away from populated areas and just run the thing in circles until we call you.'

'I thought about that. Then I thought about what might happen if we had engine trouble. Or ran out of gas. Or hit a deer. Or blew a tire at exactly the wrong moment.'

'Yeah, but—'

'Anyway,' Ben went on. 'I wasn't thinking of getting *us* trapped down there. What if . . .' He paused, already hearing how it sounded. 'What if I could make it go the other way around?'

First Floor IT raised its collective eyebrows at this idea.

Abe still wasn't sold. 'I don't know, Ben. It sounds awfully risky.'

'I got away from it once before,' Ben said. 'The thing is scary as hell, but I wouldn't call it graceful.'

'That's a long way to press your luck. *And* Charley's.'

'Charley won't be here,' Ben said. 'You either, Francesca. You two are going to get back on the road and drive south. Only stop for gas. Just keep on heading south until you hear it's safe to turn around and come back.'

'Bullshit,' Charley said. 'You need me. No way am I leaving.'

'First of all, watch your mouth. Second of all, it's not up for discu—'

'Yeah, I'm not doing that, either,' Francesca said. 'All hands on deck, right?'

'Wrong.'

'We don't have time to debate this, people.' Anabeth seemed visibly frustrated for the first time since Ben had known her. He realized they'd reached the end of her expertise on this situation, at least for the moment. Something about knowing that made him feel better and worse at the same time. 'I don't know the right answer. But Charley, honestly, I think your dad might be right-ish. This may be the best thing we can come up with on short—'

'I don't care,' Charley said. 'I don't even care if this thing kills me. I'm still staying.'

'Knock that shit off,' Ben snapped before he could stop himself. 'And don't let me hear it again. Ever.'

'That goes for me, too,' Francesca said. She hooked an arm around Charley's neck. 'Loser.'

Charley's face turned scarlet. He looked at the ground. 'I'm staying.'

Ben looked at Abe. 'Help me.'

Abe looked back at him – *How?* – then at Gordon. 'This morning. You tracked the creature's speed, right? Do you remember anything?'

'Logged the stats in my phone.'

Devon seemed to be catching a signal between them that Ben, so far had missed. 'And we know it followed us at least to Ashland.'

Jeremy: 'But we don't know where it went from there.'

Abe nodded, clapping her hands together. 'OK, Halo Team. We've got five minutes to crunch some numbers. Let's make it count.'

'Sheriff, we're getting pretty deep into theoreticals at this point,' Field Agent West said, 'but we may be up against some kind of cloaking capability.'

'Like a . . . what. Like a stealth mode, you're saying?'

'Stealth mode.' She pointed in agreement. 'That's it exactly. Something that enables the creature to remain invisible while traveling. Obviously, that could help explain the unusual shortage of reported sightings so far. As well as the challenges your search teams seem to be encountering.'

And why nobody in the bleachers can remember seeing the thing until it was halfway across the damn field, Tom Curnow thought. If the boss sensed his glance, Tom received no indication. So he sat quietly.

'But that's just a theory,' said Agent Battis.

'Uh huh.' Sheriff Prescott nodded. 'So she said. I take it you two have run across one of these gomer things before?'

'Golem,' Agent West said. 'And, no. Not in my career. Or in FDAB's case history, either – which, admittedly, only goes back to the mid-1950s.'

'Mind if I ask how we're arriving at these theories, then?' Prescott raised a friendly palm. 'Don't get me wrong – if anything explains why half the cops this side of Wahoo can't seem to locate a giant mutant freak with superhuman strength in open country, I'm all for it. But you can understand my . . .'

'Skepticism?'

'I was going to say puzzlement, but your word works, too.'

'There's precedent in the literature,' Agent Battis said. 'There have been examples of a charm or totem being used to endow such a creature with selected characteristics. Powers, you might say.'

'Uh huh. What literature are we talking about?'

'Perhaps an alternative word,' Agent West said, 'would be folklore. We know how that sounds, but bear with us, Sheriff.'

'You mean *storybooks*?' Tom blurted. 'How it sounds is like you're talking about storybooks. Fairy tales.'

'All right, then, Tom,' Prescott said.

Meanwhile, Battis had developed a smirk Tom didn't much care for. 'In our experience, Deputy, if you look hard enough, there's generally a certain amount of truth in storybooks. Maybe you should read one sometime.'

'And maybe now would be a good time for us to take a brief step to one side,' Agent West said. She produced an iPad from her satchel, opened the cover, tapped the screen a few times. Then she leaned forward and handed the tablet to Prescott. 'Can either of you remember seeing this man at any point today? Or any day recently? The photograph you're looking at is a few years old, but—'

'But he hasn't gotten any prettier,' Battis said.

Prescott fished his cheaters from his shirt pocket, put them on, grunted once, and said, 'I'd remember if I had, pretty sure.'

He tilted the screen so Tom could see. Tom thought, *What barrel of toxic waste did this one fall into?* He said, 'Also negative.'

'Sheriff, swipe to the next . . . that's it. What about her?'

'Nope. Tom?'

Bingo. 'That one, yep. She was with the paintballers this morning. Glass. It's in my notes.'

'Anabeth,' Agent West said.

'Yep. That was it.'

West and Battis exchanged looks.

'Sheriff, we'd like to have a look at that campsite,' Agent Battis said. 'If you wouldn't mind showing us the way.'

'Wouldn't mind at all,' Sheriff Prescott told him, nodding in Tom's direction as he handed back their tablet. 'That's why we hire deputies.'

TWENTY-SIX

The Grotto was a concrete and steel box about twenty-five feet square, lined on two sides with storage shelves, equipped with tank-based plumbing, AC power, and solar back-up. A narrow doorway opened into a smaller box housing a stainless-steel toilet (dry), a utility sink (calcified), and a pull-chain shower over a rusty drain grate (crawling with centipedes).

The main room had been converted into a rehearsal and hangout space, clad in cast-off carpet for acoustics. A '90s-era drum kit with pitted hardware and a hole in the kick drum sat spiderwebbed into one corner. Abandoned mic stands stood around as if waiting for a party to start. Miscellaneous reclaimed furniture sat long undisturbed, yet surprisingly light on dust. *The place must be holding*, Ben thought. He wished he felt more encouraged.

Charley flopped into a loveseat, while Ben eased himself on to the sprung, threadbare couch. They stayed there for approximately forty-five seconds before Charley said, 'It smells down here.'

'Yeah,' Ben said. 'Let's hang out up top for a while. We've got some time.'

According to First Floor IT's worst-case projections – using Ben's house as ground zero, Ashland as a last-known location, and what little they knew of the creature, its capabilities, and its current whereabouts – they had a bare minimum of two hours before the thing could conceivably reach them at the shelter, even if it came full-bore, unobstructed, in a straight line. Which was about the same amount of light they had left in the day, leaving Ben and Charley with the following two-part plan:

Part One: hang out here as a safety precaution while the others searched for the Shepherd Stone.

Part Two: If the others weren't back by sundown, leave.

But as much as it calmed his pounding head to be out of the sunlight, Ben still felt nervous down here, where he couldn't see anything. They'd need to come up with a lookout strategy. He wished they had binoculars. And a better plan.

'The signal's better up there anyway,' he said, tossing Charley the new burner. 'We need to call Mom again. You do it this time. They'll probably be able to track it somehow, but she needs to hear your voice. I can't keep . . .'

He trailed off as he realized that the phone had hit Charley in the leg and bounced away, on to the cushion beside him.

Charley was asleep.

Just like that. Dead to the world, his chest rising and falling in a clockwork rhythm. Ben could hardly blame the kid. He released a long, slow breath of his own.

Jesus, what a day. He touched his nose gingerly. It was like hitting himself in the face with a croquet mallet. He felt the swollen gash nestled down amidst the blood-crusted hair at the back of his head. That hurt, too. His bandaged neck and shoulder felt like salted road rash. All his joints ached. Even his throat hurt. Maybe he was coming down with something.

With painful effort, Ben leaned forward and hauled up one of the gas station sacks. He rummaged around through the first-aid stuff, swallowed four ibuprofen capsules with a gulp of water, tried to work up the nerve to start in with the rubbing alcohol and cotton balls.

He ended up slouching back, arms limp in his lap, and watching his son sleep instead.

It was an old cliché that children looked innocent in slumber. Like untroubled angels. Charley Edward Middleton looked like a middle-aged ad exec about to lose his biggest account. His face wore a pinched expression; his hands were balled into fists beside him; his jaw muscles stood out, and Ben could see him grinding his teeth even from across the room. Hell, he could practically hear them.

I did that, he thought miserably. *Sweet dreams, kiddo.*

It was tempting to absolve himself. After all, no parent could honestly expect to keep their children at a consistently safe distance from the world. Nobody could shield them from life's most basic, run-of-the-mill unpredictabilities, let alone the exploding curveballs, and Ben had always been of the opinion that it would be a mistake – a disservice – even to try.

Besides, this wasn't like a bully at school. Or like watching your parents split up. It wasn't even like losing one of them in a car wreck (or a hang-gliding accident, for that matter). They were facing the truly bizarre and unexplainable, here. What could *anyone* do except hold on tight and hope to survive the ride?

Except that Ben couldn't quite shake the guilty idea that today probably didn't feel like some otherworldly one-off to Charley. In his mind, Ben imagined it more like the latest step in a long progression that had started with happy Christmasses in a tidy midtown bungalow and ended in a bomb shelter in the middle of a cow pasture.

How, he thought, *did it come to this?*

But that might have been the granddaddy of all useless questions. Worse than that, a dishonest one. It had happened, Ben knew, the same way Wasserman's creature had found him in the first place:

One step at a time.

He certainly hadn't started out plodding along in his own father's irresponsible footsteps. At least Ben hadn't thought so. He and Christine had been genuinely happy together, once – a true team. And when he'd worked up his nerve, chucked the safe day job, and started, of all things, a guitar company, nobody on planet Earth had supported him more honestly, or with purer faith, than Christine.

Ben hadn't even considered himself especially prideful until he was already falling, the whole time insisting he was still on solid ground. By then he was drastically overextended, throwing good money after bad, dipping into retirement accounts. Even raiding Charley's fledgling college savings, baselessly convinced that he'd be paying it all back in spades one day. All in a stubborn attempt to deny the simple, agonizing, perfectly survivable disappointment of garden-variety failure.

He hid it all from Christine, or at least he'd tried. He started drinking more, enjoying it less, and lying about that, too. Then the drinking became its own problem (or, as Christine and any accredited counselor might have put it, merely an existing problem that finally caught him in its jaws). Either way, Ben had learned that he could avoid thinking about his problems by drinking, thus creating a self-perpetuating vortex of misery that gradually sucked up his perspective, his reputation, his self-respect, and ultimately his marriage.

Because that's what you'll do as you get older, he imagined telling Charley one day. *You'll start kidding yourself about things. Maybe it's a little thing, maybe it's a big thing, but that's how we do it. We all start building our own little monsters, and they get a little bit bigger every day. Stick with it long enough, and sooner or later, they start to wake up and chase you around.*

So, look, kid, if you learn nothing else from me, just remember . . . stop li . . . us much as you can, always . . . Charley, goddammit, I'm trying to tell you somethi—

'Dad,' Charley said, shaking him. 'Dad, wake up. We fell asleep. Oh, man.'

Ben sat up with a start, bolts of pain and panic arcing from his scalp to his toes. His head pounded. His neck had fused into an iron rod. The light coming in through the hatch from up top had changed. The shadows were longer.

'Shit.' He scrambled to his feet, scattering first-aid supplies, unsure which way to move. Was it only just this morning that he'd been waking Charley up, and not the other way around? 'Are you OK? What time is it?'

'I thought of something bad. Really bad.'

'Are you OK? What happened?'

'Those guys. They said the creature followed you to Ashland. They said—'

'Don't remind me,' Ben told him, thinking with fresh new anguish of the reports Gordon, Jeremy, and Devon had shared. Reports that now included fatalities. As if poor Jeeter weren't enough. 'What time is it?'

'Dad! It followed you to Ashland!'

'Charley, calm down. It's horrible, I know, but I can't change—'

'*It followed you.*' Charley clutched Ben's arm, his face twisted with worry. 'You came to my house! Tony's house, whatever. You came to get me.'

It finally dawned on him. The bottom of Ben's stomach dropped open like a trapdoor. He thought: *How?*

How could they have failed to think of this?

All this time, Ben had presumed that the creature must be operating on its own mystical radar – some unearthly perception that enabled it to crawl out of the ground after 150 years and locate its target from 200 miles away.

But what if it was now literally following his scent?

Ben looked at Charley. What if, now that the creature had locked on to its target, the thing was simply tracking them like some kind of preternatural bloodhound?

'Stay right here,' he said, racing toward the steps leading topside. He took them two at a time, emerging into the pasture, heart pounding in his throat.

He scanned a 360-degree circle around the hatch. Nothing but a borrowed car and wide-open grazing as far as he could see. It was still daylight, but not for much longer – the sun hung over the horizon, casting a low golden hue over everything.

He turned and called back down the hatch: 'Come on up. Grab the phone.'

In a moment, Charley appeared. He hustled up the steps, the new burner in his hand. 'What are we going to do?'

'*You're* calling Mom,' Ben said, heading toward the car. 'I'm driving.'

'What do I tell her?'

'If she's at the house, tell her to get the hell out. Don't say mud monster, but tell her she's in danger. And make her believe it.'

'How?'

How indeed? It was not lost on Ben that *Your life is in danger* were exactly the words written in the note that had started all this in the first place. What had *he* done about it?

'Tell her the men from this morning are coming back.' Ben dug Deputy Curnow's card from his pocket as he slid in behind the wheel. 'After that, call this guy. When he answers, hand the phone to me. Put your seatbelt on.'

Charley snatched the card and clicked into the passenger seat, already dialing. '*Please don't be there yet,*' Ben heard him whispering. It took him a beat to realize that Charley meant the creature, not Christine. '*Please don't be there yet. Please don't be there.*'

'Don't worry,' Ben told him, firing up Jeeter's sister's car and throwing it into gear. Pasture grass scraped at the undercarriage as he wheeled them back around, pointing them toward the fence line in the far distance, the gravel road beyond the gate. 'If you're right, it's heading toward a hospital first.'

Francesca Montecito dropped them off on the far side of the bluff, about a mile as the crow flies from Ben Middleton's property. Anabeth had expected police at the house, and she hadn't been wrong. They needed to be quick, but they needed to be quiet. Most important, they needed to slip in and out under the radar. *With* the stone. And without getting waylaid by the local law.

To that end, Francesca had rolled on to the next phase of her assignment: driving back around the section and up Ben's driveway with Reuben, who had yet to regain consciousness after his perfectly timed, short-lived rally at the motel. There she would set about creating the biggest distraction she could manage, for as long as she could manage it. Something told Anabeth that Francesca Montecito, bless her, was just the right person for the job.

'Meanwhile, if things had gone to plan, you'd probably never have met me,' Anabeth now told the others, fielding one question after another as they hiked their way in through the back timber, still decked in their paintball camouflage. 'I joined the *Arcadia* dig as a volunteer three months ago. I just ran into trouble before I could finish the job.'

'What kind of trouble?'

'Boy trouble.'

'Tell us who he is,' Jeremy said. 'We'll arrange his murder.'

'That's sweet. Maybe I should say girl trouble.'

'Now I'm listening,' said Gordon.

Anabeth swatted him. 'Animal.'

'What happened?' Devon panted. It was tough going through the heavily wooded hills and gullies. The young men of First Floor IT were tops in Anabeth's book, but they were not necessarily in peak physical condition.

'One of the other volunteers . . . how to put this modestly . . .'

'Tried to hit it?'

'Decided he fancied me. I never encouraged him. But he didn't really need any.'

'You are kinda bangin',' Jeremy said. 'For a hundred sixty-five.'

'His girlfriend didn't think so. They were interning together over the summer.'

'Uh oh.'

'Which is how the Bierbaum brothers came to find a few of their artifacts hidden in my knapsack.'

Jeremy's mouth dropped open. 'She set you up?'

'Poor Randy. Poor Dickie. If only they'd believed me when I told them I wasn't a thief.' Anabeth shook her head. 'Randy might still be alive if they had.'

'How'd you get out of it?'

'I didn't. Neither one of them had the heart to bring in the police over it, but they did bar all three of us from the project. And they set up twenty-four-hour security at the site. I couldn't get anywhere near the dig after that. Without being able to track their progress, I was flying blind. So I came up here instead.'

Devon nodded sagely. 'You skated to where the puck was going to be.'

Jeremy laughed at him. 'What?'

'It's a hockey reference.'

'You're from Nebraska, stew head. What the hell do you know about hockey?'

'Perfectly phrased, Dev,' Anabeth said, enjoying the smug look Devon then turned on Jeremy. These two. She'd miss them. 'I'd been here a couple of weeks when the job was posted at your company. Happy luck, if you believe in that sort of thing.'

'Do you?'

'Not really.' She shrugged. 'Sometimes.'

'Even luckier you actually *got* the job,' Devon said, flinching at Jeremy's shoulder punch. 'What? I'm just saying. It's a big company.'

'Actually, that part, not so much,' Anabeth said. 'The Order is connected. I faked a résumé, they pulled a couple strings, it was a done deal. But honestly, guys, it's not that hard to figure out what an interviewer is looking for once you've had a few decades of practice.'

Jeremy said, 'Do you think I could get the Order to follow me on LinkedIn?'

Gordon, however, saw the whole thing from a different angle. 'You didn't just happen to like all the same stuff we like, did you?'

'Hey, I do like all that stuff. And all of you. But no,' she admitted. 'I overheard Jeeter and Jeremy conspiring about paintball my first day in the building. I knew I had to get in on *that* invite.'

Jeremy said, 'I feel so used.'

'Don't pout. I didn't say I didn't enjoy it.'

'Unrelated question,' Gordon said. He pointed toward a flash of citron fabric a hundred feet ahead of them, nestled amidst a snarl of exposed tree roots in a dry cut bank. 'What's that up there?'

Anabeth nodded and led them on. 'Welcome to my humble abode.'

Charley pleaded on the phone for three or four minutes before giving up and handing the phone to Ben. 'She wants to talk to you.'

Ben knew he couldn't honestly have expected otherwise. He truly was making this up as he went along. He backed off on the gas, took the phone, and said, 'Hey. You're not at the house?'

'I'm all the way downtown,' Christine said. 'At police headquarters.'

'Thank god. OK, listen.'

'What kind of trouble are you in?' Her voice was surprisingly calm. Ben could tell she'd been crying. But she wasn't crying now. 'Please tell me what I need to do to get Charley home safely. Both of you.'

'OK, here's step one: if the cops are listening in right now, hang up, get somewhere private, and call me back.'

'I'm in the cafeteria. Watching the five o'clock news.'

'Alone?'

'Yes.'

'No, you aren't.'

She sighed in his ear. 'Heather and LaDonna are with me. Ben, please. Whatever is wrong, we can fix it. I'm on your side. Just tell me what you need me to do.'

'What's your comfort level with calling in a bomb threat to a hospital?'

Silence.

Then: 'I don't know what to say to that, Ben. Except that nothing's very funny right now.'

'I wasn't joking,' Ben said. 'But never mind, we can handle it. I just need you to meet us. Alone.'

'Meet you where?'

He'd been thinking about this. 'Where we got married.'

When she spoke again, there was sadness in her voice. More like pity. 'Oh, Ben.'

'It's probably not as sentimental as you think. We'll be there in ten minutes.'

'Ben . . .'

'I'll be able to see everything from up there, so make sure it's only your car I see coming. Otherwise we're gone.'

'Why are you doing this?'

'Just meet us. After this is over, the cops can have me if they want me. This is just how it has to be right now. Please trust me. Tall order, I realize.'

More silence.

'Christine?'

'Stay there when you get there,' she said. 'I'm on my way.'

The flash of fabric, of course, belonged to the Marmot solo mountaineering tent Anabeth had pitched back here upon her arrival, a thousand yards from Ben's house, well out of view of everything but the birds, squirrels, rabbits, deer, coyotes, foxes, and raccoons. A couple of weeks back, she'd even seen a bobcat. It had been decades since she'd lived rough on the land for such an extended period, and the nostalgia of it had seemed like both a hurt and a balm. It had taken her back to her younger days so efficiently that at times she could almost imagine Silas by her side. And it had been a lovely autumn, too. Crisp leaves. Crisp air. Hardly any rain.

Devon said, 'You've been *living* out here?'

'It's not so bad. People didn't always have indoor plumbing, you know.'

'But you always look so . . . clean.'

'Jesus, dude,' Jeremy said. 'Why are you like this?'

Anabeth just laughed. 'I'll admit to keeping a curling iron in the locker room at work.'

'Forget the curling iron, where do you keep your car?'

'Farmer,' she said. 'Next mile over. He rents me shed space and doesn't ask questions. Anyway, the tent is mostly just a clothes closet. After midnight I usually stay up on the porch with the cats.'

Now it was Jeremy's turn to gape at her. 'You've been sleeping on Middleton's porch?'

'Who said sleeping? I'm on watch, here.'

'Wait a minute.'

Devon said, 'You don't sleep?'

'Are you kidding? I've been outliving mattress warranties since before you guys were born. But it turns out I don't actually need it.' She shrugged. 'Thanks, Grandma.'

Gordon said, 'How long have you been awake?'

'Since I got here?' Anabeth checked the date on her phone. 'I dunno. About five weeks, I guess.'

They reached the tent. She let them stand around staring at each other while she unzipped the flap and ducked inside, returning with a small nylon duffel.

'Here,' she said, passing out water and Clif bars. 'You guys look like you could use a boost.'

Jeremy looked at the protein bar, looked at the bag, looked at Anabeth. 'You don't happen to have a spare Shepherd Stone in there, do you?'

'I wish I did. Now, listen. Once we get over that next rise, we'll be close.'

As if in response, a twig snapped somewhere in the timber ahead of them. Anabeth froze, a finger to her lips. The guys stood like suits of armor in a Halloween haunted house, moving only their eyes. Everybody listened.

Nothing.

Probably a deer.

Anabeth lowered her voice. 'I know you've got more questions. And I promise I'll answer them. As soon as we find the stone. Until then, we need to switch off the chatter, put the coms on mute, total silent ops from this point on. Be the forest.'

'Stealth mode,' Jeremy said. 'Got it.'

'Shut up, then,' Devon said.

Before Jeremy could dig back at him, another twig snapped. This time behind and above them. Followed by the crunch and rustle of dry leaves underfoot.

Gordon glanced over his shoulder and said, 'Aw, shit.'

Up on the ridge of the cut bank, backlit by a beam of dusty sunlight slanting in low through the trees, stood a man in a police uniform. He looked down on them from higher ground, a thumb hooked in his duty belt, one hand resting on the butt of his service weapon.

Anabeth thought: *So much for under the radar.*

'Look who it is,' Deputy Tom Curnow said.

TWENTY-SEVEN

Holy Family Shrine was a soaring glass chapel perched high on a hill overlooking the Platte River valley. Its arching wood timbers and limestone foundation could be seen from the interstate for miles in either direction, providing a dramatic wayside for weary travelers and sweeping 360-degree views of the surrounding prairie.

At this hour on a Saturday, Ben and Charley had the place to themselves. It would be at least twenty more minutes before Christine arrived, assuming reasonable traffic. The chapel itself was closed, but there were plenty of places outside to sit and wait.

Neither one of them felt like sitting and waiting. While Charley wandered away from the formal landscaping in search of a semi-respectable place to take another leak, Ben found a good signal and tried Abe and the guys on the prepaid.

No answer. He tried a few more times, then decided he didn't like having Charley out of his sight. After ten minutes, he went looking.

Ben found him around the back of the chapel, standing amidst the wildflowers and prairie grass, looking up at the expansive altar window. It was a peaceful spot, calm and still, well beyond earshot of the silent, slow-motion interstate far below. Ben could hear the faintest whisper of a breeze in the trees: Mother Nature's room tone.

'I'm fine,' Charley said.

'I know,' Ben said casually. 'I just realized you still have that card I gave you. I need to call that cop.'

Charley dug in his back pocket, handed the card over. Ben took it. He shoved the card into his own pocket for the moment, pausing to join Charley instead. The big glass above the altar was etched with a portrait of the chapel's namesake holy family: Mary, Joseph, Jesus as a nipper. The three of them looked happy.

'Did you know they don't even let people get married here?' Ben told him. 'Not sure how she did it, but your mom finagled it somehow. Sweet-talked the board I guess. Didn't work for me when I tried it, but she wouldn't be denied.'

'Cool,' Charley said flatly. 'Too bad she couldn't stick out the actual marriage.'

Ben felt a flash of anger at that. Or defensiveness. Or something. Whatever it was, he swallowed it and hung his arm over Charley's shoulder.

'Kid, let me tell you something about your mom. She had a hundred reasons to leave, and she forgave every one of them. You want to talk about sticking? She stuck.'

'If you say so.'

'Right up until that day I got pulled over. You remember.'

'Uh huh.'

'Why do you remember?'

'I was there, Dad.'

'Bingo.' Ben gave him a short squeeze, which Charley resisted. 'I was way over the limit, and I put you in a car. That's the *only* thing she couldn't forgive. Looking back, I don't blame her.'

Charley said nothing.

'I'll tell you something else. If she *had* forgiven me? Hell, I might not ever have gotten my act together. Where'd you get the knife, by the way?'

Charley glanced down at his own belt. Clipped to it was a folding knife with a locking blade. Just like the kind Red had used to cut their cuffs back at the River Bend Inn. Ben hadn't noticed it until they were standing here.

'Bought it,' he said, covering the knife with the tail of his shirt. 'When we stopped at the gas station.'

'I thought you had to use the bathroom.'

'I did.'

'Oh.' *Drop it*, Ben thought. *Just let it go. At least for now.* But he couldn't. 'So . . . why the knife?'

A shrug. 'Just to have it.'

'Oh.'

What else could he say? What makes you think you need a weapon, give it here? Ben put his hands in his pockets. He stood there, looking out at the horizon, now painted in pinks and reds, limned in gold. His head still ached, and his vision had gone blurry again, lending a romantic soft focus to the view. He opened his mouth to say more, then closed it again. Finally, he said, 'Charley . . .'

'Mom's here,' Charley said, already walking away through the tall grass, just as the sound of an approaching engine reached Ben's ears.

Anabeth assessed the situation to the best of her abilities. She found no immediate course of action that didn't end badly, so she chose what seemed like the quickest available option under the circumstances.

She slipped her hand into the duffel, shedding the bag entirely as she stepped behind Devon. In her hand was an object she detested: the .40-caliber Beretta Px4 she kept for emergencies. She pressed the muzzle against Devon's temple.

'Hey! What are you . . . is that thing real?'

'Whoa.' Jeremy raised his palms. 'Hey. Abe.'

Deputy Curnow had his own weapon unholstered and leveled in a flash. 'Drop it and step away. Right now.'

'Deputy – guys – I'm sorry about this.' Anabeth hooked an arm around Devon's neck from behind, arranging him to portray a more convincing human shield. 'But we're going to have to do that the other way around. I want you to throw your gun that way.' She pointed in the general direction behind Curnow. 'As hard as you can. Then do the same thing with your radio.'

Curnow shook his head. 'That won't be happening.'

'Then I start plugging Tech Support.'

'You said you liked us!'

'Dev. Shut up,' Jeremy took a step toward them. 'Abe. Come on. This is—'

She pointed the gun at Jeremy, cringing inside. She would have liked to reassure the guys with some kind of signal, but she needed to sell this. Jeremy stopped instantly in his tracks, raising his hands higher, hurt flickering in his eyes. She put the gun back on Devon, pulling the hammer back with her thumb: *click-click*. The trigger felt dreadful beneath her finger.

'For the record, everybody's making me extremely twitchy right now,' she said. 'Starting with you, Deputy. Lose that gun. And I mean lose it. Gordon, as soon as he complies, get up there and grab his cuffs.'

'Frerking!' Curnow said. 'You move an inch and *I'll* start plugging Tech Support.'

Gordon looked back and forth between them like a dog caught between owners, finally choosing Anabeth to hear his appeal. 'I sorta feel like my hands are tied here.'

'Deputy Curnow, none of us want this,' Abe said. 'Least of all me. But I can't accept delays just now. I'd accept your help, if you offered.'

'Drop the gun and we'll talk about it.'

'Sorry. I'll give you ten seconds to decide your next move.'

'Already decided. I'm calling your bluff.'

'Eight seconds.'

'What did *I* do?' Devon whimpered. 'Why are you pointing a gun at me?'

'Hush, now,' Abe told him. 'Five seconds.'

'I just paid off my student loans!'

'Glass, don't be stupid,' Curnow said. 'What do you think is going to happen if you pull that trigger?'

'I don't believe you'll allow that. But we'll find out in three seconds.'

'Even if I didn't shoot you, which I will, there's plenty more cops over that hill. Plus the two coming up behind you right now.'

Anabeth had already heard them: more footfalls rustling and crunching through the leaf litter, back left and back right. Flanking them.

'Whoever's back there,' she called, 'shooting me won't help. You'll have to take my word for that.'

'Hello, Anabeth,' a woman's voice said, just off her right shoulder. 'We heard you might be in town.'

Off her left shoulder, a male voice joined in stereo: 'That was ten seconds, by the way. Might as well let the egghead go.'

Anabeth recognized both voices immediately. She didn't know whether to laugh or to shriek in frustration. She glanced at the angle of the sunlight and thought, *this is getting us nowhere.* Another part of her wondered if maybe their luck was holding after all.

She followed her gut and uncocked the Beretta. It was a palpable relief. Like stepping away from the edge of a building, even if you'd had no intention of jumping in the first place. She lowered the gun, stood on tiptoe, and kissed Devon on the cheek before he could flinch away. 'Sorry about that, Dev. Please know I'd never have plugged you.'

'*Not* cool,' Devon blurted, stumbling a few steps forward. Jeremy reached out a hand to steady him, shaking his head, for once refraining from comment.

'Connie,' Anabeth said, turning to face the newcomers. 'Si. Long time no see. I was starting to wonder if there'd been budget cuts or something.'

Jeremy said, 'You know these people?'

'We've crossed paths.'

'Glass, you're still not listening,' Deputy Curnow said. 'Drop it now.'

Agent West offered her a friendly smile. 'I think he's talking about that weapon you're still holding.'

'Thanks.' Anabeth tucked the Beretta in her waistband. 'You're both looking well.'

'You look exactly the same,' Agent Battis said, extending his right hand.

Anabeth had just enough time to think, *But I'm obviously slipping.*

Because she'd no sooner identified the shaped-pulse Taser in the FDAB agent's hand than its electrified barbs had bitten into her like angry horseflies, instantly replacing the forest around her with a sizzling lightning storm in her brain.

Ben trudged back around to the front of the chapel to find Christine hugging Charley like he'd come home from war. The sight put an immediate lump in his throat, and he felt good for the first time since sunrise this morning. Longer.

Then Christine saw him coming.

In the time it took him to raise a wave, her face went from fury to concern to an expression he couldn't interpret. She let Charley breathe a moment, looked Ben up and down, and said, 'I thought you sounded different on the phone.'

'I had some work done.'

'I was sure you'd . . . slipped.'

'Sober as a judge,' Ben said. 'Frankie's with the others. She's safe.'

'I already told her,' Charley said. His spirits seemed noticeably lifted.

'Who is Abe?' Christine asked. 'What others is Francesca with? Where are you going?'

'I can't stick around, and neither can you guys. Head south until I call you, there's no time to explain why. Charley will fill you in. But you need to get him out of here.'

'Dad. Give it up.' Charley turned to Christine. 'He has a concussion.'

'I don't know whose car that is,' Christine called after him, 'but the police are looking for it. So wherever you think you're going, you probably won't get far.'

Shit. Ben stopped, turned, and hustled back to them, wincing with each stride. He held out Riya Mallipudi's car keys. 'In that case, I need another favor.'

'What you need is a hospital.'

'Funny you should say that. Listen, honey, here's the truth: I'm not really sure where I'm going. Maybe I can find the thing somehow. Lead it away from people. I just know I can't sit around in one place for too long, and neither can Charley. Abe can fix all this, but until then, we need to get him as far away from here as possible.'

'Again, who is this Abe person? What *thing* are you talking about? You're still not making any sense.'

'Charley knows everything. If you guys get pulled over heading south, at least you'll be south . . .'

He heard a sudden loud hiss somewhere behind him. Ben wheeled around, startled, momentarily disoriented. Then he panicked, a single thought flashing like neon in his brain: *Where's Charley?*

Then he saw Riya Mallipudi's car sagging back on its haunches. The sound came again, and a moment later, Charley appeared around the front bumper. He stooped and plunged his nifty new pocketknife into the front passenger tire: *hissss.* Then the rear. Then he straightened and walked back toward them, refolding the knife as he moved.

'Oops,' he said. 'Guess Mom's driving.'

TWENTY-EIGHT

When Anabeth came back to herself, she was on the ground, and so was Gordon Frerking. Between the two of them, Gordon was the only one with FDAB Field Agent Constance West's knee in his back. Also the only one in handcuffs. Agent Battis stood over both of them with a puffy left eye. He held Anabeth's Beretta in one hand, the Taser in the other.

Anabeth herself was still connected to the Taser's barbed leads like a problem dog on an electric leash. She sat up in the crunching leaf litter. Her old-fashioned mercury fillings felt hot in her molars. She looked up at Agent Battis and said, 'Come on, Simon. Was that nice?'

'You were instructed to relinquish your weapon,' Battis said. 'Multiple times.'

'And Connie. Why are you sitting on Gordon?'

Agent West sighed. 'He assaulted a federal agent while you were being electrocuted.'

Gordon spat out a leaf. 'He had it coming.'

'I'm not saying I disagree with you,' West said. 'Now. If I take these off and let you up, are you going to behave?'

'Probably. Are you going to let me buy you a drink later?'

'Probably not, but nice of you to ask.'

'The age difference isn't a problem, trust me.'

'You should have stopped while I was still thinking about taking these cuffs off you.'

Agent Battis scowled at them with his puffy eye, turning back to Anabeth. 'Where's Frost?'

'Tied to a bed in Missouri Valley, Iowa, last time I saw him.'

'Uh huh.'

'Get your mind out of the gutter.' Anabeth moved her right hand slowly toward the barbs stuck in her upper chest. 'May I? Or were you planning on torturing more information out of me?'

Battis raised the Taser. 'Frost.'

'He's probably in custody by now. I'm sure you can confirm

that.' Tired of waiting for permission, Anabeth winced as she grabbed the wires and yanked the barbs out of herself anyway. 'We haven't worked together in a decade and a half, Battis. You know that perfectly well.'

'Things change.'

'Not everything changes.' Anabeth stood up and brushed herself off. 'And now we've wasted even more daylight playing grab-ass out here in the trees. Agent West. Agent Battis. Please, take control of this site. Help me help everybody.'

From atop the cut bank, Deputy Curnow said, 'I'd say some good faith is in order.'

'How do you mean?'

'I don't know who Frost is. But it doesn't sound like he lives in Saunders County, so I don't much care. Where's Middleton?'

'I'll take you straight to him,' Anabeth said. 'That's where we're going as soon as we find it.'

'Find what?' Agent West said.

'There's a *shem*.'

Curnow said, 'A what now?'

'A magical object inscribed with the secret name of God,' Agent Battis said. 'It's what makes the golem go. She's just stalling.'

'No. Loew made a second one. A failsafe – he called it the Shepherd Stone. We lost it back here this morning, during the first attack. It's the only way to stop the creature.'

'You mean the only way to become its master.'

'That's what Malcom wanted. Not me.'

'So you say.'

'Battis! If you think I want to stay chained to that stinking brute for more lifetimes than I have already, then we're just wasting more time!'

Curnow: 'Say again?'

Meanwhile, Gordon rejoined his peers, rubbing the cuff marks out of his wrists. Jeremy shook his head in admiration. 'Dude. That was straight boss.'

'Come on, guys,' Anabeth prompted the agents. 'Let's let bygones be bygones and crowd-source this thing. There aren't any answers at the house. It's all back here. This is the whole ball game.'

Before anyone could respond, Curnow's phone rang. While he

was answering it, Agent West's went off as well. Then Battis's. Then Curnow's radio erupted in a sudden crackle of chatter. All at once the quiet forest was abeep with sounds of modern notification. Anabeth thought of a whitetail buck snorting to alert the herd: *Something amiss. Look alive, everybody.*

State Patrol Sergeant Andrew Yost tried to keep a flexible mind, operationally speaking. In his time with Troop A Special Weapons and Tactics, he'd seen plenty of crazy shit. You relied on your training, your instincts, your hard-won experience, and whatever actionable intelligence happened to be available. What you *didn't* do was make presuppositions before you rammed in the door.

Then again, maybe his mind wasn't quite so flexible after all.

Because he'd still been operating under the presumption – despite what they'd been hearing over the radio, and right up until it was already too late – that there were no such things as actual monsters.

They moved out of Louisville in response to multiple calls reporting 'some kind of Bigfoot' crossing State 31, along the north bank of the Platte. Yost and his team picked up a trail that included, over a twelve-mile distance: a few toppled trees; one ruptured grain silo; scads of fresh gouges in the earth; an overturned Case IH Model 4416 combine with a sixteen-row corn head; and four Polled Hereford steers with no heads at all.

The trail ran out just west of Springfield, at which time Lawler, behind the wheel of the BearCat, pointed through the windscreen and said, 'Sarge?'

'I see it,' Yost said.

Although he couldn't have reported precisely what he was looking at. Directly ahead of them, two mysterious, glowing green points seemed to hang in midair. Somehow, the points grew steadily brighter, even in the sunlight.

And then . . . there it was. Shimmering to life in front of them. Some kind of faceless, nutless, green-eyed hulk, hunching its shoulders as it charged.

Lawler let out a war-whoop and hit the gas, ramping up speed to meet the thing head-on.

'Hold tight!' Yost called to the back, bracing himself for a collision that never came.

'Holy shit, that thing can jump,' Lawler said, craning forward for a better view as he cranked the wheel around.

They lit the thing up through the gun ports until support from the Sarpy County Sheriff's Department arrived. But that time, Yost and his team had fired no fewer than a dozen 40-millimeter grenades, along with enough 5.56×45mm NATO rounds to sink a naval destroyer. All to no lasting effect. The thing just kept . . . getting up. Yost had never experienced anything like it. Except maybe in some horrible stress nightmare. And he couldn't remember ever having a stress nightmare quite like this.

They finally managed to corral the thing in a recently harvested field where it had no chance for cover; Yost piled out and ran through the stubble in a crouch, hoping to get closer with the M79 without getting shot by some freckle-faced deputy.

That was when the creature began to turn in circles like a dog getting ready to bed down.

But it didn't bed down. It just kept turning faster, then faster and faster, until it was spinning in place like some wicked cross between a garden sprinkler and a Gatling gun.

Yost hit the deck reflexively, hearing the clamorous sound of his team being pelted with their own projectiles. Recycled shrapnel *zinged* and *whanged* off the BearCat's half-inch armor and ballistic glass. Spent rounds whizzed back over his head like angry insects. Windows shattered out of county prowlers; bullet holes marched across doors. Bodies fell like spouting dominos.

Then the dust cleared, and the BearCat was somehow airborne, landing on its roof with a ground-trembling crash a hundred yards away.

'Lawler!' Yost barked into the com set on his shoulder, scrambling to his feet even as the green-eyed thing turned slowly his way. 'Johnson! Dunn! Report!'

Empty static from the 'Cat.

Also, Troop A SWAT Sergeant Andy Yost couldn't help noticing a curious dark shadow spreading around his own boots.

Ben stood at the passenger door of Christine's Highlander and waited for Charley to climb in the back. When was the last time the three of them had been in a car together? Three years? Four? He couldn't even remember. 'What the hell are you grinning about?'

'It's like we're going on vacation,' Charley said.

'If you think jail sounds like a vacation, sure.'

'You won't go to jail, I bet.'

'That's very reassuring.'

'If you do, I'll come visit you on my birthday.'

'I forgot to tell you. Your birthday's canceled. Get in.'

When everybody was settled, Christine backed out of the parking area and headed for the access road. 'Lakeside has an ER,' she said. 'We'll be there in ten minutes if game traffic hasn't let out.'

'Definitely not,' Ben said. 'Get back on 80 and head south.'

'You aren't driving, so don't try to drive.'

'I'm not arguing this, either. You can't take me anywhere I haven't already been.'

'Why?'

'Because things are bad enough already, that's why. I'm being followed.'

'By who?'

'Oh my god,' Charley said from the back. 'Mom, you should have seen these guys. They were all like . . .'

'Ben? Who is he talking about?'

'It doesn't matter right now,' Ben said. 'All that matters is keeping me and the tire slasher back there away from people until Abe calls.'

Christine turned out on to Fishery Road, heading back toward Highway 31. 'I guess I'll just keep asking, then: who is Abe?'

'I like her,' Charley said. 'She's hot.'

This raised an eyebrow. 'She?'

'Trust me,' Ben said. 'I'm way too young for her.'

'Whatever you say. We're still getting you to a hospital.'

'Go north and I'll bail. Seriously.' Ben sat up in the seat. The movement made his head pound. What was left of his nose throbbed mercilessly in response. 'Just head toward my place. I'll call Curnow on the way. Between here and Mo Valley, maybe the cops have found enough by now to actually listen to my crazy story.'

'Our crazy story,' Charley said.

It broke Ben's heart a little, how cheerful the kid seemed, now that the three of them were together. On the other hand, so what? After the day they'd had, he deserved a little cheer, even if it didn't

last. 'Anyway. Francesca's probably there. So you're duty-bound as
a responsible stepmother to follow my instructions.'

Christine was silent a long moment. Then she sighed. 'God
help us.'

Ben chuckled. 'I'm sure going to miss you.'

She put on her blinker, braked to a stop, looked both ways. 'Why?
Am I going somewhere?'

Ben looked at her.

'Atlanta is off,' she said, turning cautiously on to the highway.
'Tony called me first thing this morning. He said he turned it
down.'

Ben felt a tingle. He caught a flash in the rearview mirror: Charley
pumping his fist in the backseat. He said, 'Oh?'

'He said he couldn't do it to you.'

'To *me*?'

'He's a divorced father too, you know. He said he tried to imagine
his ex moving across the country with Frankie and decided he wasn't
going to be that guy.'

Ben didn't know what to say to that. He didn't even know what
to feel about it. So he just sat there, throbbing.

'He's a good guy, Ben. You'd like him if you gave him half a
chance. His favorite band is The Who, for god's sake.'

'Jesus, I hope this monster kills me.'

Charley laughed in the back. 'Dad.'

'Monster?' Christine said.

Ben was pondering his response as they approached the ramp.
But a curious sight stopped him:

A convoy of three National Guard Humvees, blasting north on
the interstate. Just as they rumbled past, he heard an alarming
sound overhead. Ben ran down his window, stuck his head out,
and looked up. He saw two T-38 training jets screaming across
the sky in tight formation, coming from the general direction of
Offutt AFB.

Heading toward a towering column of heavy black smoke in the
far distance.

His blood ran cold. That wasn't just a figure of speech, Ben
realized: his blood literally felt cold in his veins.

'Oh, shit,' he said to the wind.

TWENTY-NINE

What started as a rush against the sunset became a desperate race against a catastrophe-in-progress.

Even with half the leaves in the forest on the ground instead of over their heads, it got darker faster in the timber than under the open sky. And then there were half the leaves in the forest on the ground to contend with.

Despite the hastily woven search net comprising herself, First Floor IT, Deputy Curnow, Agents Battis and West, four temporarily reallocated crime scene technicians, and four eager television news reporters wearing inappropriate footwear, Anabeth had begun to despair of ever finding the Shepherd Stone, let alone finding it in time to minimize the disaster currently unfolding fifteen miles to the north of Ben Middleton's property.

They needed more bodies. They needed those pole-mounted floodbanks that turned construction sites and crime scenes from night into day. They needed a break.

Be careful what you wish for, Anabeth would think later, long after the first voice called out: 'What's that?'

Another voice: 'What's what?'

'That! It's . . .'

'Did somebody toss a cigarette?'

'Stamp it out! It's nothing but kindling back here!'

'*Found it!*' yet another voice shrieked, and Anabeth was sprinting, rushing to the stranger now holding the Shepherd Stone in her hands. The stranger happened to be one of the news reporters who'd joined in the search, her hair still sprayed almost perfectly in place, even after tromping around out here in the trees. 'It was . . . I swear, that thing was glowing. Pete! Are you getting this?'

'Give it to me,' Anabeth said. Her voice sounded hoarse, unfamiliar to her own ears.

'God, that smells awful,' the reporter said, wrinkling her nose in distaste as she handed the stone over. In the background, Pete the photographer scrambled to grab his gear from where he'd stashed it at the base of a huge bur oak. Anabeth had admonished them all: *Put those cameras down and help us.* 'I saw it glowing through the leaves. It looked like a hot coal or something. But it was ice cold!'

Not to Anabeth.

To Anabeth, the stone felt warm.

Just like always.

She sank to her knees on the forest floor. It was as if a great weight pressed her down. Her chest felt tight. Now tighter. Like a steel band constricting her ribs.

The stone had glowed. It had flared like embers, like a beacon, bright enough to be noticed in the dim, dusky light. And then it had faded.

Now a dark spot appeared on its surface, followed by another, then another. These faded too, slowly, as the cursed old clay absorbed Anabeth's tears.

Reuben, she thought, struck low by a sudden grief. She became dimly aware of Gordon and Jeremy and Devon at her side, but she had nothing for them. Nothing at all. Anabeth clutched the horrid stone to her breast and wept, knowing in her weary soul that this stroke of good fortune – this lucky break she'd wished for so keenly – could mean only one thing:

Somehow, somewhere, a water carrier had died.

THIRTY

O n the evening of Saturday, October 17, under expedited emergency authorization from the Pentagon, in conjunction with the gubernatorial offices of Nebraska and Iowa, based on classified ground intelligence submitted with highest priority by the Federal Deviative Assessments Bureau, a pair of unmanned aerial vehicles engaged a confirmed non-human combatant at an evacuated truck and container yard near Chalco Hills Recreation Area, just southwest of the Omaha, Nebraska city limits.

The MQ-9 Reaper drones – scrambled out of Des Moines and operated remotely by the Iowa Air National Guard's 132nd Fighter Wing – each carried two 100-pound Longbow Hellfire air-to-surface missiles at a unit cost of $16.9 million apiece. Range: 1,500 miles. Top air speed: 300 miles per hour. Projected media and public affairs fallout surrounding domestic drone strike policy: eight to thirty-six months. Estimated time-to-target: thirty-two minutes.

Anyway. That didn't work, either.

'Then tell them to stop shooting it!' Ben yelled into the phone, craning for a better view out the window. 'I'm almost there – you *gotta* get a message to somebody in charge. We'll be the red Toyota Highlander with its hazard lights on. They need to clear us a path. And, Curnow?'

'Still here,' the deputy said in his ear.

'Please drive faster.'

He hung up the phone as Christine raced along the wide shoulder, flashing past backed-up traffic, her knuckles white on the wheel. 'Dear god,' she whispered.

'Wow,' Charley said from the back.

'Ben, what is *happening* here?'

They were driving into a war zone, that was what: soldiers, police, armored vehicles, choppers circling overhead. They plunged into a strobing haze of drifting smoke and flashing emergency lights. An oily, acrid smell seeped into the sealed car – the smell of a gasoline tanker driving into a dynamite plant on the Fourth of July.

Ben reached out and punched the hazard button as they approached the West Omaha exit. Through the smoke up ahead, he saw barricades. Road flares. A cordon made up of military fatigues and assault rifles.

'Crap,' he said, already ringing Deputy Curnow again.

Tom Curnow kept his pedal to the floor, roaring up the wrong side of Highway 6 toward Gretna with full lights and wailers. Agents Battis and West were hot on his tail in their government sedan. I-80 was a parking lot, with Saturday football traffic backed up for miles, and 6 wasn't much better. But it was flat ground, with shoulder to work with. State patrol had everything moving south sealed off at Highway 370, with an escort of cruisers waiting to pick them up at Capeheart Road.

'I understand that, son,' he said to the Army Reserve E4 on the other end of the line. 'No, I'm not in your chain of command. But I'm telling you: if that red Highlander is at your TCP, and if the guy who handed you that phone is named Middleton, then right now, Exit 440 is ground zero. You're all sitting ducks. You bet I'll stand by.'

He glanced over at the Glass girl while he waited. She was hunched in the passenger seat, scraping furiously at her crazy rock with the multi-tool from Curnow's gear belt. 'What are you doing with that thing, anyway?'

'What I should have done weeks ago,' she said. 'Tampering with the universe.'

From what Tom could see in quick glimpses, 'tampering with the universe' appeared to mean trying like hell to scrape out the foreign-looking inscription carved into the clay.

'No,' she specified. 'Just the aleph.'

'The what?'

'The first letter.'

'Why?'

'Because *emet* means *truth*,' she said. 'And *met* means *death*.'

As crazy as it was to admit it, Curnow thought he understood. She was attempting to convert this magic rock of hers from a control module into a kill switch – not unlike converting a semi-automatic rifle into a fully automatic machine gun by filing down the firing pin. Curnow saw only one problem: all that stuff about filing down a firing pin was a bunch of crocked-up, soldier-of-fortune nonsense that only worked in the movies. 'And you're pretty sure that's going to do the trick?'

'Let's hope we get a chance to find out,' she said, scraping all the harder.

Her entire outward persona had changed since the forest. This same young woman who'd shrugged off a Taser jolt like it was no big deal between friends had become all business: terse, tense, ultra-focused, stoic as the warrior her combat boots might have suggested, were they not covered in paintball splotches.

This new mode of hers hadn't changed even after they'd gotten word from Sheriff Prescott about the teenager in the Subaru and her unconscious passenger – one Reuben Wasserman from Chicago, according to his Illinois-issued driver's license.

His pulse had been so thready and weak on arrival that Prescott had radioed immediately for medical. Wasserman had flatlined in the ambulance shortly after Tiff and Roy Webber arrived on site. They'd gotten him back with the paddles, but he'd coded again twice in traffic. He didn't seem responsive to the vasopressin/ epinephrine cocktail they'd loaded into his system. It was touch and go, with no available airlift, and Tiff hadn't sounded optimistic on the phone. Glass called Wasserman her cousin, although Tom suspected that was bullshit. Why she was lying, he couldn't have guessed.

But it didn't matter. Wasserman was Tiff's concern.

Tom's concern – though he still had trouble accepting it – was the thing wreaking havoc up at Exit 440 like some old-fashioned drive-in creature feature come to life.

That, and the unusual young woman scraping a rock with his multi-tool like she was trying to start a fire in the rain.

'Listen,' he told her. 'For what it's worth, lots of people have tried dying on Tiff. Very few ever succeed. My money says your cousin pulls through.'

Glass responded by banging the tool against his dashboard, blowing clay dust from its jaws, and resuming her scraping.

Then the corporal came back on the line.

'Still here,' Tom said. 'Affirmative. Take 'em into custody if you have to, just get them moving west on 370 and we'll meet you in the mid . . . Jesus, what . . . Exit 440, do you copy?'

But nobody seemed to be receiving just then. Tom winced and took the phone away from his ear, the conversation suddenly ended by the sudden rattle of M16 fire on the other end of the line.

National Guard troops had cordoned off Exit 440 at both ends: the off-ramp on one side, 144th Street on the other, creating a muster zone in between. While the corporal spoke to Deputy Curnow on Ben's phone, his fellow citizen-soldiers ushered them through the first set of barricades, which they closed again behind the Highlander, culling them from stalled traffic into a kind of extended sally port.

Or a holding pen.

Ben first saw the motorcycle through his open window: a big Victory bagger in full touring dress. It came over the roofline of the bike dealer's showroom directly on their right, separated from their position by a grassy ditch and a low chain-link fence. The bike sailed through the air in a flat, riderless spin, landing with a crash fifty feet in front of them. It skidded across the pavement, sending up a comet tail of sparks, scattering Guard troops like digital-camo bowling pins.

'Holy shit!' Charley cried.

Christine's eyes couldn't have opened any wider. 'What in God's name . . .'

Then everybody was shooting, drowning everything else in a chattering cacophony of automatic weapons fire.

'*Get out of the car!*' Ben shouted at them, shoving Christine toward her door as he shouldered open his own, his pellet wounds stinging along to a single, vivid picture in his mind: a memory of his own kitchen. Specifically, what had happened there this morning, after he'd unloaded on the creature with the shotgun.

He threw open the back, dragging Charley out, shoving him down to the ground. Christine appeared around the front end, her face flushed and terrified, hair flying. He shoved her down, too, shouting with as much force as his lungs would produce over the deafening machine-gun fire all around them: '*Get under!*'

Charley scrambled instantly, crawling under the Highlander on his belly, Christine following right on the soles of those sneakers she'd painted for him by hand. Ben hit the deck himself just as projectiles began slamming themselves into the body paneling above him like kamikaze June bugs, perforating the sheet metal, turning the Highlander into a colander.

The continuous static of gunfire shorted out into sporadic bursts. Ben now heard screaming. Radio chatter. Boots pounding pavement, commands to hold all fire. A long, keening wail of agony somewhere nearby.

And then he heard something else he remembered very well from this morning. A mind-erasing sound, directly behind him.

Somewhere between crashing jetliner and fallen asteroid.

Accompanied by a seismic tremor that opened up a crack in the very pavement beneath his cheek.

Anabeth first saw the motorcycle on the north side of Gretna: a race replica sport bike sitting in the long line of traffic backed up at the state patrol barricade.

They'd reached their junction; Deputy Curnow had to slow down to turn east. She shoved the stone into her right-hand cargo pocket, snatched the deputy's shotgun from its clip, and piled out of the cruiser before he could react.

'Hi!' she yelled to the guy on the bike, racking the slide as she ran up to him. 'Sorry about this. Get off. Kickstand down, please.'

The guy's eyes went wide inside his helmet. She heard him exclaim something, but his face shield was down, so she couldn't make out his muffled words. But it didn't matter; the important thing was that he got off the bike.

'Glass!' Curnow shouted behind her, already out of his cruiser and giving chase. She saw Battis and West screeching to a stop behind his car.

Abe tossed the shotgun into the ditch with a clatter, patted the guy on one shoulder, and hopped on the bike. 'Again, really sorry,' she said. 'Thank you.'

Then she swiped up the kickstand, toed the bike into gear, and wrung the throttle.

Ben opened his eyes and saw his son's face directly in front of him. Charley was pressed flat beneath the Highlander, safe for the moment, his eyes swimming with panic. Ben's head swam, too, filled with a kind of floating, disembodied hush. He couldn't hear Charley's voice. But he could read his lips:

'*Dad.*'

Ben reached out and grabbed Charley's hand. '*Don't move!*' he shouted, his own voice resonating like a muffled speaker in the bone enclosure of his skull.

Then he scrambled to his feet, Charley's fingers slipping from his. Now he did hear Charley's voice, faintly, as if from the bottom of a swimming pool. As if, God help him, from the bottom of a grave:

'*Dad!*'

Then time sped up again. Ben turned. Twenty feet behind him, he saw flames, smoke, a ring of buckled pavement. Then two glowing green lamps in the haze.

And then, through the smoke, the creature emerged. It moved almost at a saunter; brow dipped low, shoulders hunched, crude arms hanging. The thing shifted its gaze slightly toward Ben, as if catching his scent. Its glowing green eyes flared brighter.

'Fuck me,' Ben said to nobody.

Then ran.

THIRTY-ONE

The first time Ben Middleton had escaped from the golem sent to assassinate his fourth great-grandfather, it had been first thing in the morning. He hadn't slept the greatest, but still, he'd been uninjured. At least semi-fresh from the night's rest. He'd had a head's-up, thanks to Reuben Wasserman. He'd had a head start, thanks to the four guys ranked above him in First Floor IT. He'd even had coffee.

This time, things hardly seemed fair.

He'd gotten about six steps when the ground thundered. Then the creature was in front of him again, rising up from a crouch like a green-eyed Atlas pushing up the world.

Ben didn't know whether to zig or zag. He only knew that he needed to keep moving away from Charley and Christine. So he veered right, into the grassy ditch, aiming to vault the chain-link fence. He could make a break for the vacated parking lot of the filling station just beyond. Possibly find cover. Or maybe just run in circles around the empty building until his lungs gave out.

He tripped in the weeds instead, falling flat, rolling away from the shadow already spreading around him.

Ben scuttled like a crab toward the mouth of a galvanized culvert pipe running beneath 144th Street. He slipped into the dark tube like a man-sized sewer fluke, clawing and scrabbling his way through foul-smelling sludge, cobwebs, broken beer bottles, cigarette butts, God only knew what else. The ground thundered again, and silt rained down, and when he looked back he saw the mouth of the tube crimped shut behind him.

He began to lose it then, hyperventilating in the dark, his heart hammering beneath a heavy blanket of claustrophobic panic. Then, ten feet ahead of him: an open portal back into the world.

Now blocked by a crouching, green-eyed thing looking in.

He was trapped.

This is it, Ben thought. *This is how it ends.* Silently, he began to pray: *Abe. Anabeth. Anabet. Please get here with that rock. Please help my boy.*

And then, as he readied himself for whatever was to happen next, the worst thing he could have possibly imagined came to pass: The creature pulled its blank face away from the opening.

And Ben heard Charley's voice in the distance, screaming, 'Hey, you pile of shit! Come and get it! *Over here!*'

Abe quick-shifted the big liter bike, preloading the lever and blipping the throttle instead of wasting time pulling the clutch. She leaned around an oncoming vehicle, then back the other way around the center median, slaloming through obstacles, scanning ahead for gaps and spaces. She lost the rear wheel in a scatter of gravel, reflexively backing off the twist-grip and counter-steering through a yawning, bum-clenching skid. Then she rode the center line like a rail, winding the bike up until it screamed.

It seemed like she was moving in slow motion, even as the speedo crept toward 135. The crisp autumn air felt like a polar blizzard at such speed, freeze-drying her eyeballs and numbing her hands into unfeeling lumps. Her hair flapped so violently behind her that it stung her scalp. She focused on the pain and pushed the bike harder, praying against potholes, leaving each new state police cruiser behind her like they were standing still.

Before long, the cruisers stopped following. Then they seemed to be helping instead of chasing, opening up lanes in the roadway far ahead of her.

Abe pinned back the throttle, set the lock, and crouched down behind the fairing until she was draped across the fuel tank, flat as she could go. Obsessively reaching down to pat her right leg with each flashing mile.

The stone still waited there. Still snug in its pocket. The only warm thing in her life.

'*I'm coming for you!*' she shouted into the wind, cold air drying her mouth, billowing her cheeks, snatching her words and whipping them away.

And then it was nothing but smoke and madness everywhere around her.

Dragging himself frantically out of the open end of that culvert pipe, wheeling like a madman in search of his son, finally staggering back up to the haze-clouded roadway, Benjamin Allen Middleton almost could have passed, they told him later, for a second creature himself.

All Ben would be able to remember about it were two indelible images, burned into his soul like nuclear-flash imprints. The first image was the most terrifying thing he'd ever witnessed. The second one was the finest. He'd carry both around with him for all the rest of his days.

The first image:

Charley in a backpedaling sprawl, in the middle of 144th Street, at the feet of a thundering kill monster.

Ben's mind went blank and his body moved seemingly on its own, hobbling and limping and straining to reach its child, to grab Charley by the collar and drag him away. But his strength failed him, and the next thing he knew, they were on the ground together as the creature launched itself into the air. Ben wrapped Charley in one arm and raised the other in defense: a ridiculous, puny, futile gesture of protection he could not provide. A feeble pantomime of ultimate, irrevocable failure.

Then came the second image:

Anabeth Glass riding out of the smoke on the back of a motorcycle.

It might have seemed like a manufactured memory, in retrospect, if Christine's own recollection hadn't borne it out: Abe climbing up on to the seat of the bike like some Wild West trick rider; Abe launching herself toward the creature as the bike skidded and tumbled away; the ageless face of Anabet Glacz, twisted in a battle snarl, as she met her long-awaited creature in midair.

And then came the sound of a mountain cracking in half. The sound of history folding back on itself. The sound of dueling immortalities expiring simultaneously as Anabeth Glass became human again, and her creature became stone. Ben didn't stop to listen. He was too busy dragging Charley. Or maybe Charley was dragging him.

The rest came in flashes:

Charley's bloody, sweat-streaked face.

Stars winking on in the darkening sky.

Anabeth, motionless, in a craggy rubble of broken stone.

And then Ben saw nothing but boots and uniforms, felt nothing but Charley's hot breath on his neck, heard nothing but his ex-wife's voice, calling their names.

GILDED LOAM AND
PAINTED CLAY

THIRTY-TWO

I t was April of the following year before they celebrated their birthdays properly: Charley's fourteenth and Ben's fortieth, together. They planned it on the half-year anniversary of that horrible day in October, when so much life had been lost: a long-belated gathering for family and a few friends.

And then it just sort of got out of hand.

They'd started with nothing more than a small family picnic at The Grotto. Charley's idea. Then Caleb Warren canceled three club dates before Ben could stop him, crowbarring his bandmates into providing the entertainment free of charge. Francesca Montecito got wind of that and would accept no discussion to the contrary.

Ben didn't know what to think. Nobody was saying it was going to be Altamont; this was small-potatoes, home-town stuff. But he still worried. It seemed borderline disrespectful, first of all, and besides, things had just sort of started to die down.

From what Ben could tell, roughly 25 percent of the world thought the whole thing about the runaway mud monster in Nebraska was bullshit. Total Fake News. Of those that were left – at least judging by the Internet – another 25 percent thought Ben Middleton should have fed himself *and* his kid to the monster and saved a hundred other people the agony.

The rest thought all kinds of crazy things. Personally, Ben found it all queasy and unpleasant and easy enough to ignore, but what if it just started making Charley's life a living hell again?

Charley, of course, said bring it on, screw 'em if they can't take a joke. Tentative green light from Christine. And then Ben complained about it to Ajeet Mallipudi on the phone one day, and Jeeter said, 'Why don't you charge tickets and donate the money to the Ashland Fund, or something of that nature?'

He'd come such a long way, that guy. Worrisome cerebral contusions; compression fractures and nerve damage throughout his cervical spine; twelve weeks in a halo brace. Ben knew that he still got headaches, and he sometimes seemed frustrated with himself,

but Jeeter never seemed to let it keep him down. After six months
of rehab, he was looking at least 80 percent again to Ben, and
climbing fast.

And, honestly, it hadn't seemed like the worst idea he'd ever
heard. So they set up a flatbed trailer in the pasture and started
the whole thing off with a memorial. Shirley Rademacher, Big
Glenn's widow, got up and said a few words. Sheriff Dale Prescott
followed her with a few words of his own. Tiff Curnow ran a
slideshow of faces and read out a too-long list of names.

As imagined, it was a pretty somber cow pasture by that point.
To nudge things toward a lighter mood, the Saunders County
Sheriff's Department ended the service with a twenty-one-gun salute.
Using paintball rifles.

Then Crane climbed up and got things moving in different
direction entirely. Caleb said it reminded him of the old days.
The security crew said you could hear the set all the way out
on the road.

Along the way, back down underground in the semi-privacy of
the shelter itself, Ben found a moment to give Charley his present:
a custom Partscaster, cut and dried from a hundred-year-old
hackberry tree that had fallen on Ben's property during a storm
the year before. Pretty simple – a bare-bones instrument, basically
dressed up like a '54 Blackguard, with a few extra windings in
the pickups just for spice. Not a masterpiece, by any means. But
it screamed like a demon and played like butter, and it put Charley
over the moon.

Corby McLaren got plastered and sprained his ankle stepping
into a badger hole. First Floor IT set him up in the back of Gordon
Frerking's freshly restored Vandura, with the back doors propped
open, where he could watch the rest of the show with his foot on
ice. Ben doubted the incident would negatively affect his rank
on Corby's stack chart. It couldn't get lower anyway.

Frankie and her friends took so many selfies with Caleb and the
other band members that Ben wondered if Instagram would survive
the assault. At one point her dad wandered over, his face ruddy
from the margarita fountain, and plopped down in an empty lawn
chair next to Ben.

'Middleton, I'll take my hat off to you,' he said. 'You know how
to go over the hill in style.'

Ben chuckled. 'Thanks. Your wife vetoed the mud-wrestling.'

Tony Montecito raised his Solo cup. 'Happy birthday.'

Ben touched his thermal coffee mug to the rim. 'Cheers.'

They drank, then sat and watched Charley having the time of his life up on the flatbed, power-chording along with the band at Caleb Warren's invitation for a hard-driving cover of CCR's 'Fortunate Son.'

'I still sometimes wish I'd been the one to punch you in the nose, though,' Montecito said then, apropos of nothing, his eyes wistfully glassy. 'I don't know why.'

Later, after Tony had wandered off again, Ben turned to Christine and said, 'He seems to be having fun.'

Christine laughed. 'He's a little drunk, I think. Did you know he took Charley golfing today?'

'I heard. They have a good time?'

'Charley hated it.'

'That's my boy.'

'But he was very sweet.' Christine got up, stooped down, and planted a quick smooch on Ben's cheek. 'Happy birthday.'

'Thanks,' Ben said, touching the spot. 'What was that for?'

'Because I love you, dummy.'

'I *knew* it.'

'Unfortunately for you, slow learner, I also love my husband.' She tousled his hair. 'And he's better-looking. Makes a shit-ton more money. Also . . .'

'Go towel off your rock star,' he told her. 'Let me grow old in peace.'

He'd have liked it if Wasserman could have made it to the shindig. But between a brand-new nephew on the home front, and newfound celebrity on YouTube, Reuben had enough on his plate these days.

The enigmatic toxic shock that nearly ended him had gone a long way toward freshening his perspective on a few things, Reuben claimed, and he was working hard on building back some of the trust he'd wrecked with Claire. After spending four days handcuffed in a closet with only the ghastliest disjointed memories of how she'd gotten there, she'd been – perhaps understandably – uncertain about the long-term potential of their relationship.

But they were working on it. Ben could only advise him, from

personal experience, that honesty was generally the best policy. In
the meantime, at least for the moment, no more trips to Omaha.

They kept the party going long into the night. Ben checked his
phone about a thousand times, hoping for a return text to the one
he'd sent that afternoon. Just before midnight, he finally got it: a
photo with an accompanying note.

The photo depicted a fiery sunrise over a blue-domed mosque.
The note said, simply: *Today's the day.*

Ben sat with that a moment.

Then he texted back: *It sure as hell is.*

MULE VARIATIONS

vii. Farewell to Arms
Southern Kurdistan

S he finally caught up with him at a café in Erbil. He was sitting alone at a window table, sipping coffee from a dainty *fenjan*, reading the daily *Al-Mashriq*. Word around the campfire was that he'd arrived two days prior with a bottled-up *djinn* for sale. His suspected buyer: a known sleeper cell holed up somewhere in the Qandil Mountains near the border.

'Hello, Betsy,' he said in her shadow, before she'd even lowered her hijab. Frost raised his eyes from the newspaper, took one look at the carbon fiber prosthetic she wore in place of her lower right arm, and smirked. 'Have you come to give me a hand?'

'That's exactly right,' she told him. 'A helping hand all the way home.'

Frost seemed to think that was funny. 'Will you sit?'

She didn't see why not.

She watched the street traffic around the citadel through the café window as he motioned for a server. Then she watched him pour her a cup of coffee from the *dallah* already on the table. She paid special attention to his hands.

'It's bitter,' he said. 'You'll like it.'

'Just the one cup, and then we'll be going.'

Frost chuckled. It was an unpleasant sight. An unpleasant sound. She hadn't forgotten it. She doubted she would any time soon.

'So, tell me,' he said, freshening his own cup from the same vessel. 'How does it feel to be dying a little bit each day, just like the rest of us?'

'It feels glorious, now that you mention it.'

'We may see about that.'

Anabeth smiled and took down her headscarf, still pondering the coffee in front of her.

'Try me,' she said.

viii. Farewell to Ass
Kansas City

If Dickie James Bierbaum had said it once, he'd said it a thousand
times: *You can't fight city hall.* Not that he had much heart for it
these days, anyway. When it came to hunting treasure, Dickie had
liked the digging and the finding. Red tape had been Randy's job.

Now Randy was gone.

And so was *Arcadia.* They'd taken her, of course, after everything that happened. Under amended guidelines of the Abandoned
Shipwrecks Act of 1988, oversight and curation of the remaining
excavation had passed to a task force of state, federal, and international agencies. Cooperating institutions included the United
States Department of Homeland Security, the Archaeological
Institute of America, the World Council of Religious Leaders, the
University of Kansas, and the Division of Physical Anthropology
at the Smithsonian. There'd been all sorts of arguing and fighting
about the whos and whats and whens, but Dickie hadn't paid attention to any of that. At least not until it was time to talk turkey.

He'd sunk everything he had into that blasted hole in the ground,
after all. Now he was a fifty-five-year-old man with bad knees,
glaucoma, and a heart valve that flapped like a busted laundry vent.
By the time all the madness was over with, he hadn't had a pot to
piss in or a window to throw it out, unless you counted Randy's
– which Dickie couldn't anymore, since Myra and the kids had
gotten everything left of any value in what passed for his big
brother's estate.

Naturally, talking turkey with the government was more like
watching the government carve and then eating what they gave
you. And their idea of fair market value looked more like about
thirty cents on the dollar to Dickie. But it was still more than
plenty. Hell, when you counted the money people kept paying
him to go on television or talk to a group, Dickie almost felt guilty.
Randy shouldn't have missed out.

Meanwhile, he could hardly help keeping up with the reports,
even if he'd wanted to avoid them. *Arcadia* had changed the world,
sort of. Or maybe not, but the world sure couldn't seem to stop
talking about it. Dickie mostly stuck to the Smithsonian's running
web gallery, where they posted professional-looking photos and

decent little write-ups about all the new discoveries as they rinsed them off. One day he popped off so loudly that the other morning regulars at the diner stopped playing cards.

'What's the matter, Dickie?' Jerry Trauerneck called over. 'You win the lottery again?'

'Gotcha!' Dickie cried, pointing at the cracked screen of his ancient laptop. 'Thought you'd gotten away with it, didn't you? Didn't you? Ha!'

Shelly topped off his coffee as she passed by the table, pausing to look over his shoulder. 'Who got away with what, Mr Bierbaum? Ooh. Yuck. What is that?'

It was the first honest belly laugh Dickie Bierbaum had enjoyed in just about as long as he could remember, that was what it was. The old-timers set aside their Euchre hands and wandered over, too curious to stay away.

On the screen was a photograph of a rust-caked sawmill from *Arcadia*'s aft deck. Attached to the sawmill by three feet of chain: the intact, skeletal remains of a small john mule.

Dickie took great relish in recounting for them the old story, published in the paper of the day, of a Swedish trader named Frisk – the loud and proud owner of *Arcadia*'s only living casualty. Back then, Frisk had claimed he'd tried everything to get his poor mule ashore.

'I'll be damned,' Jerry Trauerneck said. 'The sorry thing was still tied up.'

'History always gets its man,' Dickie said, still grinning like a loony. He clapped his hands, wiped his eyes, and sat there shaking his head. 'Wouldn't budge, my ass.'

Somebody said, 'That guy Frisk's ass, you mean.'

'An ass is a donkey,' Trauerneck replied. 'A mule's just a mule.'

Others: 'Isn't a mule half-donkey?'

'So it's half-assed, you're saying.'

'Yeah, but which half?'

'Dickie, look it up on the computer. What do you call a donkey?'

'I ask you,' Dickie asked them, ignoring the debate. Who cared what you called a donkey? 'Is it not to laugh?'

'Sure, Dickie,' somebody else said, as the old-timers gradually got tired of looking at chained-up mule bones and wandered back the way they'd come. 'It's a good story.'

'Guess it goes to show you.'

'Just goes to show you what, Mr Bierbaum?'

Dickie thought about that, shrugged, sipped his coffee.

'Hell if I know,' he said.

ACKNOWLEDGEMENTS

Special thanks are due to the *Arabia* Steamboat Museum in Kansas City, Missouri, for providing the seeds that eventually grew into this book. Much of the *Arcadia* lore in these pages is based on the historical facts of the *Arabia*. As for historical facts, there is no evidence that the real Henry Ward Beecher ever commissioned a golem; most experts doubt that it even occurred to him to try.

Additional thanks once again to Jill Doolittle, RN, and Detective Craig Enloe, Overland Park Police Department, for providing excellent info about how far a writer might stretch the operational parameters of an ER and a crime scene, respectively. Thanks to Nathaniel G. Lew of Saint Michael's College for the Hebrew translations, and to old pal Wayne Edwards for brokering them. Thanks to Ian Hancock of The University of Texas at Austin for the Romani translations. Thanks to Victor Gischler for letting me buy him a steak.

Finally, for excellence in monster husbandry, sincerest warmth and abiding fuzziness to David Hale Smith, my longtime agent; to Steve Feldberg, Vikas Adam, and the team at Audible Originals; and to Kate Lyall Grant, Carl Smith, Leila Cruikshank, Piers Tilbury, and the team at Severn House – thank you all!